# Praise for the Underdead Books

"Kept me on the edge of my seat anxious to find out more. I was thoroughly engaged from beginning to end. This is a great story to curl up with on a rainy day."
-Coffee Time Romance

"Hilariously funny...a page-turner extraordinaire."
-MyShelf

"*UNDERDEAD* had me grinning from the first line! Off-beat, charming, irreverent and so much fun to read I couldn't put it down."
-Mary Buckham, award-winning author of *Break Into Fiction*

"*UNDERDEAD* is certainly not your typical vampire story, it's better... I guarantee *UNDERDEAD* will have you laughing out loud, while keeping you in suspense right up until the end."
-Two Lips Reviews

"Light-hearted mystery with a touch of the paranormal and a hint of romance is a recipe for a just about perfect read."
-HuntressReviews

"People of any age and from every walk of life will enjoy this intelligently written, humorous take of a normal girl's entry into the paranormal."
-*Grunion Gazzette*

"This is a funny and fast-paced read that will delight anyone who has ever enjoyed a cozy mystery, a comedy, a romance, or a vampire novel."
-BellaOnline

# UNDERDEAD
## IN DENIAL

by

Liz Jasper

TEXT © 2008 BY LIZ JASPER

COVER ART © 2011 BY KIMBERLY VAN METER

ISBN 978-0-9839450-1-7

ORIGINAL EDITOR PAMELA CAMPBELL

COVER AND INTERIOR DESIGN BY
STEPHEN JAMES PRICE
WWW.BOOKLOOKSDESIGN.BLOGSPOT.COM

# Acknowledgments

---

**T**hose who come through with help and support are like chocolate and coffee—wonderful in every way.

Thanks to L and M who are always ready and willing to talk through plot ideas and read drafts—late at night, early in the morning—and even if they've read only a slightly different version the day before.

Much thanks to Pamela, my original editor, for her wonderful input.

Special thanks to my parents who are always a generous source of encouragement and enthusiasm. And a reliable source of minutia.

Big fat thanks to contest winner Cathie M. for coming up with the perfect name for my new vampire character. And thanks to her dad for being okay with the fact that it is his name.

Thanks to D.P. Lyle for being, as usual, generous with his time and knowledge about forensics. Any too-generous liberties (AKA screwups) fitting his advice to my story are my fault. Thanks also to Nancy A. Pratt of the Long Beach Police Department for patiently explaining police procedures. She made sure I understood how things really worked and then encouraged me not to let the facts get in the way of the story. Long Beach's Finest, indeed. All errors are mine.

Thanks to the Super Tuesday group—Mary, Jen, Kat, Ginger, Judythe, Sheila, and Helen—for being a reliable source of support, encouragement, whip-cracking, advice and, best of all, spit-take-on-keyboard laughter. Thanks to my fellow Pink Fuzzy Slipper Writers for keeping me well entertained in the blogosphere.

Last but not least, thanks to my sisty ugler, who gets major credit for suggesting I put Jo in a haunted house. And especially for spending hours trapped in the car with me while I worked through the last sticky plot tangle, even if, to this day, she has no idea how she helped. You are my very favorite sister. The fact that you are my only sister doesn't diminish the favoritism in the least.

# Dedication

To my mother, who has the gift of whimsy.

# Chapter One

---

*I*f it hadn't been for the faint odor of gym socks I never would have believed I was in the theater at the Bayshore Academy.

The stage was transformed into an amazingly accurate replica of the school quad, complete with real grass (I could smell the sweet, earthy sod from my seat.) and a Broadway quality backdrop of the Long Beach shoreline. It was so impeccably rendered I half expected the Queen Mary to pull up from its moorings and glide over the horizon in a belch of black smoke. But the sets were nothing next to the actors, who were emoting like soap opera stars in Emmy Award season. I wasn't sure if what I was watching was spectacularly good or spectacularly bad, but I couldn't look away.

I gasped with the rest of the audience as a rowdy mob of football players produced a noose and went after head cheerleader Esmeralda. And as they strung her up between the goal posts and let her swing, I actually rose in teacherly alarm.

I knew from watching copious amounts of television (You grade ninety-six copies of each assignment, then judge me.) that the actress had a safety harness hidden under her cheerleader costume. Even so, it was a *very* convincing effect and as my initial tug of alarm dissipated, I couldn't help but wish the play had called for a more exciting death.

I bet the director really could have done something with a play that called for, say, a knife fight. I wondered what he would have used. Some sort of special mail-order stage blood and a pump?

I was halfway through imagineering a really good design to simulate arterial spray that involved those little packets of ketchup you get at fast-food restaurants before I realized what I was doing. Obviously, I'd been spending too much time with my middle school students. Bloodthirsty things.

As Esmeralda gave her fifth and final death spasm, someone cut the lights, plunging the theater into inky darkness. A faint breeze emanating from the back of the theater broke the stale, noisome air and as I gratefully turned in my seat, I could just make out a slight, misshapen silhouette standing in an open doorway. A spotlight snapped on, identifying the hunching figure as our hero, Quasimodo, the Chess Club Chairman. As he limped convulsively up the aisle to where the cheerleader's body lay in a pool of golden light, an unseen figure up in the balcony keened a lament.

I whispered across the seat arm to Becky, "This isn't exactly the Disney version of *The Hunchback of Notre Dame*, is it?"

Becky is the high school's hot-shot chemistry teacher. She is also one of my best friends and the reason I was spending Thursday night watching this unexpectedly artsy high school production instead of polishing my lesson plan for tomorrow. Or grading lab reports. Or surfing the net for ideas on how to make my eighth grade students interested enough in earth science that they didn't seek their own entertainment in the form of lobbing spitballs. At me.

"Shhh!" With an impatient jerk of her hand, Becky waved me to silence.

"Don't you shush me. You dragged me to this…"

Becky wasn't listening to me or the play. She was craning her neck to get a better view of the backstage area just visible from our seats at the far right of the theater. Her slim black-clad figure hummed with so much energy I could almost see sparks shooting from her spiky, bleached-then-dyed-silver hair.

I let my curious gaze follow her line of sight. She was fully checking out the director, a compact, thirtyish man who was giving stage directions with mouthed words and wild flourishes of his arms.

"Oh for the love of Pete," I said. "Not you too."

Dan Sterling—Drama Dan, as the students adoringly called him—had made another conquest. I tried to figure out what the big thrill was. I suppose Dan looked a *little* like Leonardo DiCaprio, if you imagined the famous actor redrawn with crayon colors. Dan Sterling's eyes were sky blue, his cheeks were lightly flushed with pink sherbet and his hair was yellow straight out of the basic eight crayon box. He might be a little too boyishly handsome for my tastes, but that didn't seem to be keeping just about everyone else from joining the Drama Dan fan club.

A good half of the students—roughly the female half—were wildly in love with our interim director. I hated to think what would become of all his mooning groupies on Monday when our regular drama teacher came back from maternity leave and Drama Dan returned to his job as the lead actor at the Milverne Theater.

I gave up on getting anything lucid out of Becky and returned my attention to the stage, where an anguished (I could tell from the loudness of his chest thumps.) chess-club-Quasimodo was mourning cheerleader-Esmeralda.

All at once the little hairs on the back of my neck stood up. I was trying to figure out how Drama Dan had managed that particular stage trick when Carol, my other best friend at Bayshore, slid quietly into the seat I'd reserved for her. Not wanting to miss whatever was coming next, I kept my eyes firmly glued to the stage.

"It's about time you showed up," I told Carol in a low voice. "This play is something else. You're going to have to come back tomorrow night and see it from the beginning."

"Is that an invitation?" The low, silky voice wasn't Carol's, not even close.

The stage lights went up and the audience around me went wild, clapping and whistling at whatever was happening on stage. I sat frozen in my seat, staring at the man occupying the seat next to me, watching the lights from the stage dance over the sharp cheekbones and harsh planes of his lean face. Brilliant blue eyes the color of the night sky just before the sun went down glinted with intelligence and humor.

It had been months since I'd seen Will. He hadn't changed a bit. His inky black hair was still longer than current fashion. He still favored beautifully tailored black clothes that undoubtedly cost more than I made in six months. I couldn't have clicked my heels and wished up a more gorgeous male. And as if that weren't enough, he was intelligent, had a wry sense of humor and could charm chocolate off a newly dumped woman with PMS. He was, decidedly, perfect in every conceivable way.

Except for the tiny personality flaw of wanting me dead.

Undead, actually. Like him.

For one wild moment, I considered jumping to my feet and telling everyone to make a run for it as there was a vampire loose in the theater. But I didn't. No one would have believed me. Everybody knows vampires don't exist.

As if in mockery of that thought, the very real warmth from Will's lean, lithe body radiated across the armrest. Oh, he existed all right. And, God help me, he smelled fabulous. I have no idea if it was cologne or aftershave or just the soap he used combined with his natural scent. I've never been up on that sort of thing, but whatever it was, it was making my hormones hum as hard as my nerves.

I first met Will nearly a year ago. After a whirlwind sixty-minute courtship, he apparently decided I would do and sunk his teeth into my neck. Thinking him some sort of Goth freak who was taking the vampire thing a *little too* seriously, I fought him off. But not quickly enough. Not before he'd managed to turn me nearly into a vampire.

So that's me, Jo Gartner. I have my mother's red hair (The original red-gold shade, before her colorist, Rafael, got hold of her head and sanity.) and my father's hazel eyes. I'm five foot ten and I'm almost Undead.

Last spring the secret had nearly cost me my life and I'd begged Will to leave me alone. To my surprise, he had honored that request. I hadn't seen hide nor hair of him, all spring, all summer, all fall…

Until now.

A cold rush of fear snapped me out of my open-mouthed shock. "What are you—"

Will put a finger to my lips.

"Shhh, let's watch the rest of the play. I admit to being intrigued by this…unique interpretation of the classic." As he spoke, his mouth brushed my ear, sending warm shivers down my spine. Goose bumps of terror popped out everywhere else.

He relaxed back against his seat with every indication of enjoying the play. I sat bolt upright and tried to keep the air going in and out of my lungs.

The play ended with a finale that made the audience jump to their feet in a frenzy of applause. The house lights went up and I glanced at Will. He was looking boggle-eyed at the stage.

He said, "That was…"

"I know." For a moment, I forgot he was a walking death threat and we were in complete harmony.

Becky was halfway into the aisle at the side of the theater before she thought better of leaving me, her date, without a word. Catching my eye, she pointed surreptitiously to the stage to let me know she was heading over to congratulate the director. She had taken two brisk steps in that direction before she stopped and did a double take at Will. Her black eyebrows shot into her spiky silver bangs. And then she stared dreamily at him, her urgent mission apparently forgotten.

"Don't let us keep you." I gave her a shove toward the stage before she could introduce herself. I thought it best not to widen her circle of friends to include vampires.

Becky wrenched her gaze away and gave herself a slightly befuddled shake. Meeting my eyes, she flashed me a look that said, "Well done, Jo, we'll talk later," and left for the stage, her progress slow and a little unsteady.

Will's sapphire gaze followed her retreating form. "She looks familiar." His voice was thoughtful and contained that hint of an accent that I had never been able to place.

Becky had been the one, in all innocence, to point Will out that fateful night last December. I didn't want him to think of Becky as "familiar". I didn't want him to think of Becky at all. It was bad enough he'd met my mother.

"How about some coffee?" I had no idea if he drank coffee—or ate, or imbibed anything but blood—but the crowd was relocating to the foyer and I wanted to stay with them.

It might seem irresponsible of me to encourage the head of the local vampire clan to linger in the midst of so many innocent people, but I knew Will wouldn't do anything to me, or anyone else, in a crowd. It was in his interest to keep his identity secret. Crowds, even those comprised of well-mannered prep-school parents, teachers, and students, had a bad habit of turning into a panicked, torch-carrying mob when they learned they had a vampire in their midst.

Granted, in this day and age it would be hard for anyone to locate torches and pitchforks in a pinch. But after tonight I'd put my money on finding just about anything in Drama Dan's prop room and this was a resourceful group.

With the force of a fast-moving river, the departing crowd pushed us into the foyer and dropped us off in an eddy by the refreshment table. I grabbed a Styrofoam cup of coffee and a small plate of the cafeteria's rock-hard pink cookies and pushed them into Will's hands.

We were greeted, almost immediately, by a tall, plump spinster in her sixties and a small, prissy man a couple of decades younger. The school librarians. Gossip central had arrived.

I reminded myself that I wanted to be around people. Any people.

Janice spoke first in a quiver of jowls. "Jo, don't you look lovely. It's so nice to see you in a skirt."

An unsaid "for once" hung in the air. Janice wasn't shy about voicing her—their—opinion that "the students have a dress code, and so do we". Becky had been the librarians' special project since the day she stepped on campus in Doc Martens and low-slung black jeans, and she avoided both the librarians and the library like the plague.

I usually did too, but with Will on one side of me, the junior librarian mouth breathing on the other, a wall behind and Janice blocking any chance of forward escape, I was trapped. Janice went for me like an evangelist sighting a heathen in the holy land.

"Isn't that sweater *nice* on you, Jo. Green is always handsome with red hair. So much better than that pink you wore the other day. And how nice to see you out of your running shoes. Why you look practically dainty in those tiny heels. I always say, a tall woman shouldn't be afraid of her height. And is this your young man?" She peered nearsightedly up at Will, who had her by a full half a head though she was only an inch shorter than me.

Around us, the crowd was rapidly thinning as parents herded their children to the parking lot and home for the several hours of homework they undoubtedly still had ahead of them. The wealth of opportunities this presented wasn't lost on Will, who was slowly but surely edging me away from the librarians. Reversing tactics, I dug in my feet. The last thing I was going to do was allow myself to be led into a dark corner where I would be alone with Will.

The words tumbled out of my mouth before I could take them back. "Janice, Gilbert, this is Will."

Will's eyes narrowed as he shot an unreadable look in my direction. I felt his body tense next to mine and for a moment, I thought he was going to make a break for it, dragging me with him.

He put down his untouched coffee and then his cookie plate. Smiling widely, he shook hands with both librarians before draping an arm possessively around my shoulders. He smiled lovingly down at my face. "I adore Jo."

Both librarians sighed. Oh God, what had I done? The way these two worked, by morning the whole school would be planning my engagement party.

To a vampire.

Who, as the love of my life and soon to be father of a dozen children (I should be glad they didn't know Will was immortal or it would be twenty dozen children.) would be informed immediately of my whereabouts anytime he showed up.

I was so horrified I broke my own rule and unthinkingly bit into a rock-hard pink sugar cookie.

At the thunderous crunch, Will's gaze slid from the pain-clamped right side of my mouth to the trio of pink sugar cookies on the plate I'd given him.

Our eyes met and held. Moving deliberately, he stretched the hand resting on my shoulder to gently brush pink crumbs from my lips.

Then he turned back to the librarians, who were watching as if we were the most exciting thing since the invention of the printing press. Will's polite smile turned decidedly wolfish.

"What a fascinating play. Jo and I had such a lovely time tonight. She was just taking me backstage to meet some of the actors. If any of them are still around…"

I opened my mouth to protest and choked on the cookie. Will patted me on the back.

"I think Jo needs some air." Voice thrumming with concern, Will steered me out the door and into the cool October night. His arm around my shoulders was as warm, solicitous and solid as a vise.

"I'll walk you to your car." He wasn't offering, he was telling.

There were still plenty of people milling about campus. Will adjusted his pace to maximize the distance between us and the other groups strung along the path.

I stole a glance back toward the theater. From all the excited whispering and surreptitious pointing, the librarians were busy spreading the word about my new boyfriend.

Will turned to see what I was looking at. A wicked smile curved his lips.

"You did that on purpose, didn't you?"

"Ah, she talks. I was beginning to wonder if that 'cookie' had permanently soldered your jaw shut. Why ever did you eat it?"

"I— Why are you here, Will?"

"It's been a while. I've missed you."

He lifted his hand from my shoulder to run a finger lightly down the side of my neck. His touch lingered at my jugular.

I didn't breathe. I couldn't.

He watched me for a moment and then his hand dropped back to drape negligently around my shoulders and he began telling me a story about a recently released movie. As if we really were that image of the happy, normal couple we'd sold to the librarians.

It was a very funny story. Or maybe it was the reassurance of having people in front and behind us on the path as we made our slow way across the grassy quad toward the teacher's parking lot. Somehow, by the time we reached my old boxy gray Volvo, I'd regained my equilibrium.

I dug my car keys out of a pocket and Will gently removed his arm from around my shoulders as if he really were the gentleman he professed to be.

I probably could have jumped in my car and squealed away. Instead I leaned back against the driver's-side door, crossed my arms and faced him.

"What do you want, Will?"

He stepped forward and touched his lips to mine in a light kiss that sent traitorous quivers along my nerve endings.

"I thought that was obvious."

"I see. Absence makes the heart grow fonder? A little trite for someone of your age. How old *are* you, anyway?"

His face lit with a sudden grin. "I have missed you, Josephine Gartner."

A bittersweet pang beat against my chest. Confused, I ignored it. "You didn't come to see the play? The drama kids will be disappointed. They worked so hard littering the town with posters."

"I came to see you. You decided to live in this world." A wave of his hand took in the administration building, the academic quad, and the gym hulking in the distance. His gaze remained fixed on me, suddenly serious. His mouth was drawn down in an abstracted frown. "There's a place for you in…mine, when you want it."

"Is that what you want? To be my boyfriend?"

He smiled. "Are you offering?"

A rusty Toyota idling at the gate pulled out onto the street and I realized with a start that the teacher's parking lot was deserted. So did Will. The air crackled with the awareness between us. He shifted closer. Only a fraction of an inch separated his hard, lithe body and mine.

He said, "'You meet your destiny on the road you take to avoid it.' Carl Jung."

"Better than sitting and doing nothing. Jo Gartner."

He pulled me hard against him and kissed me. I had forgotten how achingly good it felt to be in his arms. I forgot to be scared. Forgot to be discreet.

Chattering voices pealed like warning bells from the path around the side of the administration building. I pulled myself together enough to push Will away.

By the time the group (To this day I have no idea who was in it.) rounded the corner into the parking lot, Will was leaning casually against the SUV parked next to me, gorgeously unruffled, appearing every inch the chivalrous male. He wasn't looking at the group. His midnight gaze was fixed on me. He watched and waited as I somehow fit my key in the lock, got in, started up my car and drove out of the parking lot.

When I looked back, he was gone. Another black shadow in the night.

The fear I had kept at bay came back with a vengeance, shimming down deep into my gut like a filet knife. I reached up a hand to touch my neck. I didn't really think he could have bitten me without my knowledge, but then Will was capable of a lot of things I didn't understand.

The skin was smooth and dry. No new marks.

I pulled up to a stop sign and rested my forehead against the cool vinyl of the steering wheel. "Oh God. Oh God. Oh God."

Someone behind me leaned on the horn. I jolted upright and drove forward. I realized I was cold. Freezing. I started to shiver. My hands shook so bad, I had a hard time keeping them on the wheel.

At the next stop sign, I pulled to the curb to let a couple of impatient tailgaters pass and dug for my cell phone. As soon as my fingers closed around it, the shaking subsided a little and I started driving again. Maybe I should have waited until I was calmer, but I didn't. Movement made me feel less like a sitting duck. But only a little.

I desperately needed someone to talk to and there was only one person—one human—who knew my secret. I hadn't spoken to him in months, but I thought this was a good time to renew our acquaintance. I fumbled with the buttons on my cell phone.

The number rang and rang and finally switched over to a robotic recording saying the number was no longer in service. I jabbed the "end call" button and cursed technology for depriving me of the satisfaction of banging a receiver back on its cradle.

At the next stop sign, I called the main switchboard at the local police station and asked to be transferred to Detective Raines. He answered on the first ring.

"Dammit, Gavin, what the hell do you think you're doing, changing your cell phone number?"

There was a slight pause. "Jo?"

"How the hell am I supposed to reach you?"

"By calling the police station, as you just did."

I hung there in stunned silence. It'd taken me weeks of knowing him last spring to get his personal cell phone number, and I had thought it meant I could rely on him. Apparently I'd misunderstood his willingness to help me. "Why did I think you could help? Goodbye, Detective Raines."

I ended the call and cursed him until I pulled into a parking space right in front of my apartment. Go figure. The night all hell broke loose, I got the number one parking spot. There's the universe in balance for you.

Stifling a noise that was half sob, half slightly hysterical laughter, I grabbed my book bag from the passenger seat and bolted for my apartment. I took the stairs at a run, as if a dozen hungry vampires were after me. Which, for all I knew, they were.

When I got inside, I jittered around, turning on every single light and ended up in the kitchen. I had the freezer open for a full five minutes before I accepted there wasn't any ice cream inside. I slammed it shut, pulled butter and eggs out of the fridge and got to work on comfort food. After a few minutes of alternating nuking and stirring two sticks of butter into a soft fluffy paste, I started to calm down. My hands were almost steady as I measured out white and brown sugar and cracked an egg into the mixing bowl.

I had the first tray of triple chocolate chip cookies in the oven and was almost humming with denial when someone knocked on my door. I glanced at the oven clock. It was after eleven. I wiped batter off my hands on a yellow daisy kitchen towel and went through the small living room to stand in front of the door.

"Who is it?"

"Gavin."

I flicked on the outside light and opened the tiny peephole door that local builders had favored back in the twenties. It was Gavin all right. I re-latched the peephole, and after a short internal debate, let him in.

The last time I'd seen him, long hours and the strain of a murder investigation had aged him so he looked closer to forty than his actual age of thirty. A new man stood before me. He was as trim and fit as ever, but a summer of biathlons had given him what my mother would have called a "healthy glow". He was…relaxed, down to the golden stubble wreathing his jaw.

My summer had been spent cowering indoors, hiding from sunlight. I felt like a pasty, redheaded mushroom and resented every sun-bleached hair on his head.

"Detective," I said, crossing my arms and fighting the urge to drop kick his toned butt back out the door.

"Hello, Jo. Long time no see." He looked at me closely, but as usual his inscrutable light gray eyes gave nothing of his thoughts away.

He sniffed the air and headed, uninvited, for the kitchen. "You're baking cookies."

He pulled out a chair from the small table in the breakfast nook. "I don't suppose that's why you called me?" He turned the chair so he could face me and sat down, stretching his long legs into the kitchen.

# UNDERDEAD IN DENIAL

"No."

The timer went off. I pulled the first batch of cookies out of the oven, transferred half onto an inverted brown paper grocery bag to cool and the other half to a plate. I handed Gavin a napkin and the plate before I realized what I was doing.

I stood frozen at the second horror of the evening. My mother had rubbed off on me.

Gavin picked up a cookie and took a large bite. The chips were still molten and he had to breathe quickly through his open mouth to cool it.

"I was watching the high school drama club's fall production tonight. Will stopped in to say hello."

Gavin swallowed his mouthful of cookie. "I see. Had you invited him?"

I snatched the plate of cookies off the table and plucked the half-eaten one from his hand. "I don't know why I bother with you."

Gavin look mournfully at the cookie plate in my hand. "Really, Jo. You didn't used be this sensitive."

"Oh? And what makes you an authority on my character?"

His face took on a shuttered look. "Nothing." He leaned back in his chair and crossed his arms over his broad, well-muscled chest, suddenly businesslike. "What did Will want?"

I felt myself blush.

"Right. Anything else?"

I gave him *a look*, and I didn't care if it had enough uncontrolled vampire venom in it to reduce him to a pile of ashes. "If you're not going to take this seriously, why don't you leave?"

He held up his hands in surrender. "You're right. I'm sorry."

When he spoke again, he sounded more like the old, worrywart Gavin. "I assume this is the first time you've seen him in a while."

My head dipped in a tight nod. "Since last spring."

He took a small wire-bound notebook out of his jacket pocket and sighed. "Why don't you tell me everything Will said." Fishing out the ballpoint pen that was tucked inside the spiral, he flipped to a blank page.

He'd asked nicely and I was scared enough that the old maxim, "a burden shared is a burden halved" sounded pretty good to me.

Who was I kidding? I would have made him listen if I'd had to tie him up to get his attention.

"Let's see…" As I forced myself to think back over the whole evening without skipping over the more troubling bits, I nibbled on a cookie to calm myself. Gavin was watching me with a funny look on his face and I realized

19

it was the one I'd stolen out of his hand. I put the cookie down, gave him back his plate and, closing my eyes, told him everything I could remember.

"Not much to go on, is it?" he said when I stopped talking.

"No."

Gavin stood, put his empty plate in the sink and looked longingly at the few cookies left cooling on the counter before leaving the kitchen. He did his usual circuit around my tiny apartment, checking all the windows to make sure they were shut and locked. I followed him, trying not to show how nervous I was at the prospect of being alone that night.

"I think it would be a good idea if you got home before sundown, at least for a while. I'll talk to the chief and see if I can't get a couple of uniforms to drive by your place at night."

Officially, Gavin was "visiting" from a small community up north to "learn" investigation techniques from the Long Beach Police Department detectives. Only the Chief of Police, and maybe one or two other necessary people affiliated with the department, such as the coroner, knew Gavin was there to quietly rid Long Beach of vampires, and they all wanted to keep it that way. Whenever a suspicious case came down the pike, the chief made sure it ended up on Gavin's desk.

My apartment, for as much of my meager paycheck that it ate up each month, is absurdly small and in no time at all we'd circled back to the front door. Gavin dug into his back pocket and handed me a card. "My new number's on that. Call anytime."

He fixed his silvery-grey gaze on me for a long, silent moment before he turned to leave.

All at once, my nerves seemed to catch up with me. I caught his arm before he went through the door. He stopped and turned slowly back to face me.

"Do you think I should be worried?" I asked.

The hard grooves of last fall returned to Gavin's face as he dropped the pretense of trying to make me feel better. "Yes."

# Chapter Two

*L*ock your door."

As if I needed to be told. I slid home the deadbolt with enough force that Gavin would be sure to hear it from his car, where he should have been by now if he didn't, at some level, think me incompetent. When the ringing subsided, I heard the soft pad of his running shoes as he turned and headed back down the stairs.

I returned to my warm chocolate-scented kitchen and finished baking cookies, putting them away as they cooled. Precisely one third went into zip-top bags and into the freezer, against future cookie emergencies. The next third went to refilling my Disney villain cookie jar. After I formed the remaining eleven cookies into a pretty, overlapping wreath inside my favorite cookie tin to bring with me to work the next morning, I did dishes.

Every bowl, spoon, measuring cup and sheet pan got a soapy hand wash and towel dry. I put them all away, organizing drawers and cupboards as I went. It wasn't until I found myself clutching a green cylinder of cleanser as if the immediate future of the world relied on my cleaning the grout between the kitchen counter tiles with a toothbrush that I admitted I was a little rattled.

It wasn't just that Will had reappeared in my life. I had known he would, the way one knows things deep inside one's gut. What scared me was *why* he'd returned, now, after all this time.

It had not escaped my notice that vampires, at least the few I'd met, didn't have neck scars from where they'd been bitten. Becoming Undead, apparently, was quite good for the complexion. Come to think of it, I hadn't seen a vampire with so much as a hangnail.

Being Underdead, on the other hand, was crap. Sure I could still go out during the day like a "normal" person. Except that I had to slather on SPF a million and wear so many layers of clothing that a bag lady would chide me for overdoing it. But if I didn't take precautions, in five minutes my skin would be as fried as if I'd lain out from dawn to dusk on a sunny June day doused in baby oil. And it would stay that way. *My* skin didn't have those miraculous vampire powers of recuperation.

It was only recently that the seeping bite marks on my neck—the ones Will had put there last December—had completely scarred over. Why had they healed now, after all this time?

I had told myself the holy water I'd conscientiously dabbed on it every Sunday after Mass (Okay, every *other* Sunday.) had worked its magic. But what if I was kidding myself? What if my neck had finally healed because I was sliding farther along the human-vampire continuum toward the friends-and-family-are-snack side? Was that why Will had shown up tonight at the theater after five months of silence? Because I was no longer balancing on the knife's edge of normal but had crossed some invisible threshold into the vampire world?

I didn't think so. I didn't suddenly feel more…vampish.

I did feel tired. Horribly, bone-weary tired. Stumbling to the bedroom, I kicked off my shoes, tugged off my khakis and sweater and crawled under the covers. I left the lights on.

I was almost asleep when a terrible thought yanked me conscious again. What if I was vampire enough now that Will no longer needed permission to enter my apartment?

Don't be silly, I told myself, wrenching my gaze from the shadowy triangle behind my bedroom door. My eyes drifted back almost immediately and with a huff of irritation that sounded frighteningly like the noise my grandmother made when Gramps left crumbs in the margarine, I got up and pushed the offending door flat against the wall.

On the way back to bed, I grabbed my childhood teddy bear from its ornamental position on the dresser and, wedging myself between it and a baseball bat, fell dead asleep.

By second period the next morning thoughts of vampires elicited no more than a yawn. I'd like to say it was a case of logic triumphing over panic, after all, no vampire could get to me while the sun was up, but I suspect it had more to do with sleep deprivation. That and the Introduction to Chemistry unit.

Blinking hard, I glanced around my classroom at the half-asleep zombies propped cheek on elbow and admitted I needed to do something before someone fell into a coma.

Especially as it might be me. My eighth-grade students weren't the only ones finding it hard to care about the Periodic Table of Elements. I mean, I had a poster of it on the wall. Wasn't that enough to tide over young minds for a few years until Becky got hold of them?

Sigh.

"Okay, let's take a poll." My voice had a jarring note of forced brightness that made the entire front row perk up long enough to switch arms for cheek propping.

I drew a rectangle on the board and scribbled in a seven. Below that I added an N and below that wrote the number fourteen.

"How many of you think there are eight electrons in the second orbital of a Nitrogen atom?"

No one raised a hand and I experienced a small jolt of excitement. After two days of drawing orbitals on the board, they were finally getting it. Hallelujah, we could move on.

"Are you sure?" I taunted, giving them a chance to change their minds. No one did. My enthusiasm was growing like...a balloon in outer space. Already, some part of my brain was beginning to spin out ideas for the upcoming astronomy unit.

"Okay, how about nine electrons? No takers, huh?" I paused, savoring my moment of victory. "Any votes for *seven*?"

No one as much as moved an eyelid.

"How many of you are in my poll?" I demanded.

The morning break bell rang and my students sprang back to life and hustled out of the room. I sank into the hard wooden chair at my desk, put my head in my hands and sighed.

"That's a helluva way to start the school year."

"Go away," I said through my fingers.

"I have coffee."

My classroom door was ajar and a slim hand came through, waggling a giant cup of Peet's.

I grunted and Becky came the rest of the way in. She was, as usual, clad from head to toe in black. Between that and her spiky silver hair, she looked more like a hip Korean high school student than a teacher.

She handed me the cup and I drank down a quarter of it in a single gulp.

"Oh thank God." I was slumped hard against the back my chair, but at least I was upright.

She gave a nonchalant swish of her hand.

"Please. Call me Becky."

I didn't respond and she studied me, frowning. "What is *wrong* with you lately? I swear, you're turning into a cranky old lady and you're only twenty-three."

"Nothing is wrong."

I yawned hard and rubbed my face, snatching my hands away as my fingers began to search for evidence of skin damage commensurate with a new degree of vampire-ness from my sprint to and from the car that morning.

There was no change since the last time I'd checked, twenty minutes ago.

"I'm just tired."

I jerked my chin toward the Wicked Witch of Oz cookie tin atop my book bag on the high, black-topped lab counter at the front of my classroom. Equipped with a sink and gas jets, the counter was designed for lab demonstrations, but more often used as a sort of open air crap drawer. Earth Science doesn't really lend itself to demos. There's only so much baking soda, vinegar and red food coloring you can mix inside a cone before you accept the best way to showcase a volcano's explosive power is to pop in a DVD of Mt. St. Helens blowing its top. Not that that keeps me from stinking up the classroom with as much vinegar as I can heft, but you get my point.

"I made cookies if you want some. Triple chocolate."

For once, Becky ignored the cookie lure and leaned over my desk to examine me more closely. "You look terrible."

"Thanks so much."

"Something's going on with you." Crossing her arms, Becky gave the demo counter a quick, automatic check for spills and leaned against it. "And I think I know what it is."

I started in disbelief. "You do?" It came out as a whisper.

"Yes. Let's look at the symptoms, shall we?" She ticked them off on her fingers. "You haven't gone on a date in months…"

The fact that she hadn't yet heard I had acquired a boyfriend last night—Will—wasn't particularly unusual. Becky's disdain for the school grapevine was legendary. But having forgotten seeing him last night was. I wasn't sure whether I was more alarmed at the idea of Will having secret mind-altering powers or excited by the idea that I might finally have stumbled upon something on the plus side of turning Undead.

Did I have mind-altering powers I didn't know about?

Apparently not.

"You get here at dawn, leave at dusk and spend your weekends sitting alone inside your apartment eating nothing but takeout burgers and chocolate, when you eat at all."

She narrowed her dark almond-shaped eyes and delved into my soul. I swallowed convulsively, unable to look away.

"You've got chronic PMS," she said.

"What? I do *not* have—"

She grinned and then her expression sobered. "I am worried that you're depressed."

I grunted in dismissal.

"Not that I blame you," She looked around my classroom at the solar system dioramas, sagging volcano posters, and dusty mineral display and curled her lip. "Teaching eighth grade earth science would depress anyone. But I have a plan."

"Oh no." I knew her plans. It was because of one of them that I now occupied the strange and lonely world between normal human being and vampire. I sank deeper in my chair and closed my eyes, trying to ignore the sharp bite of disappointment. I longed to tell her—tell her what? I couldn't explain what was really going on. It was too fantastical.

I was too tired today to make one of my usual excuses. Maybe if I fell asleep she'd go away.

"Better yet, I've already set the wheels in motion."

My eyes snapped back open. "Becky, what have you done?"

Her cheery smile vanished under my glare as if someone had pulled a plug and I felt sick. I must have inadvertently given her the vampire stare. I didn't have much control over it. I refused to practice it for fear its use would hasten my slide into permanent vampire territory.

I quickly looked away.

"I signed us up for a charity event."

Becky's voice sounded strange and I sneaked a glance at her from half-lidded eyes. Her zombified look had disappeared once I broke eye contact, so I knew whatever was going on now wasn't to do with me. I struggled to identify the odd note in her voice. Uncertainty?

"We're going to help the Milverne Theatre with their annual fundraiser."

"What?" I sat upright in my chair. "We? Why in the world would I want to do that?"

"Well, first off, it'll get you out of your apartment for a few hours on a Saturday afternoon, which you *desperately* need." The sarcasm was back. I must have imagined the strained note in her voice. "More importantly, it should be fun. It's—" She stopped abruptly.

I stopped fiddling with papers and risked another look at her. She didn't meet my eyes and her cheeks were pink. I forgot about my vampire problems and stared at her in surprise. Then it hit me. Becky, Ms. if-I-believed-in-serious-relationships-I-would-let-my-ultra-traditional-Korean-grandparents-arrange-a-marriage, didn't just have a crush on Drama Dan. She had fallen. Hard.

"Oh no," I groaned. "Not him! Becky!"

Her delicate pixie face turned hard and mulish. Before she could respond, my classroom door flew open and Carol staggered in, out of breath. Carol was the only other person in our department to give Becky competition for best high school teacher. In her mid-thirties, Carol was a plump, brown-haired mother hen who had taken me under her wing when I'd arrived, fresh out of college, to teach at Bayshore last fall. Such sweetness was typical of Carol. I probably would have detested her after five minutes if she hadn't had a sharp sense of humor that had slipped out after only three.

Becky handed Carol the third cup of Peet's.

"Why can't you have a classroom on the ground floor with us?" Carol said between gasps. "Did I miss anything?"

"Just break," I said, eyeing the clock. We had about four minutes until the bell rang. I pointed to the tin on the counter. "I brought cookies, if you want some."

"Of course I want some." As her glasses glinted toward the Wicked Witch tin, she clucked her tongue against her teeth. "One of *those* days, is it?"

"Where were you last night?" I said, a little too harshly.

Carol didn't seem to notice my fishwife impression. She busied herself with the tin. "I'm sorry. I needed to take care of something at home. How was the play?"

She bit into a cookie, rolled her eyes in ecstasy and passed the tin to Becky, who put the tin down without taking one.

"The play was unlike anything I've seen before," I said.

Becky stood half twisted away from us, uncharacteristically quiet and glum, staring unseeingly at the UV-proof blackout blinds over my classroom windows. I chided myself for being such a bad friend. It wasn't as if I had anything better to do tomorrow afternoon. Except sit inside my apartment with the blinds drawn tight and worry about what Will had in store for me.

I told Carol, "You'd better watch Hunchback tonight if you want to join us tomorrow and not feel like an idiot."

Carol reached around Becky for another cookie. Her hand paused over the tin and she muttered, "I might as well slap these right on my thighs." She took one and bit into it. "Damn these are good. What's tomorrow?"

"Becky and I are going to a fundraiser meeting at the Milverne. Wanna come?"

~*~

I got home as the sun was going down, feeling as worn as a limp dishrag. I had given my all to teaching orbitals, and while a commendable number of my students had cottoned to the logic, I knew there was more Introduction to Chemistry in my future. Each step up to my apartment seemed six inches higher than the last.

As I neared the top, a pair of high-heeled shoes came into my line of vision and I looked up to find my mother standing in front of my door. Her suit—made of some silky tweedy material—told me she'd popped by after showing a home. Chances were, she'd sold it too. My mother was a frighteningly good real estate agent.

As usual, even after what I'm sure was a long hard day, she was impeccably dressed and made up. If I weren't so obviously the outdoorsy "before" version of her, I would wonder if the stork had delivered the wrong baby.

I didn't know why she was there, but I was ridiculously glad to see her. I went over to hug her before I realized I couldn't because she was holding a large brown box. As I stood there staring stupidly at the box and wondering why she had brought it, she thrust it into my outstretched arms.

"Here. Your Aunt Bertha would have wanted you to have this."

"Aunt Bertha's dead?" My arms went slack with shock and the box slipped toward the ground.

"Careful!" My mother stuck a manicured hand under the box and pushed it more securely into my arms. "Of course Bertha's not dead. Whatever would make you think that?"

She reached into her huge leather purse and pulled out a key ring that was the duplicate of my own, down to the tiny key to my bike lock. I have no idea how she acquired any of the keys beyond the emergency set I'd given my parents when I'd moved into my apartment. I do know that I'd stolen back every unauthorized key the last time I'd been home.

She unlocked the door with an expert downward jiggle of the key at just the right time. As if she did it every day. She stepped into my tiny hallway and, aware of the growing fall of night, I followed her inside while I debated which issue to tackle first.

I had opened my mouth wide to tackle them all at once when the box in my arms moved.

"Jesus! What the hell is in here?"

"Josephine Gartner! How dare you take the Lord's name in vain!"

I put the box on the floor and squatted next to it. The box hissed. I opened the top flap and a pair of angry green eyes stared back. I quickly closed the box and moved back a respectful number of inches.

"It's Fluffy."

Fluffy was Aunt Bertha's long-haired beast of a cat. Fluffy had a well-earned reputation for loathing everyone but my aunt, who was oblivious to the cat's mean streak. Aunt Bertha doted on her Fluffy-kins.

"Of course it's Fluffy," Mom said.

The box jerked and swayed. A huge white paw scrabbled through the flaps I'd left gaping.

"No, Fluffy! Stay!" I lurched forward and sealed her back in. A box-muffled yowl of frustration filled the air.

"Bertha wants you to take care of her while she's away."

My mother's voice was steel grating on steel. I shifted my attention from the box to her and realized Mom was missing a little of her usual polish. Her pale teal blouse, though impeccably color-coordinated with her hair (Currently some shade approaching crimson via the pink family), was saggy and askew. Her lipstick was hanging in there by sheer willpower.

She still looked gorgeous. Perhaps it was time I took a leaf from her book and tried to dress a little better. Maybe get a haircut that had more than one length to it. I bet Rafael, her beautician, would find a way to fit me if I called him tomorrow morning.

Fit me in? Hell, he'd show up on my doorstep with makeup, hair dye, and an army of clipper waving minions to hold me down while he *re-imagined* me.

The fact that I had considered letting that man within ten feet of my person was disturbing. Obviously, mere proximity to Fluffy addled the brain.

I backed away from the box as if scalded. "I can't have a cat here. I'll get thrown out of my apartment."

"Don't exaggerate. Trust me, it would take more hassle than it's worth for your landlord to evict you."

"Why can't Fluffy stay at your place?"

"Really, Jo, you know how your father is about cats."

My father probably wouldn't notice if Fluffy hawked up hairballs on his lap as long as she didn't interfere with his reading of the newspaper.

"If Aunt Bertha wanted me to take care of her cat, why didn't she ask?"

"I'm sure she tried, but you're never around."

"Exactly! I *am* never around. What kind of life is that for a cat?"

"It's certainly preferable to spending a month in a kennel."

I opened my mouth to protest but I couldn't think of a good rebuttal to that.

A few seconds ticked by and my mother said, "Come down to my car and help me with her things."

Replaying the conversation in my head to try to figure out where I'd gone wrong, I followed as she clicked down the stairs in her three-inch heels without a wobble.

Three trips later, the floor of my tiny living room had disappeared under Fluffy's things. As I dragged an alarmingly heavy bag of cat food into the kitchen and saw how tiny was the bowl Mom was placing on Fluffy's placemat next to my fridge, I started to wonder exactly what she'd roped me into.

"Twenty-five pounds is a lot of cat food. How long did you say Aunt Bertha's going to be gone?"

"Oh, just five or six weeks."

"I thought you said a month!"

My mother's purse vibrated with sudden abandon. She pulled out a sleek phone, looked at the suspiciously dark screen and clucked her tongue in disapproval.

"That offer is far too low. I'd better talk to him in person." She turned and gave me a hug and a peck on the cheek. "Sorry, dear, but I've got to run."

"But…"

She gave me an extra squeeze before letting me go. "I'm so pleased you'll have some company, Joey dear. I do worry about you being so alone."

She disappeared like the wind, leaving me with the cat. I let out a loud sigh. "Damn."

I went back to find a better place for the giant carpeted cat condo than the exact center of the living room, but found I couldn't move it. The cat had parked herself inside and somehow managed to make her fifteen pounds feel like fifty.

Fluffy, it seemed, had moved in.
Great.

~*~

At four o'clock Saturday afternoon, I prepared to head out to meet Becky. The Milverne Theater is a short drive from my apartment, but even so, I was going to be late. It had nothing to do with my new roommate, who didn't appear to have moved in the past twenty-three hours. I might have worried a little had I not noticed a decided dent in the mound of kitty kibbles I'd put in her bowl.

My tardiness was deliberate as, thanks to Will, I no longer had the luxury of spontaneity. I couldn't just walk into a place I'd never been before—not during the day. I had to check it first for perilous health hazards, such as skylights and floor-to-ceiling windows.

Or worse, mirrors. I lived in dread of mirrors. Most people take their reflections for granted. Mine is about as clear as one of those hitchhiking ghosts in the Haunted House ride at Disneyland.

So far, a combination of deception and luck had enabled me to keep my Undead vampire traits a secret. Beyond the occasional weak joke, no one had connected my new "sun allergy" with vampires.

Some of my luck was doubtlessly due to our current hyper litigious, politically correct culture. No one wanted to risk a lawsuit by disrespecting my "disability", so they pretty much turned a blind eye to it. And yet…

If I walked into a room of a thousand people and announced I was turning into a vampire, nine hundred and ninety-nine of them would roll their eyes and keep talking. But that last person might believe me. They'd wonder and ask questions and dig for answers. And when they learned the truth, which they would eventually, I would have no choice but to find Will and beg him to finish the job. My life would be a living hell anyway and at least Will would know where to hide when the people with pointy sticks started after me.

As I tugged on gloves and donned one of my less dorky oversized sunhats, I became aware of an odd, rhythmic grating noise. I stopped dead and listened for the source of the sound before I realized it was emanating from me. Thinking about Will had me grinding my teeth.

After five months of silence, he reappears back into my life, all cryptic warnings and hormone-fanning kisses, and then—nothing. For two nights I'd huddled inside my apartment with all the lights on, eyes and ears trained on the front door. Listening for his footsteps. Waiting for his knock…

"Oh my God!" I said aloud. "He has me waiting by the phone!"

Well, no longer. Grabbing my keys from their dish, I wrenched open the front door and strode out to my car. Ten minutes later, I pulled open one of the thick wood doors of the theater and stepped into the cavernous lobby.

The Milverne was the sort of second-tier landmark that made it onto Long Beach postcards but wasn't quite important enough for the Los Angeles ones. It goes without saying that as a local, I'd driven by the theater a hundred times but never been inside.

I pulled off my hat and sunglasses with a defiant yank and *then* looked around to assure myself there were no mirrors. (The lobby was empty of people, but that was beside the point.)

As I took in the chipping gilt paint, velvet-papered walls and yellowing posters of Hollywood luminaries who'd gotten their start on this very stage, I realized how popular the Milverne must have been in its heyday.

Following the murmur of voices I headed across the faded red carpet to a set of double doors on the right and stepped into the theater. It was smaller than I'd expected, with seating for about five hundred.

The front few rows of the center aisle were filled with attentive volunteers. Becky's spiky silver hair made her easy to spot in the crowd.

"What did I miss?" I whispered as I sank into the plush red seat she'd saved for me.

"Shhh!"

Her attention was riveted on Drama Dan's compact form as he paced the stage soliciting fundraising ideas from the group. A man who looked like a faded copy of Dan was taking notes on a giant pad of paper. If not for the occasional squeak of his marker as he wrote, I would have forgotten he was there.

As I watched Dan, I began to realize that Becky's ridiculous crush might not be so ridiculous after all. Dan Sterling was worth a drool.

I gave myself a mental shake. Evidently my lack of sleep was getting to me.

No. Something about him was different. I studied him critically. He looked the same as he'd looked every day at school for the past month and a half. Same yellow hair, same sky-blue eyes. And yet, there was an undeniable new magnetism to him…

"That's an awesome idea, Shelley! You got that, Tom?"

The guy wielding the marker looked as if the better part of his brain was engaged elsewhere. "Yup. Carnival in the parking lot. Got it right here, next to bake sale in the parking lot."

Dan beamed at the teenage savant in the front row, who blushed crimson with pleasure, and then spun on his heel and headed toward the other end of the stage, arms wide.

"C'mon people, I know each one of you has a good idea. Let's hear 'em all."

I realized that I'd seen Dan in the coffee line at break and Dan at lunch, but never Dan on stage. Today his natural charisma was set to eleven, the better to pull money out of pockets and time out of schedules. And Dan fully "on" was pretty impressive. He was a man made for the stage, the sort of man who could read the back of the cereal box and have women falling at his feet. Men too, if the dog-like expression of adoration on the face of the guy sitting next to me was any indication.

I leaned toward Becky. "Are you sure Dan's straight?"

Becky tore her eyes away from the stage long enough to shoot me a look of disgust.

"Right," I said, barely managing to hide my grin.

My interest in the theater's fundraising plans hovered around zero. Tilting back in my seat, I entertained myself by checking out all the junk tucked in the metal scaffolding overhead. The house lights were up, giving me a new appreciation for the nuts and bolts of putting on a play. There were all sorts of fascinating plugs and lights attached to the bottom of the scaffolding. The scaffolding itself was crammed with what I can only assume were props that didn't fit in the other storage areas—a pair of Doric columns, a pretty good rendition of a larch tree, an anatomically correct David. Directly up over my head were a pair of canoes. The scaffolding must be stronger than it looked.

"There was a canoe in *Tom Sawyer*, wasn't there?"

"Shhh!" Becky said.

The meeting ended a short time later. Becky popped up from her seat like a Jack-in-the-box.

With a quick, "I'll be back," she took off toward the stage. Or, to be precise, toward Dan. Her small form wound quickly through the crowd and when she reached the stage, she somehow displaced the other hangers-on to stand to stand by his side. There was some further conversation and then the whole group tramped off somewhere backstage.

I had no idea where they were going, or why. I gave myself a congratulatory pat on the back for staying out of the whole thing and pulled a stack of papers and a red pen from my bag. The last thing I needed was to get sucked into another thankless, time-sucking activity. Given the time/pay trade-off of teaching, I felt I was doing enough charity work.

I was on my second pile of density labs when Becky returned.

"I volunteered us!"

"Mmm-hmmm. Mass *divided* by volume, Tyler. Sheesh. The stinking formula's right there." I took off three points and looked up at Becky, who was radiating excitement. "Sorry...what?"

"I volunteered us to help out with the haunted house."

"What? Why would you do that?"

"Don't worry. I didn't think you'd want to put in rehearsal time, so I signed you up to collect tickets inside the door."

I opened my mouth to tell her what she could do with her sign-up sheets and realized our discussion was drawing the interest of departing volunteers, including a couple I recognized as Bayshore parents. Later, I promised myself.

Becky thrust a brown paper bag into my lap.

"What's this?"

"Your costume."

I reached into the bag and tugged. The costume kept coming. Yard after yard of black material inlaid with occasional flashes of red. Despite my best intentions to remain indifferent, the idea of dressing up in a real theater costume was making the volunteer job sound kind of fun.

"What did you get for me?" I tried to make sense of the heap of black cloth. "A witch's dress? A bat's wings? A Harlequin?"

A pair of false, pointy incisors tumbled onto my lap.

"You've got to be kidding me," I said weakly.

"You're to collect tickets dressed as a blood-sucking vampire." Becky rubbed her thumbs against her forefingers in the universal sign for money and greed. "Get it?"

She grinned conspiratorially. "With your sun allergy, I bet we can get some of the more gullible students to believe you're the real thing. Ooh! I bet we can rig some sort of trick mirror so you don't have a reflection. Won't that be a hoot?"

"Yeah. Hilarious."

She plunked herself down next to me, dug into her own brown paper bag and held up her costume. There was definitely less of it than mine.

"I'm going to be a sexy Frankenstein's monster and guess who's Frankenstein?" She leaned close and whispered, "Dan!"

I stuffed the vampire costume back in the paper grocery bag, neatly folded the top shut and dumped it on Becky's lap. "No."

"What do you mean, 'no'? The whole point in coming here is to help out."

"Sorry, Becky. I'm just too busy."

All at once, she dropped the bravado. "Please?" Her eyes were pleading. "I can't do this without you. I'll feel like a fool."

This insecure, Dan-smitten person was so unlike the Becky I knew, I couldn't help myself. The words tumbled from my mouth as if pulled by an invisible string. "Oh, all right."

"Great!" She grabbed my wrist and yanked me to my feet. "I'll tell you the details over dinner. My treat."

I glanced at my watch. It was five thirty. Sundown. Time to go home like a good little almost vampire and call Gavin to let him know I was safe. Not that he'd answer his phone and actually talk to me. I would leave a message on his voicemail like I'd done the night before and would continue doing until, what? I grew old and died cowering in my closet?

I turned off my phone and consigned it to the bowels of my bag. "Dinner sounds good."

"Dinner" somehow became a double date at the diner next to the theater. Becky and Dan quickly became completely engrossed in each other, leaving me to make conversation with the Dan copy who'd been on stage flipping pages on the easel.

He was just as forgettable closer up. Our conversation dwindled and died shortly after I learned his name was Tom and he was indeed another member of the Long Beach Players, the acting company that performed at the Milverne Theater.

I ate slower than a snail crawls on dry pavement just for something to do. After what seemed as if days had passed, the waiter finally came by to take our plates.

"Hey guys, how about dessert?"

The look I gave him sent him back a pace.

"I'll have the, um…apple pie," Becky said, tearing her attention from Dan long enough to glance at the laminated dessert menu on the table next to the catsup.

I knew for a fact that Becky hated apple pie. I jabbed her sharply under the table.

"Ow!" She rubbed her side and scowled at me.

"I'm sorry. Did I get you?"

"Decaf for me," said Dan.

Tom frowned slightly and ordered bottled water. "It's important for actors to keep their vocal cords moist. Most people eat far too much sugar and don't take proper care of their vocal cords. For instance, a teacher like you should drink *at least* eleven glasses a day. I'll bet you—"

"One Death by Chocolate, please," I told the waiter. I didn't need to look at the dessert menu. I'd memorized it an hour ago.

"Sorry, we're out."

"Of course you are. Got any Murder by Ice Cream? Hari Kari Killer Cake? Fudge Oblivion?"

The waiter shook his head. "I'm sorry, you must be thinking of another diner. Maybe you'd like a Chocolate Avalanche sundae? It's pretty popular. It has brownie crumbles on top."

"Milk products are bad for vocal cords," Tom said.

I ordered the Chocolate Avalanche with extra brownie crumbles and hot fudge sauce.

I wondered if anyone would notice if I disappeared under the table and escaped. Probably not. Becky and Dan were so absorbed in one another that Martians could beam down inside the diner, waving anal probes, and they wouldn't notice. And Tom was so enthralled by his own conversation that, by the time he realized no one was punctuating his pauses with an occasional "Really?", "You don't say" or "How interesting", I could be halfway home.

I shifted experimentally in my seat and realized the glory of crawling to freedom through limp and dusty French fries, straw wrapper curls and Coke spills would be denied me. I'd sat in something sticky and the booth's cheap red pleather trapped me like flypaper.

"And that's when I joined my high school drama club," Tom said.

"Really? How very interesting."

Our waiter reappeared with our dessert orders. In front of me he placed a giant glass packed full of chocolate ice cream and oozing hot fudge. The brownie bits were packed so high atop the mound of whipped cream I couldn't see over the top. Picking up my sundae spoon, I took a small, tentative bite of Chocolate Avalanche.

"Oh my God." I immediately shoveled in a larger spoonful. As the heat of my mouth fused the rich hot fudge sauce with the sweeter chocolate of the ice cream, I passed Tom my unused dinner spoon. "Best dessert ever. You have *got* to try this."

"I'm fine with water," he said with a quick glance at Dan's decaf. "My vocal chords…"

I realized Tom had stopped talking and was looking at the sundae the way my mother looked at jewelry store windows.

"So, Tom, do you have any hobbies?" I asked.

He was so absorbed in watching me dig through the whipped cream to the hot fudge that his mouth parted a little as I took another bite.

Tom picked up his water bottle, took a sip and tried to collect himself. He lost the battle as soon as my spoon dipped back into my sundae glass.

"Actually I do." His voice was soft and conspiratorial. "On the weekends, I like to get up early, really early and..."

"Yes?" I prompted, looking up from arranging the perfect Chocolate Avalanche bite on my spoon. I realized I actually wanted to know what this boring man did, really early, on Saturday mornings that was so secret he hesitated to tell me about it.

Tom forcibly shifted his gaze from the sundae to me. And then he leaned closer, unaware his sleeve was resting in a pool of fudge sauce.

"I go to garage sales," he told me. "And last weekend I found—"

I took another bite of Chocolate Avalanche. His mouth clamped suddenly shut. He was so close I could see a pale pink flush spread across his face. His eyes glittered with deeply buried excitement.

"What did you find?" I asked, putting my spoon down. This rapt attention as I ate my dessert was a little unnerving. I didn't know why he didn't just order one of his own and be done with it. His lean frame could easily handle a few more pounds.

As if I'd spoken the criticism aloud, his attention shifted firmly away from my sundae. His eyes met mine. His voice was low, a hum of excitement strung into words.

"An unfinished script. Some guy inherited his late father's house and dumped all the junk his family had collected over the years onto the lawn for sale. Crates and crates of *National Geographic*. Newspapers from the 1960s. And then I found a box of junk, like someone had pulled out a desk drawer and dumped in the contents without looking. There were scraps of paper and leaky pens and a couple of half-full boxes of envelopes...and then, the script! I haven't had time to read more than a few pages, but it could be a lost masterpiece. People find them all the time at garage sales. The poor dumb fool didn't even realize what he was selling."

"Really? What's the playwright's name? Anyone I might have heard of?"

"Solaire. I doubt you'd have heard of him. He didn't actually publish any plays..." Tom's upper lip curled in a sneer, as if publishing one's work was selling out.

My enthusiasm waned. I was pretty sure there was a poor dumb fool in the scenario, and it wasn't the garage sale guy who'd made a cool ten dollars off the contents of his grandfather's junk drawer. But it was better than listening to more sleep-defying stories about Tom's serpentine path to becoming a professional actor.

I opened my mouth to ask him more about garage-sale treasure hunting when a hand clamped down on my shoulder, pinning me to the bench. My stomach clenched and my lungs stopped working. Every thought left my head except for one—the sun had set two hours ago. And I was outside the safety of my apartment. I twisted slowly around and came eye-to-stomach with Gavin.

# Chapter Three

---

**J**o Gartner. What a delight running into you here, just as I've been trying to get you on your cell."

I shrugged Gavin's heavy hand off my shoulder and struggled to my feet.

My voice matched his in fake charm. "Gavin. How lovely to see you. And on a Saturday night. What a surprise." I swept a smile over the table. "If you'll excuse me a minute. Let's go chat at your table, Gavin. You're in the wait staff's way."

I grabbed Gavin by the sleeve and pulled him away before Becky came out of her Dan trance enough to invite the detective to join us. I didn't slow until we were out of hearing range. "Where *is* your table?" I asked, looking around.

Gavin put a hand to my back and steered me out of the dining area and into the waiting area at the front of the restaurant. The early bird diners had finished and gone home and the next dinner shift was in its infancy so we were the only occupants besides a couple of high schoolers, who were using the wait time to get a jump on the after dinner make-out session. I gave them an automatic once-over, but I didn't know them.

"What the hell do you think you're doing?" Gavin positioned himself with his back to the wall and managed to glare down at me even though he was only a couple of inches taller.

"Me? What about you?" I looked him up and down. He was wearing comfortably broken-in jeans and a Long Beach Marathon t-shirt with a long-sleeved tee underneath. The slight jog in his nose from an old break that hadn't healed quite right kept him from being strictly handsome. But he looked…good. Very good, as a matter of fact. I couldn't help thinking bitter thoughts about the way my life was going. The only thing my "date" wanted to be alone with tonight was my sundae and Gavin had never thought of me as anything more than an annoying chore on the order of filling out tax forms.

"You're not on duty." I stepped around him to go back to my booth before my sundae melted and all joy was taken out of the evening. "I don't have to answer your questions."

Gavin put a hand on my shoulder to stop me. "I'm always on duty."

The hostess returned to her station and regarded us curiously. Gavin ignored her and shifted closer so we couldn't be overheard. "I thought you were scared to be back on Will's radar." His voice drummed low and tight in my ear. "And yet I find you out after sundown eschewing safety precautions and I have to wonder—"

He bit off the rest of the sentence and studied me carefully. I felt as if I were being pulled apart and evaluated piece by piece. And found lacking.

"Wonder what?" I demanded.

"Do you know what time it is?"

"No. Wonder *what*?"

"It's eight o'clock. You were supposed to call me over an hour ago to check in, remember?" He scrubbed a hand over the back of his neck. Gavin kept his brown hair cut short and I could hear the soft scratchy noise as the little hairs rubbed against each other. "I don't like it any more than you do, but it's a decent system. It works."

Little fingers of guilt let the air out of my sails. As Gavin was leaving my apartment on Thursday night, we had agreed to reinstate the system we had set up last winter when it seemed I had half the population of Long Beach gunning for my hide. And Gavin was right. It was annoying to the point of insult to have to check in with him each night, as if I were a little kid instead of an adult. But it had saved my life.

"I'm sorry," I said, and meant it. "I didn't mean to worry you."

"That isn't the point. Shit, Jo. Get some common sense, here. It's not safe for you to be out alone at night. Not anymore. And before you tell me you're fine because you're with a group, isn't that your car parked right out front? Why not just stick a 'Come get me, I'm in here' sign on it?"

I whipped around, half expecting to see a half dozen vampires waiting by my car, ready to take me out.

Right. As if I had the slightest chance of distinguishing a vampire from anyone else who happened to be in the parking lot. From my experience, vampires looked just like everyone else, until the pointy fangs popped out. And when that happened, it was already too late to run.

Gavin was right. I'd let my frustration get the better of my common sense. Will wasn't just *a* vampire, he was the local leader. If he'd retaken an interest in me, I was on all his minion's radars. And, as had been made abundantly clear to me last spring, not all the interest was positive. A motivated vampire could run me over with a car or pull the trigger on a gun just as well as anyone else.

I needed to be more careful. I wouldn't get the advantage of a warning. Unless the vampire coming after me was Will. I always knew when he was nearby by my hormone fluctuations. And besides, Will didn't skulk. If he wanted something, he took it. Me, for example? Is that what he wanted? To finally finish the job he'd started?

I shoved my dark thoughts away. Gavin was just being melodramatic to make a point. I was perfectly safe. No one would think to look for me in a restaurant I'd never been to before.

"How did you find me?" I asked.

"Your car. Parked right out front. Under," he pointed with a tanned finger, "a street light."

There went that theory. My teeth started to chatter. I bit down hard so he wouldn't notice and then my hands began to shake.

Gavin's gaze dropped to my hands. He took a half step closer.

"Gavin!"

I turned to see a pretty brunette heading our way and realized with a start that Gavin was on a date.

"Brady's on shift all night," Gavin said quickly. "Give him a call at the switchboard when you're on your way home and he'll send a patrol out to walk you to your door." It wasn't a request, but an order. I bristled, but didn't want to argue in front of his…girlfriend?

I didn't wait to be introduced (I was business, after all, not a social acquaintance.) but headed back into the seating area. I almost looked forward to the mind-numbing boredom of trying to have a conversation with Tom again.

Dropping back into my sticky booth seat, I picked up my spoon and blindly plunged it into my sundae glass. The Chocolate Avalanche would go a long way toward soothing my nerves. My spoon came up empty.

"It was melting and I didn't want it to go to waste," Tom said, looking happy and relaxed for the first time that evening.

I gave him a look so dirty he didn't say a word for the next ten minutes.

By the time Becky was ready to go, a long joyless hour later, Gavin and his date were gone.

Tom made me pay for the sundae.

# Chapter Four

H elp me!" Becky entered my classroom at a jog and shoved a plate of orange-brown blobs under my nose.

"What are these?" I picked one up. It was remarkably heavy for something a little wider than a quarter. "A density experiment?"

"I made ginger cookies last night. What do you think?"

I raised the cookie and opened my mouth to take a bite.

Carol, following in behind Becky, opened her eyes wide in horror at the sight of the cookie on its way to my mouth and violently shook her head in warning.

I lowered the cookie and looked at it more closely. It resembled a soft hunk of sandstone. I rapped it sharply against my demo table. And there the sandstone resemblance ended.

"I think it dented the table," I said incredulously, rubbing a finger over the spot where the table and cookie had collided. "What possessed you to do this to a cookie?"

Becky put her hands over her face and peered at us through her fingers. "I don't know," she moaned.

Carol and I exchanged a glance over her head. This behavior—the attempt at domesticity and the self-doubt—was so unlike Becky that neither of us knew what to say. Carol put a motherly arm around Becky's shoulders.

"It was nice of you to bring them, Becky." As Carol said that, she surreptitiously slipped the cookie half in her free hand into the trash.

"What, um, made you decide to bake last night, Becks?"

Becky shrugged and started picking at a dusty model of Saturn that one of my students had made last fall for the astronomy unit. It was one of my better classroom props, but as Jim Baxter had liked glue and shellac as much as he liked Saturn, I let her pick.

"This your way of saying you're getting tired of my cooking?"

I wasn't sure how I wanted Becky to answer that question. Nearly two

41

weeks had passed since Will had suddenly reappeared in my world and I hadn't seen him since. The stress of waiting and constantly looking over my shoulder would have turned me into a crazy person if I hadn't started baking like one. Cookies, brownies, cakes, mousses...if it contained chocolate, I'd made it.

I had also eaten it. My lust for chocolate had, if anything, increased since I'd become Underdead. At the rate I was "testing" my baked goods, I'd soon have to bump up my running to five miles daily or shop for larger clothes. As it was, I barely had time for my three-mile running loop between sunrise and the time school started. And I hated shopping. Hated. They do not design clothes with tall people in mind. Cute on a five-foot-two woman is not at all attractive stretched out on my five-foot-ten frame.

"God no. I love everything you make. It's just that..." Becky's face suddenly crumpled in misery. "On Dan's site it says they're his favorite cookies."

"You've been stalking his blog," I said incredulously.

"I knooow! What's wrong with me? I'm so pitiful."

"No, *that's* normal." I scowled at the lumpy blob in my hand. "Your cookies are what's pitiful."

"Becky, you know you don't need to impress Dan with cookies," Carol said firmly. "You are smart and beautiful and a wonderful person."

I agreed and said so. Becky nodded but she didn't look convinced.

She looked panicked.

"Oh, for crying out loud." I rolled my eyes. "If it's that important, *I'll* make them for you."

It was hardly selfless. It would help me pass the time in a non-chocolate and thus non-fattening way, until I had to show up at the theater tonight for the "dress rehearsal" for the haunted house. We were having a test-run for friends, family and anyone who had noticed our ad in the local free paper. The big crowds would start tomorrow—Thursday—when the early Halloween guides came out in the daily papers. In Southern California, Halloween season ran from mid-October to the end of the month, and the Milverne was taking full advantage of the trend.

Becky sniffed back a tear. Another thing I'd never seen her do. "Thanks, Jo."

Carol crossed her arms over her twin set-clad chest and gave me a disapproving over-the-top-of-her-glasses look. "You're helping her? I am washing my hands of the both of you."

"Oh come on, Carol. You would do the same thing except your cookies aren't any better."

Carol tightened her coral-colored lips and harrumphed.

"What time is it?" Becky looked up at the clock over my whiteboard and let out a gasp. "I'm late! Dan wants us there at four for our pre-dress rehearsal run-through."

"It's barely three," I protested to her departing back.

"Becky is going early so she can primp," Carol said. "*Becky.*"

"Don't look at me like that. It's just cookies. She's fine." I stepped out into the hallway in time to hear Becky muttering to herself about needing to stop by the mall for more makeup as she pushed through the door onto the landing. I turned back to Carol, who didn't say anything. She didn't have to. "I've helped create a monster, haven't I?"

~*~

Looking in the mirror of the women's dressing area at the back of the theater, I adjusted my black sateen bodice for the fifth time and finally accepted that it wasn't going to go any higher. There was not a doubt in my mind that my Halloween costume had been designed by a male. A filthy-minded male who had watched way too many bad Hollywood vampire movies.

"I can't go in public like this," I muttered, wondering if it was too late to come down with food poisoning.

"Did you say something?" Next to me, Becky, dressed in what looked like scraps of old army togs, leaned forward and smudged on ghoulish black circles under her eyes with black eyeliner. She widened her eyes, squinted, and widened her eyes again. "This mirror sucks! I can't see a darn thing. It's like putting on makeup by Braille."

"It's not so bad." That was a lie.

While Becky had been in a final pre-haunted house meeting with the rest of the "cast", I'd sneaked into the tiny "guest star" dressing room Becky had nabbed for us and swapped out the pair of hundred watt bulbs with a single forty-watter. I'd also rubbed a thin layer of cheap hand cream on the mirror. It was an effective trick—usually. The brand of hand cream I'd brought was new and untested in this capacity. Instead of being merely blurry, our reflections had gained a wavy quality. It was a little like looking in a fun house mirror.

She tugged a piece of her sleeve down over her elbow and rubbed at the mirror.

It didn't help. Glass cleaner might have done the trick, but there wasn't any in the building. I'd made sure of it.

"Please," Becky said. "It's almost as bad as that crap mirror in the girl's room by your classroom."

I kept an industrial-sized tub of lotion hidden in a cupboard in my classroom, just for that mirror. The janitorial staff and I were in a constant secret battle over the state of the mirror. Mr. Rushall, the aged janitor, came by regularly to my classroom to take a breather and complain about how it mysteriously fogged up all the time and I listened and guiltily fed him cookies.

With a grumbled curse, Becky gave up on the mirror and rooted around in her bag for her compact.

"Ocean air is hard on mirrors," I said lamely, aware that at a mile from the coast, the ocean air would have negligible caustic effect. Especially on a mirror in a small room in the bowels of the theater.

She turned to me with a what-kind-of-scientist-*are*-you? look but her scowl disappeared as she took in what the underwire bustier was doing for my cleavage. Or rather, what all the chocolate I'd been eating lately had accomplished, once it had been redirected from around my waist into my bra cups by virtue of tight corseting.

"Wow, Jo, you look great. Here, turn around."

I did and she wolf-whistled. "See? Look at how good you look when you're wearing something sexy instead of those shapeless khakis and button down shirts you always wear to work."

"I teach eighth graders. No one cares what I wear to work."

"You keep telling yourself that."

"Oh come on, Becky. Who even notices what I wear? Besides you. And the Bayshore librarian dress code police. Though you're hardly on the same page."

Becky made a noise of disgust at my mention of the librarians. "Trust me. The students notice and care what you're wearing. Are you going to tell me you didn't make fun of your teachers' outfits? Look me in the eye and tell me you don't secretly keep count of the number of plaid golf shirts Don Goodman has in rotation."

Three, my brain immediately supplied. It was bad, even for a math teacher.

"And what about when you leave school? What if you run into some hot guy in the supermarket on the way home, and you're wearing Dockers and your hair's in that stupid bun with disgusting classroom pencils sticking out the back? Speaking of which..."

She reached up and yanked at my hair. I dodged her hands.

"Stop it! Why do you always do that? It hurts."

"Well, let your hair down. You look like you're hosting a schoolmarm version of The Weakest Link. Or like you're going for dominatrix teacher of the year. Actually, that's not so bad, if you want to become the newest fantasy in the high school boy's locker room."

"That's disgusting." I pulled the remaining two giant bobby pins out of my hair and down it all came. I have a lot of hair, which is part of why I keep it up most of the time. It wasn't a bun so much as a hair restraint system. "Fine. You win."

Grinning smugly, Becky leaned toward the mirror and added another coat of mascara to her lashes. "By the way, you never said—what happened with that incredibly hot guy sitting next to you at the play the other night? He looked familiar."

Great. Just when I thought I was out of the water, Becky comes out of her Drama Dan hormone fog and remembers Will.

"Huh. No idea." I pulled a disposable plate, piled high with cookies, out of my bag. "Here are the gingersnaps you made Dan. I gotta go. I'm supposed to be manning the door to make sure no one sneaks into the haunted house before it opens at seven."

I headed for the door in a swirl of black cape. It was long and heavy with a silky crimson lining and I couldn't help but feel oddly powerful in it. If some little punk thought he could get by me tonight, he had another think coming.

"Hold on! You forgot these."

I turned, and with a fumble of hands, managed to catch the object Becky threw at me. Immediately, I wished I'd missed. It was the plastic vampire teeth.

"Thanks."

I stood stupidly for a moment, wondering what to do with them. I was *not* putting them in my mouth. My costume didn't have pockets. Not that I could have put anything in them if it had. The tight black satin shorts were just as form-fitting as the bodice.

Holding the teeth by an incisor, I headed down the hallway toward the shallow staircase leading down to the theater. Any noise coming from the tiny one or two person dressing rooms was dwarfed by all the giggling and chattering in the large community style women's dressing room. Though to be fair, the volume from the men's changing room at the other end of the hall was just as loud.

The door to the women's changing area was open, and as I passed I was greeted with a few wolf whistles from Bayshore students.

"Go Ms. Gartner!"

"Woo woo!"

I paused in the doorway. I recognized nearly everyone inside, either from working with them the past couple of weekends constructing the haunted house or because they were students. A few amateur thespians were industriously packing on makeup and adjusting costumes, but most everyone inside was killing time before the event. Fast-food bags and drink containers littered most surfaces and someone had brought in a platter of supermarket cookies to share.

The Bayshore Academy was a small school and I knew most of the teenagers in the room by sight, if not by name. "Hey, girls, you all set?"

Heads nodded. "Oh, yeah."

"We've got cookies if you want some," someone offered.

"We're going to scare the pants off people. I bet Conner Wong twenty bucks we'd get more people than the boys."

Conner was the high school drama club's co-president.

"How're you going to keep count?" I asked, curious.

"Screams."

"Number of people wetting their pants."

"That'll work." Laughing, I continued on down the stairs.

I realized I was having a good time. The hum of excitement backstage before a performance, even for a silly haunted house, was infectious. Instead of continuing down the corridor to the lobby, I hooked a left into the theater.

The Long Beach Players, with the considerable help of an enthusiastic volunteer crew, and some less enthusiastic volunteers dragged along by their lovesick friends, had done an amazing job transforming the space into a haunted house. If I hadn't been there to see the theater disassembled, I never could have imagined how impermanent every part of it was. The whole audience seating area had been cleared in about an hour. Each row of seats was set on a movable platform, and it was only a matter of flipping a few security bars and rolling row after row of velvet seats into a storage space under the stage.

From another storage area had come dozens of plywood sets, of which they seemed to have an endless supply. They used these to mark the haunted house's route, which started at the double doors off the left side of the lobby, wound through the theater in a meandering horseshoe-shaped path, and ended at the theater double doors on the right.

The path itself was varied, alternating eerie narrow passageways and wide room-like sections that housed the usual selection of scary dioramas. Coffins with dead bodies popping back to life. Cackling witches swirling cauldrons full of dry ice. Ghosts that materialized out of walls, or in this case, from behind opaque black sheets that, in the dim light, looked like walls.

And then, because this was a playhouse and actors couldn't just let stuff be, there were little vignettes along the way. Becky and Dan's Frankenstein bit was one example. Dan, dressed in a lab coat and a fright wig, would "zap" Becky to life, and then as she got up, zombielike, off her lab table to go get Dr. Frankenstein another body from the crowd to experiment on, the tour guide would hurry the group along to the next thing. Along the plywood lined route, they'd left hidden gaps big enough for actors dressed as various ghouls and goblins to randomly pop in on the groups, waving things like death scythes, axes and absurdly large knives.

They'd deliberately worked some of the Bayshore drama club kids into the act. My favorite was when a student pretending to be a regular paying customer got eaten by a giant spider, only to get spit back out at the end of the haunted house.

It probably would have taken regular people weeks to set up and rehearse something of this magnitude, but for this group, putting on a haunted house was like holding an improv night, only more fun because they got to scare the audience. Over and over. The last groups of the night would be in for it.

I walked through slowly, delighting in the fact that I was in a position to see the proverbial zippers in the monster suits. As I reached the start of the haunted house, I threw the vampire teeth into a witch's cauldron "steaming" with dry ice and pushed through the double doors into the lobby.

The moment I appeared, Marty Milverne, the portly third-generation owner of the theater and acting House Manager, summoned me over with an agitated wave of his arm and a loud sigh of relief.

"Good, you're here."

I hadn't quite decided if Marty was the glue that held the Milverne together or a tornado threatening to tear it apart. Probably a little of both. Holding a checklist in one plump hand, he looked me up and down. His brow wrinkled under what was either a terrible haircut or a cheap toupee.

"What are you supposed to be?"

"A vampire."

"Where are your teeth?"

I made a show of patting myself down looking for them. "I don't know. I must have lost them somewhere."

"That's okay. We have tons in the back. In fact…" He went behind a desk and rummaged in a drawer. "Here we go."

He held out a fresh pair of plastic vampire teeth, identical to the ones I'd tossed into the witch's cauldron.

"A Halloween costume store donated all their leftover stock to us for the tax break. Unfortunately, most of what they had left was teeth. We had so many bags of them we gave them away as door prizes when we did Dracula last year. Did you see it? Excellent reviews. Well, put 'em in. Let's see how you look."

I fit the plastic vampire teeth over my own and gave him a weak smile.

"Perfect." All at once, his roly-poly form came violently to life. Legs shaking, body quivering, he reared back in an owl-eyed travesty of fear.

I understood now why he was behind the desk and not on stage. Chortling in delight, he dropped the pose, winked and proceeded to remind me in painstaking detail exactly what my duties were.

I couldn't possibly have forgotten anything since his equally lengthy instruction the night before but there was no way of stopping him.

I tried anyway. "They pay for the tickets outside and come in here to wait. When the next tour guide is available, he or she will come through the doors to collect the next group. I take tickets and let no more than fifteen people through at a time."

"Exactly. Now, you must be sure to not let any more than fifteen through, otherwise, we might have stragglers, or some won't be able to see the tableaux, or…"

Why had I bothered? I was trying to maintain a look of rapt attention, lest he feel the need to start over, when a loud, shrill scream came from somewhere in the haunted house.

Marty glanced at his watch.

"Final rehearsals, right on schedule." He rubbed his hands excitedly. "This is going to be good. Look!"

One of the theater's ornate front doors was propped open, giving Marty a view of the box office outside. He pointed at the crowd gathering behind a velvet rope.

"Did you see that? The girl at the front practically fainted at the scream. If all goes well tonight, that crowd will come back again tomorrow." His voice rose an octave. "And bring all their friends. This is going to pull in more money than a Rodgers and Hammerstein musical!"

Humming to himself, he crossed the lobby, moving remarkably fast on feet too small for his embonpoint frame. In his flapping black suit, he looked a little like one of those cartoon penguins when they do that sprinting tiptoe thing. Throwing open the other outer door with a flourish, he worked the crowd for a few minutes until it was precisely seven o'clock, and then let them in. The first ones came at a run.

I positioned myself behind a velvet rope strung a few feet in front of the double doors leading into the haunted house.

"Stay here. A tour guide will—" I forgot I still had the fake teeth in my mouth. I pulled them out. The saliva that had puddled in the incisors sprayed out in a wide arc that effectively stopped the crowd.

There was a brief moment of shocked silence and then someone said, "Eew!"

I grinned. "If that's more than you can handle, you might as well go home right now."

A couple of young high school boys near the front made barking military noises of man power and stepped to the front. Just then, the doors opened behind me and Tom, my erstwhile double date, stepped slowly out. If he noticed me, he didn't show it. I wasn't sure whether to be insulted or relieved.

The crowd quieted a little. He was dressed impeccably in top hat and tails. His shirt and gloves were gleaming white and his black patent shoes shone like they'd been rubbed with Vaseline, which they probably had. The only thing marring the look was his face, which had been made up to look like a zombie. He had deep circles under his eyes and his freckles were hidden under a convincing three-day-underground pallor. He scanned the crowd and a flapping hunk of flesh nearly fell off his face. By some miracle of makeup—probably involving crazy glue—it held. When he spoke, his voice was slow and as low as a foghorn.

"Come with me."

Without looking back, he walked stiffly through the doors. I collected fifteen tickets and re-hooked the velvet rope. A short time later I heard fifteen people scream.

In a few minutes, the next "tour guide" lurched out from behind the double doors in a halting crab-like step, hunched over and dressed as Igor— the Young Frankenstein variety. Ian was one of the principals at the theater. I knew him only slightly but wasn't surprised he'd had gone the comic route. He was the class clown of the theater group, always playing the jokester in any production.

"Walk this way," he said, and scuttled back toward the door. He gave me an exaggerated, lascivious wink and disappeared inside. A couple of eleven-year-olds near the front mimicked his hunchback impersonation and the rest of the crowd followed.

The third and last tour guide was female, dressed as a witch. Or rather, like Marcia Brady dressing as a witch. Frankly, my outfit, which, truth be told, was only recognizable as a vampire costume by the fake teeth, looked almost professional next to hers. I recognized her immediately as Angelina James, the lead female in the company, but she wasn't wasting any of her acting skills on a haunted house. She came out, collected her group, and led them inside. I might have been invisible.

By the time the three tour guides had cycled round again, the crowd was straining against the ropes. It looked as if Marty wouldn't have to wait until everyone went back to school and work tomorrow for word to get out. The cell phones were doing the job.

As I re-hooked the velvet rope, someone tried to shove their way forward enough to guarantee a spot in the next group. The crowd heaved and a kid at the front of the line went sprawling at my feet. I helped him up, invited him to wait on my side of the rope and, furious, faced the crowd.

I crossed my arms and raised my voice, which from years of yelling to teammates across soccer fields, basketball courts and running tracks was loud enough to be heard clear out to the back of the lobby. "All pushing will *stop!*"

You could have heard a pin drop.

For a moment, I reveled in my success. And then I realized what I had done. I'd used my vampire glare. Not just on one person, but on a whole crowd. That vampire power was popping out of me with unsettling regularity of late, but I'd never done it to so many people before.

I quickly turned away to break the spell. And found myself staring into the mirror that hung on the wall next to me.

As I stared into it, the crowd disappeared. My stomach clenched and couldn't seem to draw air into my body. My reflection wasn't just dim, it was gone. Completely.

It had happened. I'd turned.

A squeaky voice at my elbow said excitedly, "Cool mirror. How do they do that?"

The boy I'd pulled up from the floor was pointing excitedly at the mirror. "Look, I've disappeared."

My breath flooded back with a sudden whoosh.

"Trick mirror," I whispered. I'd forgotten.

The door opened behind me and zombie Tom waltzed out for his next group. I had to try twice to unlatch the velvet rope before the mechanism opened properly, but by the time I'd taken fifteen tickets I had myself back under control.

Marty came through the crowd and stepped around the barrier to stand beside me. I could almost see the dollar signs in his eyes as his gaze roved over the crowd.

"This is going so well!" Dropping his voice and leaning in closer, he said, "Another night like this and we'll be able to hire more equity actors and take the Playhouse to the next level." His beaming smile faded abruptly. "No, no, no! Where are your vampire teeth?"

I schooled myself not to look in the corner where I'd tossed them. "I took them out to talk and they must have fallen off the desk."

"Well, we'll just get you another set!"

Stepping behind the desk, he rummaged through a drawer for another pair. Handing them to me, he waited expectantly for me to put them in.

I didn't. "Really, Marty, I'd prefer not to wear them. They're uncomfortable and they make it very hard to talk.

The genial host disappeared. "You're part of the haunted house experience, Jo. The face of it. The front man. The first person everyone sees. You set the tone for the whole thing." He stabbed a finger toward the reflection-free trick mirror. "People want to see a vampire."

I closed my eyes so he wouldn't see them roll. Reminding myself this was for charity, I put in the teeth.

He opened his arms wide. "There! Now you look like a proper vampire."

All at once, goose bumps rippled down my arms and the sweat froze on the back of my neck.

"Indeed," said a low voice, behind me. "The fangs and cape give it verisimilitude. Without them, who would know?"

Slowly, I turned around. Will, wearing black Armani, leaned negligently against the will-call desk. A wide smile cut grooves into his lean cheeks and his blue eyes gleamed with laughter. He was positioned in front of a small gilt mirror—a real one.

I was the only one who seemed to notice that he didn't reflect. At all.

I had never seen Will near a mirror. I had just assumed from my own reflecting issues that that part of vampire lore was true. Having my theory confirmed was hardly vindicating.

Marty said to me, "See? *He* gets it."

I ignored him. How had Will gotten *in* here? As if in answer, the singsong voice of the volunteer manning the box office rang through the lobby. "Thank you, here's your change. Go in and be haunted!"

Will was saying something in a low voice to Marty. I was moving forward to intercede when my step was frozen by the prick of something sharp against the base of my neck. A musky perfume hit me like a blast of ammonia.

"All it would take is one swipe," a soft female voice whispered in my ear. It was the voice of my nightmares. "By the time anyone in this crowd realizes you aren't playacting, you'll have bled to death on the floor."

"Will would know." The husky timbre of fear in my voice belied my brave words.

The prick pushed deeper into my neck and hovered, vibrating, at the exact point of breaking skin.

"You're lucky Will protects you."

With a little shove, she let me go. I whipped around to face her.

Natasha. If a horny twenty-five-year-old male were to imagine a vampire seductress, Natasha would be it. She was curvy—very—in all the right places, somehow managing to be both long legged and petite. Tonight she wore a black, barely there dress and strappy stilettos that left no one in doubt of those curves. Her long, streaky blonde hair was tousled into artless perfection that normal people could only achieve with the help of a skilled hairdresser. The only things marring the picture were her eyes. They were as cold and hard as ice.

Nothing and no one scared me more than Natasha. Will might have bitten my neck last fall, but since then I'd seen something…honorable…in him. A throwback kernel of gentlemanly conduct. It might just be wishful thinking, but I didn't believe he would look me in the eye and stick a knife in my back.

Natasha, on the other hand, would do it in a heartbeat. If she could get away with it.

To the gasping delight of the teenage boys at the front of the line, Natasha was adjusting her cleavage. Either she was hiding an insultingly small pocket knife down her front or she'd just threatened me with a fingernail. Neither scenario filled me with a sense of relief. The smart mouse knows not to relax when the cat is "merely playing".

Marty broke off from his rapt conversation with Will and Natasha melted unseen into the crowd. Under Will's genial blue gaze, Marty stepped purposely in my direction.

"Jo, why don't you take a break? I can handle it here for a while." Winking broadly, he took the ticket basket out of my hands and steered me toward Will.

I pulled out of Marty's grasp and slid behind the will-call desk. Will might lack Natasha's nasty streak, but that didn't mean that keeping a solid hunk of wood between us wasn't a good idea.

"What did you say to the house manager?" I demanded.

Will's grin spread across his face as he focused on my mouth. "No need for those, love. If you're interested, I would be happy to—"

I wrenched the fake teeth out of my mouth. "What are you doing here?"

In reply, he looked me slowly up and down in masculine appraisal. "I always thought the Hollywood portrayal of vampires a bit overdone, but now I'm beginning to like it."

He reached out a hand to fiddle with the ties of my cape. As his fingers grazed my collarbone, a rush of heat pounded through my body and I made the mistake of meeting his eyes. Everything became blue and serene. All the stress and worries left my body as if I were floating in a Tahitian lagoon. Barely conscious of what I was doing, I planted my hands on the desk and leaned toward him. The haunted house, the room full of people, it all faded away.

His lips gently brushed mine. I leaned into the kiss as naturally as a wave is pulled back into the sea. The little hairs on my neck whispered warnings. I ignored them. The warnings grew louder and then rose to a shout, jolting me upright. As I blinked my surroundings back into focus, Natasha strolled up with a seductive roll of hips. Boom-shiska-boom-shiska-boom. She wrapped her arm possessively through Will's and gave me a wolfish smile that turned my legs to ice.

"Hello, Jo," she purred.

Her welcome might have been more convincing if she hadn't just threatened to kill me.

We were both surprised when Will gently unwound Natasha's arm from his. She flashed me a venomous look that practically singed my eyelashes and batted her own curly, mascaraed ones at Will. Her smile would have had most men dragging her off to the bedroom but Will was not most men. It bounced right off him.

"Leave us," he told her softly.

Every human male in the room started to drool as she dutifully moved through the crowd, rounded hips swaying like a siren's call. Boom-shiska-boom-shiska-boom.

Only she wasn't heading away toward the exit but toward the front of the line.

Marty was no match for her. Grinning like an idiot, he waved her forward through the crowd. A hunky young blond who looked like he'd stepped out of an Abercrombie and Fitch catalog turned in annoyance when he felt her cutting up through the line. But his irritation melted away, replaced by a look of devoted wonder as she slid her arm through his.

"Oh, no," I whispered. I had to call someone. Gavin, my brain slowly supplied.

I patted around my waist for what seemed like hours before I remembered my cell phone was in the women's dressing area. I cursed myself for being so stupid and vain as to wear something without pockets.

Marty was smiling and nodding and reaching for the door handle to let Natasha and her new arm candy into the haunted house. Somewhere in there still were a few dozen kids and their parents. I fought to shake off the strange lethargy that clung to me like spider webs. She could bite a dozen screaming victims and everyone would think it was just another performance.

"Marty, don't!"

It was too late. Or maybe he didn't hear me. He tugged at the closest double door and when it didn't open, tugged harder.

"Always a pleasure, Jo, love," said a laughing voice in my ear.

I spun back toward Will, but he was no longer there. His parting caress lingered on the bare skin at the nape of my neck like a brand.

With a shiver of awareness, I searched the crowd. How did he disappear like that? Was he exceptionally light on his feet or was it another inexplicable, irrational vampire trait? And what the heck did he mean with that cryptic goodbye? Why had he come? To see me…or was he looking for new recruits?

A grunt of frustration brought my attention back to the present. Marty was tugging hard now on the stubborn left double door to the haunted house. A renewed sense of fear lent wings to my clumsy feet as I pushed through the waiting group of fifteen, trying to get to Natasha.

All at once, Marty gave up and reached for the other door, which opened so easily he stumbled a little. Regaining his poise, he waved Natasha through with a small bow. As I hurtled over the rope, she and the Abercrombie knockoff disappeared through the gap into the darkness.

Marty shut the door firmly behind them.

I was too late. "Marty," I panted. "You need to let me—"

"Hey, buddy, fix the darned door so the rest of us can get through!"

Marty shook his head, looking as if someone had splashed water on him. Frowning, he grasped the left door handle with both hands and gave it an experimental tug, then a sharp yank.

The door opened. Tom, deathly pale in his zombie makeup, stood in the doorway, glassy-eyed, looking back at the crowd. Slowly at first, then gathering speed, he toppled to the ground like a felled tree. His top hat rolled to a stop at my feet.

Grinding to a halt, I stared in growing horror at Tom's unmoving form stretched out across the entranceway to the haunted house. His right hand was a frozen claw suspended in mid-scrabble toward his chest. If he was playing dead, it was remarkably convincing.

"Look. Dead zombie." A young teenage boy standing behind me let out a high-pitched giggle and pointed at Tom.

His buddy beside him snickered. "Didn't know you could kill a zombie. Thought they were already dead."

It was a setup no actor could resist, but Tom didn't bounce back to his feet. He just lay there.

"Oh God." My words were a silent puff of breath.

The boys stopped high-fiving each other over their wit, their giggles replaced by a wide-eyed silence that galvanized me into motion.

I reached for my cell phone before I remembered I didn't have it.

"Someone call 9-1-1!" I said aloud and positioned myself as a barrier between Tom and his tour group. Twenty people reached for their cell phones.

Marty sprang to action as if someone had stuck a pin in him. Squatting with a vast creaking of knees, he reached two fingers toward Tom's neck.

His arm stopped halfway to its goal. He made a strange noise deep in his throat and tried for a pulse in Tom's wrist instead.

Gulping at the acid rising in my throat, I craned forward to scan Tom's neck for bite marks. Hoping, to my shame, that the telltale marks wouldn't be too obvious.

Marty gently let go of Tom's wrist and placed it neatly along Tom's side. Meeting my intent gaze with a look of heart-wrenching disbelief, he barely shook his head. It was the first time I'd seen him unsure of what to do.

I felt dizzy with disbelief…and guilt. It was my fault Tom was dead, as surely as if I'd killed him myself. I knew what Natasha was and yet I'd let her go in the haunted house. I should have fought harder to stop her.

I stood there, staring at Tom's neck, unable to look away. His skin was chalky and waxen and just a tiny bit green.

Odd.

I couldn't see any blood. Or teeth marks.

Marty hadn't felt for a wrist pulse because Tom's jugular was destroyed, but because his neck was encased in thick zombie latex. I was so relieved I nearly laughed aloud.

One of the boys tapped lightly on my shoulder. His voice cracked so badly up and down the register with nerves and hormone changes that I could barely understand him. "Um, what's the address here?"

"It's…here, give it to me." I took the phone from his clammy outstretched hand. "We're in the front lobby of the Milverne Theater on the corner of Sixth and Long Beach Boulevard. One of the actors has collapsed on the floor."

I cupped my hand around the phone and lowered my voice, wanting to protect the boys from knowing what they could undoubtedly see for themselves. "He has no pulse and he's not breathing."

A calm, authoritative female voice replied, "Thank you for reporting the emergency. We have already logged the incident and an emergency vehicle is on the way. Please stay on the line in case we need further assistance. Your name is…?"

I handed the phone back to its young owner who provided his name in an excited squeak.

The emergency operator wasn't kidding. The EMTs must have been right around the corner, for the red fire department truck screeched to a halt in front of the theater with a blare of sirens, flooding the lobby windows with flashes of orange and yellow lights.

"Stand back, please!"

A paramedic parted the crowd at a jog, followed by two more paramedics carrying a stretcher. As we backed up to give them room, a black-and-white police car pulled up behind the ambulance and two patrol officers got out and came inside.

With practiced efficiency, the EMTs fit a mask over Tom's nose and mouth and gently pumped in air with what looked like a small blue rubber football. As they lifted him onto the stretcher, the door from the haunted house opened and a bored looking Angelina stepped into the lobby to collect her next group.

She stopped, irritated, when she realized there wasn't one waiting for her. It was only as she looked around for someone to blame that she noticed the paramedics. Her eyes fell to the stretcher.

"Is that Tom? What happened? Tom!" She rushed toward him but one of the officers intercepted her. Wailing, arms flapping like windmills, she tried to resist. "Noooo!"

The officer snapped a curt command and to my surprise she stopped at once and stood docilely where he placed her. Her witch's hat had gone askew. Reaching up a slim hand to right it, she watched quietly with the rest of us as the EMTs whisked Tom's unmoving form out to the ambulance and drove off in a blare of sirens.

Into the hushed silence, Ian, dressed as Igor, listed comically through the theater doors for his next group. He halted with a wide-eyed suddenness that might have been funny under different conditions.

"What's going on?" Ian asked. His fake Marty Feldman accent was gone, replaced by a faint New Jersey twang.

Ian's dropping character jolted the crowd back to life. People turned to each other, and when they didn't get answers to their questions, shouted them at the police. One of the officers set Ian to the side in a small cocoon of isolation with a sharp admonition to stay put while the other got to work doing the crowd control thing.

Angelina didn't seem to realize the officers had deliberately kept Ian and her apart. Crossing to him, she fell upon his shoulder and started crying in loud racking sobs.

"Tom collapsed! He's dead!"

Ian's shattered countenance showed every emotion. First, confusion and grief as he watched the ambulance turn out of sight. Then disgust, as his gaze flicked to Angelina, racked with heartache in his arms.

Apparently I wasn't the only one wondering at her anguish. The few times I've seen her in Tom's company, she'd treated him more like a piece of furniture than a dear friend or lover. Which was the acting?

Marty hustled through the crowd toward her. His face was as blank as a mask, but I caught the look in his eyes as he passed me. He was furious.

The officer was looking pained as he tried to remove Angelina from Ian's person and escort her back to her spot. "Miss, please. The paramedics will take the best possible care of your friend. Now, if you wouldn't mind..."

A blast of cool air cut through the stuffy lobby as the outside doors opened. Gavin stepped into the room and strode quickly toward the officers through the gap in the crowd left by the paramedics.

I tried to blend into the crowd, but my height and hair color make that difficult at the best of times, and tonight I was wearing a bustier and skintight black satin hot pants. And a cape.

Gavin's long, athletic stride faltered when he caught sight of me. I thought I saw his lips move in a bitten-off epithet, but I must have imagined it for his face was as impassive as ever as he came abreast of me. His pale gray eyes gave me a quick once over and then locked on my right hand. I was still holding a pair of the fake vampire teeth. In my nervousness, I'd hooked my thumb and fingers through the back and was making the teeth snap together like little castanets.

I offered up a weak smile, which he didn't return. He didn't stop to talk to me either but continued straight to the patrol officers. I was too far away to hear what they were saying, but from their body language and gestures, I gathered the officer was filling Gavin in on what had happened. His expression as he spoke to Gavin was an odd combination of irritation and wariness, and I deduced Gavin was still posing as a visiting detective. I wasn't sure exactly how long Gavin and the Long Beach Chief of Police had been working that story, but from his reception tonight, I would say it had been a little too long.

From their perspective, Gavin was either the slowest detective ever sent down for training or some sort of ultra-secret narc. As had been the case last spring, his fellow officers, professional to the last, instantly gave him the backup and support required of their positions, but they were considerably less free with their friendship and respect.

Marty had gotten Angelina to shut up and was talking in a low voice to Gavin and the officers. After a quiet but impassioned discussion, Marty broke stiffly away, hands clenched at his sides. He managed to smooth his large square face back to good-natured blandness as he pulled the chair out from behind the will-call desk, hefted himself up onto it and waved his arms to get the crowd's attention.

"Ladies and gentlemen," he boomed. "We regret to inform you that due to the illness of one of our actors, the haunted house is closed for the evening."

He raised his voice a notch to be heard over the fussing crowd. "Your tickets are valid through the run of the haunted house or..." A pained expression flitted across his face and was quickly mastered. "You can bring your tickets to the box office for a full refund. Thank you for coming to the Milverne Theater haunted house!"

He raised his hands like a preacher and smiled beatifically over the crowd. I decided I had misjudged his acting ability.

As he got down heavily from the chair to hover anxiously on the outskirts of the police activity, I shifted over a few feet until I was by his side.

"What's going on?" I asked softly.

He didn't look at me when he answered. His gaze roved from the police, across the lobby, to the box office, and back again in a constant cycle. "They took Tom to the hospital, but more for form's sake than anything. They'll probably pronounce him dead on arrival. These gentlemen," he tipped his head toward the police, "are deciding whether or not to close us down."

"I thought they already had." By now, the police had completely cleared the theater end of the lobby where Tom had lain.

One of the officers stepped through the open theater doors and flipped on the house lights. The haunted house had that shabby disillusioning look of a swank velvet-papered hotel in the daytime. It was hard to believe anyone had been scared by a bunch of actors in a horseshoe-shaped tunnel of plywood sets and black bedroom sheets.

Marty spared me a glance. "I mean shut down for good. It depends on whether they want to carry on as if foul play happened here tonight or accept that Tom died of a heart attack. The way his father did at that age."

The second officer had a notebook in hand and was asking Angelina gently probing questions along the lines of "Did Tom do drugs? Was he acting strangely tonight?"

Marty followed my gaze. "Damn fools." The words came out in a low, angry hiss.

The policemen turned and looked sharply in our direction, as if we were colluding about how we'd killed off Tom. Marty moved immediately to his side, smiling like a man only too eager to please. "Officer, if there's anything we can do to assist you…"

Taking out a notebook, Gavin broke away and headed toward the front of the lobby where looky-loo visitors foolish enough to have stayed were huddled in groups of two and three.

I reached out and touched Gavin's arm as he passed. He drew to a halt and raised sun-bleached brows in a look of bored curiosity. I swallowed hard against the golf ball of guilt and fear that remained lodged in my throat.

"Is it…" I looked around to make sure no one was in eavesdropping range and lowered my voice to the barest whisper. "Vampire-related?"

"Why would you think that?"

"You're here."

Impatience flicked briefly across Gavin's face and was gone. "I don't see anything out of the ordinary. Unless…"

"What? I finally crossed over to the dark side and celebrated with a rampage?" I held out my wrists to be cuffed. "Yeah. That's it. Detective, look no further. I'm turning myself in."

Gavin grabbed my wrists with one hand and pushed them down out of sight. His voice was low and hushed. "Jesus, Jo. Do you always have to be so melodramatic?"

We glared at each other for a moment and then I pointedly dropped my gaze to my wrists, which he still held. He let go.

I rubbed my wrists. "Will was here," I said curtly. "With Natasha."

"Why didn't you call me?"

"I don't have my phone."

He looked at me as if I were the most irresponsible person on the planet. I yanked open my cape to display my satin bustier and skintight black pants.

"Well where was I supposed to put it?"

Gavin crossed his arms as if he had to do it to keep from strangling me. His voice, when he spoke, was rigidly controlled. "When was Will here?"

"He and Natasha showed up around eight-thirty."

"And?"

"They bought tickets and were welcomed in like everyone else. Actually, I don't know if they bought tickets. I never saw them. Will stayed out here but Natasha went inside."

"You *let* her go in?"

"Of course I didn't *let* her go in. She just went! You don't seem to understand how she works. She's like Obi-Wan Kenobi with the Stormtroopers. Every male in the place was stumbling over himself trying to let her get to the front of the line. Our own house manager, Marty, opened the door for her and the tour guide—Tom—hadn't even shown up yet."

The memory of Tom being carried away by paramedics doused my anger like a bucket of ice water.

"And then?" Gavin asked.

My gaze went to the spot where Tom had fallen. I wrenched it back up to look at Gavin. "The left double door was stuck. Marty pulled it hard and when it opened, Tom came with it." I turned my palms up as the feeling of helpless frustration returned. "I couldn't follow her, not after that."

"What about Will?"

"I already told you. He stayed out here."

"And did what?"

"He was just talking to me. Until Tom…" I swallowed. "Then Will left."

"Did Will say what he wanted? Why he was here?"

I shook my head and shrugged. "No, nothing."

The inadequacy of my response irritated me and yet I don't know that I could have learned more, no matter how hard I tried. I never seemed to have control of things when I was with Will. Being with him was like driving too fast down a dark mountain road in the rain—you just hung on and hoped you made it around the next turn.

Gavin's mouth drew tight. Whatever was clicking through his head, he didn't share it with me. One of the officers looked in our direction.

Gavin pitched his voice a little louder. "Thank you, Miss. You're free to go."

"That's it? You're not going to ask me any more questions?"

"Not unless you saw or heard something pertaining to Tom Langley's collapse."

"Do you really think he had a heart attack?"

The patrol officer, slogging his way through the onlookers with his own pen and notebook, shot Gavin an irritated look.

"Go home," Gavin told me. Clicking his pen open, he made his way to the group at the front of the lobby.

~*~

When I got back to my apartment, I tried to get Fluffy out of the kitty condo, thinking a little purring comfort would be nice, but she was having none of it. I was learning, at the cost of several bandaged fingers, that the cat and I had an unwritten contract. I would feed her and clean her litter box and in exchange she would sleep a lot and look cute—from a distance. Petting, much less picking her up or any form of cuddling, was a clear violation of the "no touch" rule.

I went to bed alone and tried not to be disheartened by the fact that a cat in the next room might be the closest thing to nighttime company that I would ever have. As soon as the self-pitying thought entered my head, I chased it away in disgust. What kind of person was I to worry about my social life when Tom was in the intensive care unit in the hospital?

I punched my pillow into a more comfortable rectangle and let out a frustrated sigh when sleep still was not forthcoming. Deep down, I knew my focus on petty things *and* my self-flagellating responses were merely my way of distracting myself from thinking about unpleasant things. Such as why had Will and Natasha been at the haunted house tonight? And had they done something to Tom?

A million possible answers to those questions kept my mind spinning until the wee hours of the morning and when my alarm went off at dawn, one thing was clear. I needed to get off Will's radar.

There was a perfectly logical explanation for why he never seemed to run into me by chance. He could simply follow my car. Or, as was the case last night, Becky's car. And yet, he seemed to be able to find me as easily as if I wore some sort of homing beacon.

And if that were the case, there was only one place to go for help.

I skipped my usual morning run and went straight to the shower. Fifteen minutes later—clean, dressed and SPF'd, hair towel-dried and twisted into its usual knot—I made my way through the morning twilight to my car. The traffic was light and in no time at all, I was standing in front of my church.

The church was locked, the adjacent vestry dark. I checked my watch. Daily crack-of-dawn Mass wouldn't be said for another hour and a half. Trotting quickly up the well-worn marble stairs, I ducked into the shadowy archway and made a beeline for the statue of Mary that watched over the right side of the building. I said a quick, silent prayer for forgiveness for stealing and pulled a small test tube out of my windbreaker. In one swift motion, I dipped it into the dish of holy water at Mary's side, corked it, and shoved it back in my pocket.

Everyone has seen a movie where someone flings holy water at a vampire, who then skitters away, skin smoking, howling with pain. My experience with holy water was a little different. It stung, but only for a moment, and it was really no worse than drinking orange juice with chapped lips. It had healed the sun damage to my skin and eventually, the bite marks on my neck. More importantly, it had, for a while, kept Will from being able to find me with his usual intuitive ease. Or so I believed.

I was giddy with relief and halfway down the steps, going back to my car, when behind me I heard the faint but unmistakable swish of clothing.

"Josephine?"

I whirled on a gasp of air to find old Father Stevens standing under the shadow of the archway. His thick glasses glinted opaque in the pale morning light.

"It is you!" He held out a blue-veined hand and I trotted back up the stairs to clasp it.

"Good morning, Father."

"Josephine Gartner." Father Stevens was one of the few people who knew and used my given name. I'd been too young to protest when he'd baptized me, and it had stuck. "What a delight to see you."

"I…uh…"

His faded blue eyes twinkled behind the heavy lenses. "It's been a while since you've joined us for Mass."

I felt the heat go to my cheeks. "Yes, Father."

"It's a little early for daily Mass. But if you'd like, I can let you into the church. The kneeling pads are a little more comfortable than the cold cement out here." He inclined his head toward the flat bit of cement in front of the statue of Mary that some people used as a place to kneel and pray.

As I had done, moments ago. I felt the heat drain from my face as quickly as it had arrived. How long had Father Stevens been here, watching me? Had he seen me take the holy water?

He didn't seem to notice my distraction, just prattled cheerfully away. "Or if you have time, you can join me for a cup of tea in the vestry? A nice cup of Earl Gray wouldn't go amiss." He leaned toward me and said confidentially, "I make a very good cup of tea, if I say so myself."

I relaxed, realizing he wanted company, nothing more. "Thank you, Father, but I'm afraid I need to get to work."

"Yes, yes, of course. Still teaching, are you? Schools start so early these days. Another time then." He held out his hands and gave mine a squeeze.

On impulse, I kissed him on the cheek before jogging down the steps and hurrying to my car before the sun got any higher. The vial of holy water weighed heavily in my pocket. And the reason I needed it weighed heavier still.

# Chapter Five

"When do we get our labs back?" Danielle Gamble demanded without first raising her hand.

I didn't bother to utter a reprimand. I'd learned if I gave my students a few minutes of anarchy at the beginning of the class, when I was doing maintenance stuff like checking homework and passing back papers, they tended to behave better when I needed them to focus. And today I needed all the good behavior I could get. Running into Father Stevens at my early morning holy water raid had left me with the energy of a wet noodle and it wasn't even half past seven. It was true. There was no situation exempt from Catholic guilt.

"Tomorrow," I said.

The room rang with theatrical groans. "But you promised!"

"Something came up," I said shortly. "John, why don't you draw the answer to number two on the board."

I made a mark in my grade book that Lisa Wilcox had done her homework. As I moved on to the next row, she stopped me with a question.

"Ms. Gartner, did you see that guy get axed at the haunted house last night?"

There was a chorus of hushed, indrawn breaths and the room went so silent I could hear Alan lecturing about physics across the hall.

Carefully modulating my voice to something between boredom and a verbal eye roll, I said, "No one got axed," and motioned for the two troublemakers in the back row to show me their homework. Only one of them had done it. "I want to see this done *tomorrow*," I told the slacker softly.

Behind me, Lisa Wilcox shifted impatiently in her seat. "But, Ms. Gartner—"

"A man had a heart attack. Now, if you'll turn to page one hundred twenty-five in your texts..."

Someone, I couldn't tell who, for he dropped his voice low enough that I could hear the words but not the characterizing features, whispered, "He died. My mom was working the ER last night and I heard her telling my dad this morning."

My step faltered as I progressed back up the aisle. Dead? Tom was dead?

I shouldn't have been so surprised. I knew Tom was in bad shape when the EMTs took him to the hospital. A hot rush of tears clouded my vision. Breathing in through my nose, I ruthlessly blinked them back. The chain of whispers went silent as I regained the front of the room and turned to face my class. Nineteen pairs of eyes waited for me to say something.

Normally I would have made an attempt to soothe to the class, but if anyone in that classroom needed the comfort of a reassuring natter about Tom's death, it was me. Moreover I didn't even know if it was true. Until I had confirmation, I intended to brazen it out.

"Texts. Page one twenty-five. Now. Or would you prefer to get out a pen and a piece of paper for a pop quiz worth twenty-five percent of a test grade? Actually, that sounds pretty good. See how much chemistry you really know before the exam."

There was a harried zip of backpacks and the thunk of books being opened on lab benches. It was a full-on hack teacher maneuver. I knew from experience that students quickly grew inured to threats. I repressed a shudder as I imagined what it would be like when spring fever hit and I had no tools left in the toolbox.

About a hundred years later, the end of period bell rang. I deliberately spun out the homework instructions, keeping them a minute or two over so they had no time to linger with questions. As they slung their backpacks over their shoulders and raced off to their next classes, I followed them out and over to the computer room down the hall. It was empty but for a couple of high school students working on nothing that looked like science homework. I turned a blind eye to whatever they were doing and they returned the courtesy as I powered up the computer at the other end of the room and went online.

Our local paper had the news. Tom had indeed died last night from heart failure. They'd given his death two brief, matter-of-fact paragraphs that talked more about the Milverne Theater than anything else. In its infinite wisdom, the newspaper had decreed Tom's death sad but not headline-grabbing.

I shut down the computer and returned to my empty classroom. It was a free period for me and I had plenty of grading to do. I sat down at my desk, pulled a stack of lab reports and got to work.

With the sort of single-minded efficiency one only gets when desperate to ignore something else, I managed to get through all of third period's labs in a fast-moving half-hour. It was when I reached for the next stack that my focus slipped and Tom took over my thoughts.

I couldn't help but remember that I'd spent my last moments with him angry over the fact that he hadn't even offered to pay for my sundae after eating most of it. I'd gotten huffy over a little hot fudge sauce and now he was dead.

The bell rang for morning break. I popped up from my desk and reached for my sun protection gear. Coffee. I needed coffee. Studies showed that caffeine improved moods in women and if there were days I desperately needed a mood improver, this was one of them. If I didn't get out of there and pour some caffeine down my gullet right away, chances were good I'd face my next class with watery eyes and a bright red nose from our crappy institutional-grade classroom tissues. Giving my eighth-grade students that kind of ammo was like stepping up in front of a firing squad and yelling, "Go for it!"

Tugging on gloves, I wrapped a scarf around my face and neck, plunked a wide-brimmed sunhat on my head and bolted down the outside staircase to the first floor of the science wing. The high school students milling around their lockers in the hallways didn't give me as much as a glance. I wasn't sure whether to be relieved or offended.

The two-story science "wing" is on one end of a rectangular building. The English department occupies the other end and the school theater is a buffer in between. From the eye-watering stink in the air, it was a lab day for Becky's chemistry students and painting sets day in the drama classes. The background pong of the lockers (I hated to think what foul things were incubating in them after almost two months of school.) wasn't helping matters. I picked up my pace and hurried past the theater and out the far end of the building. Instead of heading out to the grassy quad with the rest of the crowd, I took the rainy day route under a network of covered walkways and entered the cafeteria through a side door.

The industrial-size coffee urn was on the cafeteria terrace. Most of my colleagues considered it one of the few perks of the job that we could catch a few rays near the beach over a cup of coffee every morning. I used to, too.

No one spared me a glance, which meant I'd correctly judged the gossip lull. Tom's heart attack might have been good for a few moments of "did you hear" in the faculty room before school and a sad headshake about the unpredictability of life between morning classes, but as no one here particularly knew him, interest would wane unless fed. No one but me would have read that tiny newsfeed that Tom had died.

I looked around for Becky or Carol, but if they'd been to coffee break, they'd already come and gone. Careful to keep to the deeply shaded section under the thick overhang, I forced myself to wait while the football coach fumbled for a Styrofoam cup, instead of reaching across him and sticking my mug under the spigot. Not because it was rude—Greg wouldn't have cared—but because it was as good as broadcasting that I didn't just want coffee but *needed* it. And if you thought no one would notice you are laboring under a misconception that teachers are somehow more high-minded than other adults. They're not. On the contrary, teachers can take grade school playground one-upmanship to a new level.

"Come *on*, pokey!" I muttered under my breath.

After what seemed like hours, it was finally my turn. I leaned forward trying to get a buzz from the fumes as hot coffee streamed into my cup.

I felt a tap on my arm. The head librarian had joined me in line.

"Jo, how nice to see you outside."

How Janice managed to imply in a simple greeting that I was antisocial to the point of being unfit to be around children was beyond me.

Mustering up a smile, I turned around to find myself facing not just Janice but Gilbert as well. *Both* librarians. Great. This day was getting better by the minute.

I snapped the lid on my travel mug in a businesslike fashion. "Beautiful day, huh?" I sidled toward the cafeteria door. "Too bad I can't stay to enjoy it. I have a—"

"I bet you're a little behind in your work," Janice said, reaching out to pat my hand.

"No, really, it's just that I promised to meet—"

"And tired too, poor thing," chimed in Gilbert. "I bet you got back *very* late last night."

"I...uh..." I blinked and stared at him. Had he really just said that? And with the school chaplain right there? Not to mention the head of HR.

Janice clucked sadly. "Poor dear, it must have been awful for you..."

*What?*

"That young man dying practically at your feet."

Oh. I glanced around, but no one had an ear cocked to our conversation. I'd been right that the teachers hadn't yet seen that small article in the paper, but I'd forgotten the librarians read *everything*.

They were almost right. I was tired, and it had been unpleasant for me. But the only people it was awful for were Tom, his close friends and his family. A surge of outrage on Tom's behalf filled me, overriding my usual meekness when confronted by the librarians.

I rose to my full height, stared down at them, and spoke quietly but firmly. "Actually, Janice, Gilbert, Tom didn't die 'practically at my feet'. He died in the hospital after having a heart attack. He was a nice man and a dedicated actor and I'm sure he will be sorely missed by his friends and family."

It shut them up. The end of break bell blared into our small corner of silence.

I don't know if their recollection of the good manners they prided themselves in having lasted beyond the moment I sailed back into the cafeteria, as I didn't see them again that day. I had so much work to do that I skipped lunch in the cafeteria and made do with an energy bar at my desk.

Even so, I still had a depressingly thick stack of ungraded lab reports requiring my attention when school ended. I also had a couple dozen students with a sudden burning interest in chemistry. Amazing how this lust for knowledge coincided with tomorrow's test.

After I answered the last student's questions, I spent a couple of hours writing the rest of the chemistry test and lost track of time coaxing the copy machine to spit out copies. I'd just pulled a stack of lab reports to me and wearily uncapped my red pen when Becky appeared in my doorway.

"There you are. Haven't seen you all day. Did you want to hitch a ride to the theater with me?"

Twice a week, parking in my neighborhood was banned on one side of every street from four to six a.m. for street cleaning. Anyone who wasn't in for the night by seven on a Thursday wouldn't find a parking spot in our zip code.

"Surely we're not having the haunted house? You did hear that, um…" I struggled over the wording and then just came out with it. "Tom didn't survive his heart attack."

She nodded, sniffed and yanked a tissue out of the box. She blew her nose and dabbed at her eyes. "I know. Dan called me with the news this morning. I really tried to make it up here today to tell you, but I got swamped.

"Anyway, we're still doing the haunted house. You know how theater folks are. The show must go on. If anything, they're more determined than ever to do a good job, in Tom's memory."

There was no way I was getting out of going to the haunted house. I would just have to stay up late tonight to finish the lab reports after I got back. There was only one more day left of the work week. I would survive.

"Right." I recapped my pen, shifted the labs into my book bag and slung it over my shoulder. "Carpooling would be a lifesaver. Why don't you follow me home and we'll go from there? I—"

Stepping into the hallway, I got a good look at Becky.

"Your hair is green."

The spiky tips of her hair were as verdant as the football field.

She ran a hand guiltily over her hair as if trying to tame its exuberance. I realized Tom's death had hit her hard. With all the time she'd spent at the theater the past couple of weeks, she'd probably gotten to know him pretty well.

"I did it yesterday before the haunted house started. Gave my costume a bit of pizzazz, especially after I added a little glow-in-the-dark hair gel."

"When? I was with you a half-hour before it opened."

She shrugged. "It only takes ten minutes."

I studied her critically. "Actually, I like it." I turned off the lights and locked my classroom door behind me. "Maybe I should try it with my hair."

"Don't you dare! Once you dye it, you'll never get that gorgeous red-gold color back. And don't you cut it short, either."

"I thought you hated my bun."

"Everyone hates your bun. You should wear it down."

"And have Roger write me up for being a fire hazard?"

Our department chair lives for officious little power trips like that. In the fourteen months I'd been teaching at Bayshore, he'd been after me for everything from the color of pens I let my students write with—"Blue or black only. Red is for teachers. Students must correct their work with green ink or get a demerit."—to the number of essay questions on my tests.

As I'd hoped, the inane turn of conversation helped temper her grief and she let out a snort of laughter. "Oh my God, he totally would!" She pushed open the outside door. "Roger's such an ass."

"I know. All the joy I've given him, all those times he's written me up for things and never once has he said 'thank you'."

Becky's laughter rang across the quad. I kept my gaze focused on the terrain around us, scanning every doorway and shadowy arch for signs of something lurking. Every inch of the school was pretty well lit after dark, but my skin pricked uncomfortably. I didn't usually leave this late. The sun went down early in October.

"Hey, slow down, lanky legs," Becky complained. Grabbing my elbow, she tugged me toward the low-slung administration building. "Let's go this way. I need to stop and get my mail."

"Sorry." I'd instinctively led us away from the buildings toward the wide open, visibly vampire-free quad.

Stepping into the faculty room, we rifled through our mailboxes. I didn't have anything that couldn't wait until tomorrow. Becky tucked a couple of pink phone messages in her bag and we exited through the handsome parquet lobby and out the front to the faculty, staff and guest parking lot. Becky had to run a quick errand and get gas and I needed to check on Fluffy so we agreed to meet in front of my place in a half-hour.

Fluffy was curled in a tight ball in the bottom room of her cat condo. I wouldn't have thought she'd moved at all that day except as usual the food level had gone down as if I were feeding a St. Bernard. I reached a hand through the hole of a doorway of her kitty condo and gave her soft fur a pat just make sure she was still alive. She woke with a start, shot me a dirty look, yawned and went back to sleep.

Feeling guilty about leaving her alone all day, I dangled a mouse with a tinkly bell for a nose in front of the condo door. Fluffy shifted so her back was more firmly to me.

As I got back to my feet, the vial of holy water in my jacket pocket knocked against my waist like a nagging child. I glanced at my watch. I still had fifteen minutes until I was supposed to meet Becky. Plenty of time to douse myself before going out.

Taking the holy water into the bathroom, I stripped down and uncorked the vial. Remembering that nip of discomfort from the last time, I poured a few drops into my cupped palm and quickly rubbed it over my cheeks and forehead.

This time was different. The holy water sank into my pores like fire and acid. A fierce animalistic rage tore through my body. Screaming with pain, I scrabbled for the glass vial and lifted it high above my head to shatter it against the floor.

As suddenly as it had come the moment passed, leaving me sweat-soaked and trembling. Lowering my arm, I returned the vial gently to the countertop. Fumbling for purchase to hold my shaking body up, I leaned close to the mirror, expecting to see my face blistered with red, raw skin.

My reflection was oddly imbalanced. Atop my ghostly body, perched a near photographic-sharp image of my head, the skin soft and dewy. A confused sob broke from my chest and I collapsed on the little foot stool by the shower and put my head in my hands.

I made myself get back up. Grasping the vial of holy water, I pulled the cork out a second time, my hands shaking hard against the desire to slam the cork in tighter. A terrible, cowardly part of me wanted desperately to avoid the pain, to stop fighting what was so clearly inevitable. But my anger at being manipulated by something outside my control was stronger. Drop by drop, I rubbed the holy water over every inch of my body, gritting my teeth against the pain.

I let the empty vial fall into the trash and stumbled out into my bedroom. I don't know how long I stood there in the dark.

The ringing of my cell phone jostled me out of my stupor. Following the mechanical strains of Beethoven's Ninth, I padded back into the bathroom and pulled it out of my book bag.

It was Becky. "Hey, I'm here. Get your butt downstairs or we're going to be late."

Her voice was...normal. It flowed through me like a warm, healing tonic.

Half-formed plans of bailing on her so I could stay inside where it was safe receded as I realized I wanted to be, needed to be, out with friends. "I'll be down in two minutes."

I got back into my work clothes. Stowing the vampire costume in my book bag, I made a quick stop at the kitchen to refill Fluffy's food and water bowls and called goodbye to the furry bit of her back that was visible through the hole.

Becky was double parked out front, her pristine 1965 black Mustang gleaming in the glow from the streetlight. The car was decades older than mine and in far better shape.

"How many miles do you have on this thing?" I asked as I sank into the remarkably comfortable passenger seat. Becky made an effort to maintain the car's original equipment as long as it didn't interfere with comfort or speed. Which meant the seats had been re-sprung, there were seat belts and the engine was powerful enough to tow a tanker.

"'Bout a hundred fifty thousand. I can't turn left here, can I? I hate these stupid one-way streets."

"That's a lot of miles. Don't you worry about breaking down on the freeway?"

"Nah. I've got a guy."

"A guy?"

"Rene. He's a genius with engines. I hear the tiniest noise and he fixes it for me during his breaks at the garage. I get parts at cost and half-price labor."

Of course she had a guy. Becky knew everyone from all walks of life and she had the gift I associate with cheerleaders and prom queens of getting males to trip over themselves lining up to do things for her. Only, Becky wasn't manipulative about it. They just liked her.

"How come I don't have a guy?" I muttered, jealous.

She grinned and downshifted around a corner. "You really want me to answer that?"

"No."

"Good. Because I don't have an answer. You're gorgeous, smart and nice. And you bake."

I was touched. "Thanks, that's very—"

"And not all men are put off by a granny bun, frumpy clothes—"

"Hey!"

"I mean, was there like a *giant* sale on old lady cruise wear? They do make *attractive* clothes in your size, you know." Becky scowled down at my feet. "And don't even get me started on your shoes."

"Gee, I feel pretty."

"And yet for some reason, hot men still flock to you." She threw up her hands then refit them on the steering wheel with a smack.

"What men?"

She flashed a glance at me as she shifted to third. "Your problem is *not* that you can't get men. Your problem is you keep turning them down."

"What men? Where are these men?"

We pulled up to a stop sign. "Why are you shouting?"

She didn't wait for an answer. "Let's see. There was that gorgeous hunk of masculinity sitting next you at the play, for one. In fact, there doesn't need to be any more. He's enough. You couldn't make a man sexier than that." She pursed her lips and thought about it a second. "Yep, he's perfect."

He *was* perfect. He was also a vampire.

The dreamy look on her face sharpened into a thoughtful frown. "I swear I've seen him before somewhere..." She shook her head. "No, I guess not. A guy like that makes an impression."

I let out the breath I was holding and relaxed back into the seat.

"So?" she prompted.

"What?"

"What about tall, dark and sexy?"

"What about him?"

Becky blew out a long-suffering sigh. "No wonder you're always home alone on Friday nights."

"Light," I said, pointing at the traffic signal.

She slowed to a stop. "I don't get it. Why in the *world* aren't you dating him? I mean right this second. He's movie-star gorgeous and he's obviously interested in you. I mean he sat through a high school drama production for you. If that doesn't say 'ready to go the mile', I don't know what does."

Becky's sharp black gaze dug into me.

"You're shy, aren't you?" Dawning surprise tinged her voice. "That's okay. We can overcome that. Here's the plan. I'll call him for you and we'll—"

"No! He's um..." For the life of me, I couldn't think of an excuse to give her.

"Please don't tell me he's gay."

Will was so patently heterosexual that I didn't bother to answer.

"Oh God, I'm right aren't I?"

I started to correct the misunderstanding but caught myself in time.

Her chest heaved in a sigh of disappointment. "I knew he was too good to be true."

She was right about that. My stomach rumbled. "I'm starving. Where are we going for dinner?"

"Marty's providing dinner for us. We're having a pre-haunted house memorial for Tom."

"Really? That's nice." I was surprised at the expenditure. Everything I'd seen about Marty Milverne pointed to cheap.

"At least I assume he's providing food. Dan only told me about their trip to Costco for alcohol. Apparently it's going to be an Irish wake."

"Tom was Irish?"

She grinned. "He is tonight."

After the day I'd had, working the haunted house drunk was sounding pretty good. "Glad I'm not driving."

"Hah! Why do you think I offered to carpool? You can drive home."

She parked and we collected our costumes from the backseat and circled up the path to the front entrance of the theater. The heavy double doors were closed tight.

"That's odd," Becky said.

"They're probably all back in the rehearsal room."

"Mmm, yeah. You're probably right. You know how Marty is about that threadbare old carpet in the lobby."

We headed back the way we had come and wound around to the rear of the theater. Hearing the faint sounds of music, we pounded on the door. Golden-haired Angelina opened it.

"Oh." Her smile of welcome was frankly unconvincing.

"Hey, the brain trust's here!" Dan called from across the room.

Angelina's gaze flicked from Dan to Becky and the wattage of her smile faded from dim to barely on.

Dan made it to Becky's side with the speed of a lovesick swain. He was wearing his Dr. Frankenstein costume—lab coat and fright wig—and his face was blanched and aged with makeup. He handed us each a class of punch that, from the fumes, had more than a splash of alcohol.

"Here. You can catch up while you're getting into costume." He raised his glass. "To Tom!"

We clinked plastic and headed into the makeshift girls dressing room off one side of the rehearsal stage. I speed-changed, eager to get to the tiny cold cut tray I'd spied before all the roast beef was gone.

"Hold on." Becky grabbed hold of my cape as I was about to dart out. "What about your vampire makeup?"

"I'll get vampire teeth from Marty later. Trust me, he has a whole drawer of them in the lobby."

"No, I mean the rest of it." Pushing me down onto a folding chair, she pulled out of her bag a fresh makeup sponge and a large compact with divots of white, green and black makeup. "I use this for my Frankenstein's monster look, but it should work for vampires as well. One color palette fits all when you come back to life after being dead."

"I don't want it." I pushed the makeup away.

"Too bad." She dabbed the sponge in the face whitener and blended in a little green.

Regarding me critically, she frowned, squinted, and leaned toward my face for a closer look. "You're skin's positively glowing! It's like you've been sprinkled with fairy dust. Did you buy some new base or something?" She rubbed a finger across my cheek and sat back in astonishment when it didn't come away covered with makeup.

"My...um, mother brought me some sort of experimental face stuff from Europe."

"Shit, next time, have her get some for me."

"Are you going to vamp me up or not?"

It didn't take her long. She set the makeup with a thin layer of a translucent powder, which she applied with a huge fluffy brush.

"Ta da!"

She passed me her compact so I could admire her expertise in the mirror. The transformation was startling. The heavy makeup had crisped my reflection even more than the holy water, and for the first time in over a year, I saw my face almost clearly in the mirror. Or, rather, I saw *a face*. The milky coating of greenish-white base made me even more pale than usual. My hazel-green eyes looked huge under a thick coating of eyeliner and mascara and my lips were blood red.

I looked like a B-movie vampire. All I lacked was the requisite fangs. I snapped the compact shut and handed it back. "Ready?"

"God no. I still need to do all my scars. You go ahead. You've got that look."

"What look?"

"Like you're going to kill someone if you don't eat soon."

I stared at her in horrified silence.

She frowned. "Kidding. Geez. What is *with* you lately." She shoved me toward the party. "Go. I'll catch up."

Kicking myself for my overreaction, I made my way to the food table for some serious comfort eating. What I *wanted* was a big plate of the roast beef, but I made myself a proper sandwich with lettuce and tomatoes and even added a couple of carrot sticks to the side of my plate. I was going to eat like a regular person if it killed me.

Despite my good intentions, I went a little overboard on the roast beef. I could barely open my mouth wide enough to get a corner in my mouth. But I managed somehow and was maneuvering in for a second mouthful when Marty burst through the connecting door from the main theater and swore aloud.

Conversation stopped. Marty wasn't a public swearer.

"Sorry. Didn't mean—" He was sweating as if he'd been running laps in a sauna. He pulled out a handkerchief and wiped his brow. It only added to the oddness of the moment. I didn't know about anyone else, but I hadn't seen someone use a real handkerchief since my grandfather Gartner had last whipped one out. And even he had given them up a good ten years ago in favor of disposable tissues.

Visibly pulling himself together, Marty announced, "I regret to tell you all that the haunted house has been shut down."

"The health inspector finally realized those rat-sized cockroaches aren't stage props?" someone quipped, to a chorus of tipsy giggles and guffaws.

Apparently the drinking part of Tom's wake was well underway.

A man I'd never seen before came to stand behind Marty in the doorway. He had on the same plain-clothed cop "uniform" of slacks, button-down, and tie that Gavin always wore. His watchful eyes scanned the room like lasers. *Detective*, I thought, clutching my sandwich hard. I put the sandwich down before the roast beef dropped down my front.

"No," Marty said. There was a quality in his voice that made the room go silent. "The Long Beach Police Department has shut us down because Tom didn't die of a heart attack last night. He was murdered."

# Chapter Six

ir, I'll thank you to leave the explanations to us." The detective stepped past Marty into the rehearsal room. A soft paunch pressed at the belt of his gray slacks, suggesting too many fast-food meals behind a desk. The pear-like shape, together with his sallow complexion and thick unibrow, made him look a little like Bert from Sesame Street. Which made his solemnity all the more chilling.

"The Milverne Theater will be locked until further notice. We'd like to ask your patience while we ask each of you a few questions." He was immediately barraged with questions, protests, and the occasional whining complaint.

A second detective followed in through the door but remained in the background, silently watching us.

"Why would anyone kill *Tom*?" Becky asked me in a low voice, under the noise.

"Hate, unrequited love, money, fame…"

Her eyebrows rose with each word I uttered. "Have you met Tom?" She winced. "That didn't come out quite right. I didn't mean to be disrespectful, it's just that…"

"I know." Tom was the kind of guy you cast as the hero's younger brother Chip, who had to stay behind. He didn't exactly inspire strong emotions. Unless you happened to be the one whose dessert he'd swiped.

Our whispered conversation came to a halt as the detectives quieted the room and gave out general instructions that basically amounted to "hurry up and wait, and don't even think of talking to one another". Becky and I exchanged surreptitious looks but dutifully moved apart and headed to the side of the room as directed.

Wishing I hadn't left my sandwich on the table, yet sure I couldn't have eaten a bite, I leaned back against the wall and pulled my cape around me, grateful for its warmth. Marty might have opened his wallet for the liquor portion of Tom's wake, but he wasn't wasting precious dimes turning on the heat. I closed my eyes and tried to make myself comfortable. If my experience with police investigations last winter was any indication, we would be here for a while.

To my surprise, I was questioned briefly and hustled out the door in about half an hour. As Marty himself hadn't let me leave my post anytime close to the moment of Tom's death, I was a person of little interest. I would have cheered my good luck, except that now I was banned to the even colder parking lot. Not sure what else to do, I went and stood by Becky's car.

Becky was still inside, waiting for her turn. At least I assumed she was. If she was hiding in a dark corner making out with Dan Sterling, I was going to kill her. The last thing I needed to be doing was hanging around a deserted parking lot at night, wearing something from Elvira's closet.

If I'd had on better shoes—and a bra—I would have jogged the three miles home. I was digging in my bag for my cell phone to call a cab when I heard someone coming around the side of the building.

It was a man. I wasn't sure how I knew, but I did.

"Okay," I told myself, scrabbling in earnest for my cell. "No need to panic. It's probably just the next person who's been questioned and released."

Except, if it was, they'd be exiting through the back of the theater, not coming around the side.

I couldn't find my phone. I was about to dodge behind the sole minivan in the parking lot when the footsteps stopped.

A voice came from the shadows. "Jo? What the hell are you doing out here?"

Gavin separated from the darkness and strode toward me. My breath rushed out in a combination of relief and irritation.

"You scared me!"

"Go home."

"I'm working on it." I jerked my head toward the theater. "They've got my ride in there for questioning."

"I can take you." He pulled car keys from a pocket in his slacks.

"Thanks."

I didn't bother to pretend I wasn't thrilled to get out of there. I scribbled a note for Becky, snapped it under her front wiper, and followed Gavin to his Jetta.

"How come you're able to leave? Aren't you in charge of the case? First detective on the scene or something?"

"This isn't my particular area of expertise."

"No vampires," I said, relieved.

Gavin beeped open his car and circled around to the driver's side. He studied me over the roof of the Jetta. "I wouldn't say that, exactly."

It was like he'd punched me in the stomach. I realized when he looked at me, he didn't see *me*. He saw a woman who was turning into a vampire.

"Why are you standing there?" Gavin said irritably. "Get in."

"Are you sure? I wouldn't want to compromise your integrity. Or endanger you. Halloween's around the corner and the moon's almost full. I could turn on you at any time."

"Jesus. I don't have time for— Get in the damn car, Jo."

I wouldn't. I couldn't. Not when he thought of me as…some sort of monster.

With a snarl of exasperation, Gavin came around to my side of the car. "What the hell is wrong with you? Standing there like that when it's dark out?" Yanking open the passenger door, he unceremoniously shoved me into the seat, got in his side, and told me to put on my seatbelt. We drove off in silence.

My stomach rumbled.

"Have you eaten?" he asked.

"Yes." Two bites of roast beef sandwich.

"I haven't." Gavin pulled into a drive-through and ordered himself a number six and an orange juice without consulting the menu. "Sure you don't want anything? Raw meat on a bun? Steak tartare milkshake?"

That was low. It had been a moment of weakness that I'd never repeated. I wanted to tell him what he could do with his steak tartare shake, but my stomach growled again. I leaned across the console to call my order out to the microphone. Gavin pressed back into the leather of the driver's seat and tightened his hands where they rested on his thighs, as if I had cooties.

"I'll have your thickest burger. That restaurant one, plain, very rare. I like it raw in the middle."

Gavin's mouth grew tighter at the last, but all he said was, "Wrong chain."

I flopped back in my seat. "Please. They all have some giant burger now."

"You shouldn't order like that. You'll get E. coli."

"Like *that's* my biggest worry."

Gavin drove to the next window and, ignoring the ten I waved in his direction, paid and dumped the bag in my lap. I had it open before we left the parking lot, intending to snitch a few of Gavin's fries.

There weren't any.

I crumpled the bag shut and twisted in my seat to face him. "What is it with you and fries, Gavin? The first person who orders always gets them. Supersizes them. The whole point of coming here is for the fries."

"I thought it was to get something to eat."

I rolled my eyes and kicked the bag under the dashboard. "You'd better get with the program or your girlfriend isn't going to stick around for long."

He braked for a red light and turned to face me. "Who?"

"What do you mean *who*? How many girlfriends do you have? The woman you were with last Saturday night."

"Oh." Comprehension dawned. "You mean Sara."

"Try to have a little enthusiasm for the woman you like, Gavin."

He stared at me for a beat. The air in the car seemed to disappear. "I have plenty of enthusiasm."

The light turned green and we drove the rest of the way home in silence. It was not companionable.

Gavin followed me up and in to my apartment without asking. I threw my shoulder bag in the direction of the table by the door, but it got tangled in my cape and landed instead on the floor by my feet. I stepped over it and headed for my bedroom. "I'm getting out of this stupid costume. Don't eat my dinner."

"Wouldn't dream of it. Hold on, who is this?"

He pointed down at Fluffy, who was rubbing a cheek on his ankle. Not once had she done that to me.

"You are such a little turd," I told the cat. "That," I informed Gavin, as I headed down the short hall to my bedroom, "is Fluffy. I'm babysitting her for my Aunt Bertha."

A few minutes later, dressed in jeans and a thick yellow Pooh sweatshirt, I joined Gavin at my kitchen table. He was halfway through his grilled chicken sandwich. Fluffy was splayed bonelessly on his lap, purring like a steam engine.

Ignoring them both, I dug into my burger with relish. They'd done a nice job of barely cooking it. Most places were too concerned about health code regulations to leave it really rare. It must have been a new guy at the grill. I made a mental note to go back and find out his shift schedule.

When I was done, I wiped my hands clean on a stack of napkins. Fluffy had fallen asleep and Gavin had moved on to wordlessly making his way through a side salad. The silence was grating on my nerves. I was tempted to lick the juice off my burger wrapper just to annoy Gavin, but I was afraid I might enjoy it too much. Besides, I wanted him to stay so I could ask him some questions about what was going on. I gathered up my trash and threw it in the bin under the sink.

Gavin might eat annoyingly healthfully but he never said no to homemade cookies. I put enough gingersnaps on a plate for both of us and brought it back to the table with me.

He stared at the plate as if it contained coiled cobras. And then he stared at me.

"You made gingersnaps?" His voice was oddly strangled.

"As you see." I jiggled the plate.

"You always make chocolate chip."

"There *are* other cookies, Gavin. Do you want some or not?"

He leaned back in the kitchen chair, crossed his arms over his chest and narrowed his eyes at me.

"That depends. Do these have cyanide in them?"

"What?" The plate tilted and the cookies began to slide.

Gavin caught the plate and put it on the table. He did not take a cookie.

"Is that what killed Tom?" My voice seemed to have shrunk by half. "I thought he had a heart attack. Marty said—"

"Marty Milverne would say anything to keep that theater open. We might have believed it was a heart attack, except Tom cut his arm at some point and his blood was the wrong color when it came out. Too red. They fast-tracked him at the coroner's office. Found cookies in his stomach and some in his pocket with what appeared to be traces of cyanide powder. They'll need the tests back to be certain, but…" His shrug told me they were pretty darn sure what the tests would say.

"Are you going to arrest me?"

"Should I?"

"Do you think I did it?"

"No." He grinned suddenly. "If you wanted to kill him, you would have beaten him to death with your sundae spoon that night at the diner. You wouldn't have poisoned your own cookies. You're not that stupid."

"*That* stupid? I'm not *that* stupid?"

I stood, hands on hips, and if he could have expired from a look he would have keeled over.

Putting Fluffy gently on the floor, he got to his feet with the speedy grace of an athlete. He ate up the distance between us in two large strides, grasped my shoulders and shook me. "What is wrong with you tonight?"

He was so close I had to tilt my head back to look at him. His eyes had gone silver. A strange warmth coursed over me, robbing me of my breath.

Gavin released me. He moved past me with as wide a berth as the small kitchen allowed and headed for the front door. "I'll call you tomorrow around dusk to make sure you made it home safely. Try to stay out of trouble."

"Why do you keep saying that?"

"You noticed? Good. Maybe it will stick. Make sure your windows are locked."

And he was gone.

~*~

I had to hit the snooze alarm twice before I was able to haul myself out of bed the next morning. As I drove my seven-minute commute down the peninsula to Bayshore, I fought hard against the impulse to pull a U-turn and go back to bed. Calling in sick was a luxury I couldn't afford, now that I was involved, however peripherally, in another murder. If I didn't show up, everyone would think I was in jail.

The first bell rang as I squeezed the Volvo into a compact spot a few inches wider than the rectangle of the car. I had five minutes to get up to my classroom and let in my homeroom kids. I made it in four and a half, and that included a pass through the faculty room to get the morning announcements out of my mailbox.

Wheezing, I stuck my key in the lock and pushed open the door just as the bell rang. There was a chorus of disappointed groans as my eighth-grade advisees followed me in. We'd made a deal that if I was late three times I had to bring doughnuts, and my count was already at two.

I handed the still-warm half sheet of school announcements to one of my advisees to read. "Stop your whining," I told them. "You've already gotten doughnuts three times."

"Four," someone corrected.

Jeez. "Listen to the announcements. Go ahead, Quentin."

Quentin was a slow speaker. By the time he finished the announcements, the bell rang and our five minutes of homeroom was over. I sagged in relief as they hefted backpacks and scurried to their first classes without mentioning the haunted house. Apparently, the news of Tom's murder hadn't yet made the rounds.

My first class came in and sat down with the usual quiet distraction of a test day. While they drew atom orbitals and made density calculations, I sifted through my astronomy notes from last year. With all the things vying for attention in my head, my opening lecture wasn't fine tuned beyond, "The universe is really, really big."

My students and I worked industriously on our respective tasks right up to the bell. They left without comment, aside from the usual fretful moaning from the A students about how hard the test had been.

A few hours later, when the lunch bell rang and my students didn't bolt for the cafeteria, I knew the first feelers of gossip had made the rounds. I distracted them with a comment about needing to grade tests and kicked them out. I gave the hallways five minutes to clear, donned my protective sun gear and ran downstairs to find Becky. The next wave of students wouldn't be so easy to put off and I needed to brainstorm ways to shut them down.

Her classroom was locked. Again. I caught a glimpse of movement in the back of the room through the little window in her door and knocked. She hurried over and let me in.

"Lock that behind you, will you?"

I followed her to the back room where she stored the chemicals. She was wearing a fitted lime green lab coat and elbow length rubber gloves in preparation for scrubbing glassware at the sink. In a sudden spurt of jealousy, I forgot why I had come.

"Where did you get that lab coat?" Mine had come with my classroom. It was standard-issue white and made for a much shorter, stouter person. It had mysterious stains. And a burn mark on the left cuff, but that was mine.

"You can have them special ordered in any color," Becky said, plunging a bottle brush into a test tube.

"And Roger will pay for it?" I asked, surprised.

"How much sleep did *you* get last night?"

"Oh right," I muttered. Our department chair wouldn't pay for a new set of whiteboard markers without a fight. Like the sleek lab goggles she wore instead of the bulbous classroom ones, Becky had paid for the coat herself. As she often said, if you had to spend ten hours a day somewhere, you might as well look good.

She broke from cleaning and I stared back in surprise at the fatigue etched on her unusually pale face. Becky bragged about how she didn't need more than four or five hours of sleep a night, and it was a fair claim. She could—and did—go clubbing on a school night before a day of double chem labs, and when school ended, she would stay for another couple of hours cheerfully cleaning and grading.

"What time did *you* get home?" I asked in concern.

"They didn't let me go until four." She put the last test tube on a rack to dry, pulled off her gloves and slumped wearily against the spotless blacktopped counter. My concern grew. Becky leaned coolly, if she leaned at all. She didn't slump.

"Four? Why? Who's 'they'?"

This earned me another flash of impatience for a slow mind. "The police. Who else?"

"Are you kidding me? I was home by nine."

"Yeah, I got the message that hunky cop drove you home." Her black eyebrows danced suggestively under the green spikes. "I always wondered if there was something going on with you two last spring."

"Please. Gavin thinks of me as an annoying little sister. He's very happy with his girlfriend." *Plenty of enthusiasm*, he'd said. I pushed away the thought and the unexpected flash of jealousy that accompanied it. His social life was none of my business. I certainly didn't care whom he dated.

"Uh-huh."

"Trust me. He barely thinks of me as human." That was all too true. And if I slid any further into the gray area between normal person and vampire, the honorable Detective Gavin Raines wouldn't think twice before plunging a stake through my chest. "Stop changing the subject."

Becky stared unseeingly at a *The Far Side* poster of a fat kid trying to push his way into The School for the Gifted through a door marked "pull". She was silent so long I began to wonder if she'd fallen asleep with her eyes open. Yet another critical teacher's skill I needed to master as soon as possible. Without it, I didn't think I'd make it through another year of faculty meetings with my sanity intact.

"Becky?"

"The police think I tried to poison Dan."

"That's ridiculous! Wait…Dan? Drama Dan?"

"Yes, Dan. Tom died from cyanide poisoning after eating some of Dan's gingersnaps."

"How the hell do you know all this?" I demanded.

"The police aren't exactly a model of discretion."

"In my experience," I said, "they're pretty good at keeping things to themselves in a possible murder investigation."

"I don't think they realized how good the acoustics are in the theater."

Becky looked a little guilty. I was pretty sure what the police hadn't realized was that Becky had been eavesdropping.

She waved an impatient hand through the air. "My point is—"

"It doesn't make sense. I made the cookies. If you're right, I should be the primary suspect."

She looked offended. "I didn't tell them *you* made the gingersnaps."

"Becky!"

"Like I was going to sic those idiots on you when you had nothing to do with it."

"What makes you so sure I didn't do it?" I was genuinely curious.

"Whoever did it probably used potassium cyanide or sodium cyanide. You can order either over the Internet pretty easily. They're both white powders. You know as well as I that you rolled your cookies in those big pieces of clear crunchy sugar. What's that called?"

"Turbinado," I answered automatically. "But that hardly—"

She shook her head to silence me. "If you'd put cyanide on the cookies, we'd both be dead. We transferred them to the Frankenstein tin I got for Dan, remember? Cyanide absorbs through the skin into the bloodstream like that." She snapped her fingers.

"Becky, you need to tell them. Gavin—Detective Raines—knows I made the gingersnaps. I offered him some last night."

She stared at me wide-eyed and then started to laugh. "Only you, Jo."

"How was I supposed to know? Anyway, I still could have done it. You don't know for sure that it's cyanide. The police still have to get the autopsy results back."

"Please. The tests are just official pieces of paper to cover their asses for when they go to court. Cyanide's easy to identify, especially if your medical examiner is one of the fifty percent of the population who can detect the almond smell. Even if he lacks the gene, I'm sure someone on his staff has it."

"Exactly how long were you eavesdropping on the police last night?"

I had a passing thought that she knew an awful lot about this, and chided myself for even thinking it. Becky hadn't killed Tom. It was too sloppily done, for starters. If Becky wanted someone dead, she would have come up with something that was undetectable by police labs and absolutely untraceable to her.

"I still don't see why you think someone was trying to poison Dan. If someone sprinkled cyanide powder on the cookies, anyone could've eaten one. It's just Tom's misfortune that he's so piggy and he got to them first." I couldn't keep a note of disgust out of my voice.

Becky leaned forward, her face earnest, her dark eyes intent. "You don't get it. I know Dan usually puts food out to share, but he's crazy about gingersnaps. He hid the tin under his sweatshirt and it was still there when the police went to look for it. Tom must have found the cookies by accident, snitched a few and put the tin back so Dan wouldn't know."

"If cyanide is so toxic, why didn't Tom keel over in the dressing room?"

"Don't you remember his zombie costume? He wore gloves."

Oh. I sat heavily on a stool and looked up at her, not sure whether I believed it or not, but quite sure I didn't want to. This was getting uglier by the moment. "But who'd want to kill *Dan*?"

# Chapter Seven

**A**pparently, *me*." Becky tried to look as if she didn't care, but it was about as convincing as her green hair.

"Oh please. The police are clueless if they think you tried to kill Dan. Have they seen the way you look at him? It's sickening."

My jollying got me a ghost of a smile that lasted only a second before it twisted beyond recognition.

I blew out a sigh. "I wish I could tell you it's going to get easier, Becks, but I can't. You're on the police radar and until they figure things out, you're going to get treated with suspicion."

"I know." She pulled a cheap brown paper towel from the holder over the sink, swiped a couple of times at her nose and flung the wadded ball into the trash. "Which is why we're going to find out who did this."

"What do you mean, *we*?"

"C'mon, Jo. It's obvious the police aren't going to figure it out. They still half think Tom was the target and that Dan and I did him in."

"You don't know that."

Becky shot me the same look Fluffy had given me that morning when I'd tried to foist on her a can of Chicken Dinner instead of the Tuna Delight she favored.

"We can start sleuthing tonight. They're setting up another haunted house in the parking lot."

"What?" I sputtered. "Why would anyone want to do *that* after what happened to Tom? Is it even legal?"

"Marty already has the permits. He wanted the hunted house out there all along. All those people tromping through his theater, wearing out that ugly, forty-year-old carpet?" She snorted. "Point is, 'His Cheapness' doesn't want all the advertising to go to waste, *especially* the free advertising. After the news of Tom's murder hits the papers, people are going to come in droves."

Her voice took on a pleading quality. "All the haunted house workers will be there tonight, setting it up. We ask a few questions—"

I held up my hands and backed up. "No. No way. Not a chance."

"It gets dark at six, Jo. There won't be any trouble with your sun allergy."

"This isn't about my sun allergy and you know it. We are not going to do any sleuthing. That's called interfering with an investigation." I wasn't sure if that was strictly true, but I didn't really care. "Trust me—you want to stay far, far away, before people start labeling you a love-crazed mass murderer."

"Don't be ridiculous."

"You're not love-crazed?"

Becky didn't respond.

"It's stupid and dangerous, Becky. Let the police do the investigating. It's their job."

"Tell me you believe that if you'd left things to the police last spring you'd still be alive right now." She crossed her arms over her chest and leaned back against the edge of the sink.

I opened my mouth to protest, but no words came out. What was I supposed to say? Well, Becky, I would gladly have left it to the police. But it was a little hard to avoid them, seeing as I had a detective sleeping in my living room so the vampire who tried to turn me didn't finish the job. And now the vampire is back again, with Lord only knows what on his agenda, and spending time in a parking lot at night *really* isn't a good idea for me right now.

"Didn't think so. We can do this, Jo," she pleaded. "We're scientists, trained to look at evidence and draw conclusions. And since we're not police, people will tell us stuff. All we have to do is apply our talents to the problem and we'll figure it out in no time."

"No."

"I can't believe you don't want to help, especially after what you went through last year. You were a social pariah for months! You know you're going to be one again if this doesn't clear up fast. It's going to get around that you made the cookies."

I didn't respond.

"You're going to sit by and let other people go through the same horrible things you went through," she said incredulously.

"It's hardly the same thing, Becky!"

"Isn't it?"

"No! You have no idea what happened to me! You dealt with a few suspicious looks for a few hours. That is nothing! I—"

It was pointless. Becky would never understand because I would never tell her what was really going on. I forced myself to take a breath and calm down. "It's a bad idea," I said finally.

Becky stood facing me, hands clenched, her eyes luminous with disappointment.

"Fine. I'll do it alone. You're free to follow your conscience. I have to follow mine. Now, if you don't mind, I have some prep work to finish before my next class comes in."

"Becky…"

She turned her back to me and busied herself putting clean glassware in the cabinets.

I stomped out, shut her door with exaggerated care and strode rapidly through the maze of indoor hallways and covered corridors to the cafeteria. It was obviously pointless to reason with Becky. She couldn't recognize reason right now if it bit her on the butt. Otherwise, she'd realize that the police must believe the cookies were poisoned *after* she gave them to Dan. Or else she'd be talking to a lawyer right now and Gavin would never have let me off so lightly when he learned I'd made them.

They'd questioned Becky, not because they thought she'd murdered Tom, but because they hoped she could direct them to the person who had.

And speaking of faulty logic, I wasn't so sure I agreed Dan was the intended victim. From what Becky had told me about cyanide, using it to kill someone required a lot of planning. And yet the killer had carefully targeted Dan by…doctoring cookies left under a sweatshirt where anyone could have found them?

It was too random. I wasn't buying it. And if Becky was her usual logic-minded self instead of this half-crazed emotion-driven Dan groupie, she wouldn't be buying it either.

"Hi Laurel. Could I trouble you for some more…ah, that's it. Thanks."

As I took my slab of pot pie, with an extra spoonful of gravy, from the grandmotherly woman who ruled the lunch line, Carol waved to me from the back of the cafeteria.

I slammed my tray onto the table and sat heavily in an orange plastic chair across from her.

"What's wrong?"

I poked at my pot pie, assessing the beef to vegetable ratio. "Is it just me, or has the student health club gotten to them again?" The cafeteria made lunch from scratch, mostly. "This is all carrots and peas."

Carol pursed her lips in disapprobation. It was a little like watching Glinda the Good Witch try to look angry. If the Oz witch had had brown hair, gold rimmed glasses and a few more pounds around her middle.

I pushed a bright green pea to the side of my plate, the way I'd corralled onion slices in my mom's spaghetti sauce as a kid.

"I swear, you're worse than the seventh graders. Eat your veggies. They're good for you. Now, what's wrong, *besides* lunch? Your students been giving you a hard time about the haunted house?"

Carol was just as tuned in to the school gossip network as the librarians—if not more so. The difference was that she used her powers for good, keeping abreast of the rumors to correct the stupid and hurtful ones where she could.

"Not really," I said. "Chemistry test. But we start astronomy tomorrow."

She nodded, immediately understanding that our grade-obsessed students wouldn't waste time gossiping on a test day, but they would waste time like crazy at the start of a new unit, especially when that unit was astronomy. Tomorrow, I was doomed.

"Not the easiest of units," Carol mused. "I wonder sometimes if it might be better to switch that unit to the spring, when eighth graders might be better able to grasp abstract concepts like light years and Doppler shifts."

"Yeah, but then I'd have to contend with spring fever."

"Mmm," she nodded thoughtfully. "I can see how that would be worse." She popped a bite of dressingless salad into her mouth and chewed with all the enjoyment of a forced march.

"Not to mention, I'd have a dozen parents calling to complain that I was teaching in a different order than in the book."

"They don't do that."

"They do to me."

Carol bit back a grin.

"It isn't funny."

"I know." The grin lingered a moment longer before she was able to wipe it off her face.

I carefully arranged a bite of potpie on my spoon. A hunk of beef, half a carrot slice, one pea, a bit of crust and lots of gravy.

"And Becky's mad at me," I said.

"Becky?" Carol looked surprised. "Why?"

I stuck the loaded spoon into my mouth to buy myself time. I wasn't sure how much to tell Carol. It's not that I was worried about her spreading gossip. Things I told her went into the vault and stayed there. But telling her about Becky's plan to solve the mystery of Tom's death to protect her would-be boyfriend seemed like tattling. Especially as I wasn't sure I would be able to phrase it in a way that wouldn't have Carol barging into Becky's room to pound some sense into her.

I shrugged and skirted the truth. "They're putting up another haunted house in the theater parking lot. I think it's a bad idea and I don't really want to volunteer there anymore."

Ignoring the carrots and peas, I scooped up a hunk of beef and gravy. As I chewed, I caught myself swirling the gravy on my tongue and wishing I was eating juicy, raw beef instead. Disgusted with myself, I made myself eat three carrot wedges in a row. My "this isn't meat" gag reflex instantly kicked in, which so annoyed me that I ate some peas.

Carol reached across the table and squeezed my forearm. "You had a rough time of it last spring. The last thing you'd want to do is be anywhere near another investigation."

"Exactly."

For some reason, her support made me feel worse. Weren't friends supposed to put themselves out a little for friendship's sake? I remembered how Becky and Carol had rallied around me last year, even when it had been a vastly unpopular way to go. Becky and Carol and Jo. All for one and one for all.

I ate another carrot.

~*~

When the last of my students left my classroom at the end of the day, I shoved on my sun hat and went downstairs. I wasn't sure what I was going to say to Becky, but I needed to make things right.

"Ms. Gartner!"

I whipped around to find my department chair haring toward me from the left branch of the hallway. He was so angry his face was purple. He lowered his voice in deference to eavesdropping high schoolers, but still somehow managed to shout at me.

"What is the meaning of *this*?" He shook a newspaper under my nose.

"I have no idea, Roger."

He thrust the *Press Telegram* into my hands and planted a stubby index finger under a photograph of the haunted house on the front page. It was a little grainy, but behind the crowd of people in the foreground, I recognized myself. I was turned away from the camera, but it was still me. A lot of me. I was going to kill Becky for encouraging me to wear that bustier in public.

"This is absolutely appalling!" Roger said.

My mouth flopped open a couple of times but I couldn't get any words out, even if I'd known what to say. The picture of me in the bustier, while not my usual style, was perfectly decent. But as I stood in the judging presence of my ultra-conservative department chair, the neckline of that bustier seemed to drop another inch. I pulled the collar of my unisex button-down shirt a little tighter around my neck.

He stabbed the paper again. "Read that."

Swallowing, I read aloud, "'Local Haunted House Proves Deadly'. What an incredibly insensitive headline," I said, outraged on Tom's behalf. "Imagine how his family will feel when they see that."

Roger ripped the paper back out of my hands and shoved the picture in my face. "This is an embarrassment to everyone here."

My eyes focused on the shot of my cleavage. "I *beg* your pardon?"

"*We* have a reputation to uphold. *I expected*, after your experience last spring, that you would have learned *something* about the appropriate conduct of a *Bayshore Academy* faculty member. And yet here you are, involved with another sordid—"

I turned away before I said something that got me fired, and strode rapidly back down the hall. Roger would have to jog after me if he wanted to keep insulting me. Without thinking, I headed for Becky's room for comfort instead of returning to my own. Rounding the corner like a bullet train, I plowed smack into Dan Sterling.

# Chapter Eight

*D*an reached out to steady me. "Whoa, speedy! You okay?"

"Yeah. You?"

We were about the same height and had narrowly missed knocking each other out.

"Trust me—I get battered worse than this on a daily basis." At my blank stare, he explained, "We do drama exercises in the mornings to improve our craft. Last week it was physical comedy, this week it's sword fights."

"That must be fun," I said enviously, thinking of the astronomy lecture I'd be giving while Dan was swashbuckling around a stage in the Milverne rehearsal room with his colleagues.

"It is, until someone's sword slips." He gingerly rubbed a shoulder and his mobile face pulled into an exaggerated grimace of pain. "They're not sharp but they can leave impressive bruises."

"Ouch."

Dan's charm was a relief after Roger's venomous arrogance. My shoulders started to climb down from around my ears.

"How come you're on campus?" I hadn't seen him at Bayshore since our regular drama teacher had returned from maternity leave.

Dan's wince was genuine this time. "Picking up my last paycheck. With the haunted house closed, it's going to have to last."

"I thought you guys were going to whip up a new one in the parking lot."

He shrugged. "It was a nice idea, but…"

"A lot of work."

"Yeah."

"Does Becky know it's not happening?"

"She knew it was a possibility. I was on my way to tell her." He started walking toward Becky's room and I fell into step beside him.

"I didn't know you were getting paid for the haunted house. I suppose it makes sense. After all, if you weren't doing the haunted house, you could be making money acting elsewhere."

Dan shook his head. "The haunted house was a labor of love for all of us. All the money went into the general fund. But now that our fall fundraiser's kaput, the Milverne can't afford to put on as many plays, which means less work and fewer paychecks for us."

His words had a slightly canned ring to them. I had a feeling I would have known all this if I had been on time to that first volunteer's meeting. Or paid a lick of attention to his speech after I finally did arrive.

Becky was at her desk, grading. Her face lit up when she saw Dan. The smile faded when she saw me.

Dan said, "Hey, Becks. I see you made it through the day okay. Sorry about the late night."

"Like it's your fault." Becky put down her grading pen and came around her desk to join us. "How's the new haunted house going?"

"Canceled," Dan leaned back against the counter. "Not enough volunteers."

"I'll bet the drama kids will help. If *you* ask them." Becky batted her eyelashes suggestively.

He said, "Actually, that's not a bad idea. The kids can help with…"

We all turned as Roger thundered into the classroom like an angry bull and shut the door behind him. I braced myself for the rest of his "teachers represent the school, even when they're not on campus" speech, but Roger's anger had a new target. He rounded on Dan.

"Do I understand that you plan to use Bayshore Academy students to do something that will financially benefit your theater?"

Becky opened her mouth to respond, but Dan beat her to it. "Hello, Roger. Nice to see you again. Yes, I'm going to ask students to volunteer some time at the theater."

"It's completely inappropriate. You are no longer a teacher here." The way Roger said "teacher" made clear his opinion of the arts program. "Which, given your poor judgment, can only be a good thing."

Becky said, "You're taking it the wrong way, Roger. Dan—"

"*That* is for the administration to decide." Roger spun on his heel and left.

Dan dropped his friendly veneer. He rubbed his eyes tiredly. "Damn," he said softly. He looked at us with a small, twisted grin. "That went well."

"Don't worry," I said. Ten minutes ago, I would have stopped there, but Roger's pigheadedness had cleared a few things up for me. "It'll work out.

You've got Becky and me to help. Well, you get me as soon as the sun goes down, but in the meantime, I'll help you hunt down the drama kids. I'm sure they'll lend a hand."

I got the full Becky grin. "I'll go find the headmaster and remind him that Roger's full of shit." She grabbed her keys off her desk. "Diplomatically, of course."

We both stared at her.

"Hey, I can do diplomacy. I've learned a few acting tips hanging around the theater all week. Might as well put them to use."

~*~

I decided it was a good time to put one of *my* new resources to use—a functioning cell number for Gavin. If I was going to do some sleuthing, or, as was more likely, spend an evening reining in Becky, I needed to know as much about what was really going on as possible.

"What you want?"

No, no, don't shower me with warmth. I might get a swelled head. "Did you tell the other detectives that I made the cookies?" No sense beating around the bush.

"Are you suggesting I withheld evidence from the principals on the case?"

Someone was in a bad mood. "Of course not. I just wondered if it was important."

"Everything's important."

I made myself count to ten. It was the only way to keep from saying some rude, and I didn't want Gavin to hang up on me. One, two...

"Is that all?" he asked.

"No. I wondered how seriously the police are considering the theory that someone was actually trying to poison Dan."

"It's a theory, is it?"

"Oh, come on. They were Dan's cookies. It's not too big a stretch to imagine Tom taking something that wasn't his."

"Sounds as if you haven't forgiven Tom for eating your sundae at the diner."

For a moment, the only sound was the grating of my teeth.

"I assure you, we consider all options when we investigate a suspicious death."

"Glad to hear it, Detective."

"Anything else?"

"I wouldn't dream of taking up any more of your precious time," I said. "Thank you so much for easing my concerns."

"I knew giving you my cell number wasn't a good idea," he muttered.

"Actually, I think the cell phone was a very *good* idea. If I were talking to you in person right now, you'd have to throw me in jail for police brutality. And think of all the tiresome paperwork *that* would generate." I punched off my phone, forced a smile on my face, and went to find some high school drama kids to help with the haunted house.

~*~

Becky had left school a half-hour before me, but I caught up to her three blocks from the theater as she was wedging her Mustang into a microscopic spot. I lucked into a parking place big enough for the Volvo only a half block farther down the street.

Becky waited for me and we walked to the theater together. She was still fuming from no-parking road rage. "Remind me never to be late for a play here. There is zero street parking. I feel like I've been circling for hours. What were they thinking, setting up the haunted house in the parking lot? Where's everyone supposed to put their cars? Sometimes I think theater people take the 'show must go on' philosophy a little too far."

She pointed a finger at me. "Don't even think of reminding me that I supported this crazy idea."

"Wasn't gonna."

We reached the theater and followed the sounds of activity around to the back.

"Holy cow," I said, squinting against the brightness.

A long row of floodlights amped up the light from the streetlights, illuminating...nothing. Unless visitors were supposed to imagine a haunted house in place of the chalked-in track snaking through the parking lot, we were in trouble. It occurred to me that the storage rooms with all the leftover plywood screens, black sheets and Halloween props were also behind locked doors that were covered with yellow crime-scene tape.

Houston, we have a problem.

Just then, a couple of pickup trucks, fully loaded and riding low, turned into the lot. A couple of burly guys descended from the truck cabs and started to unload old plywood sets with impressive efficiency. Another truck pulled in behind them. It looked as though whatever had been taking up space in theater storage rooms around town was getting trucked to the Milverne. I wondered who'd called in the favors.

Becky spied Dan coming around the dark side of the theater and sped to his side. I followed her. For a moment, I thought they had decided to admit their feelings and publicly embrace, but as I got closer, I realized they were arguing.

"All I'm saying is, be careful."

"You're nuts," Dan told her. "Tom died, not me. No one's secretly trying to kill me."

His response surprised me. Not only had I assumed he was on board with Becky's theory, I'd expected he would enjoy the attention.

Hearing my footsteps, Dan turned and placed a sympathetic hand on my shoulder. He admonished Becky, "The person who needs our support at this time is Jo."

Huh?

Someone called for Dan's help over at the trucks. He gave my shoulder a sympathetic squeeze and jogged over to help unload sets. Becky watched him go, a worried frown on her face.

My expression was one of bewilderment.

"What the hell?" I noticed then that a lot of people were shooting surreptitious looks of concern in my direction. "What the hell?" I repeated, a little more vehemently.

"I think…" Becky cleared her throat. "Everyone thinks you and Tom were dating."

"What? I barely knew him. The only time I really spent with him was that one night at the diner when you dragged me along so you and Dan could date. That's it, isn't it? Becky, what did you do?"

"Nothing…I… Oh, fine. I might have mentioned that Dan and I were only there because you and Tom wanted to meet."

My mouth flopped open. "I can't believe you did that. You know how I hate being the center of attention. These people are just as gossipy as teachers."

"Why do you think Dan and I were trying to keep it quiet? A lot of the female fans come because they like to sit in the audience and dream up scenarios where they and Dan meet and fall instantly in love, like a scene out of Cinderella."

"You sold me out for personal gain? I feel so much better."

"I didn't think you'd mind. You know no one would have cared if Tom hadn't been killed, and I could hardly have anticipated that!"

She was right, but that was beside the point. A group of volunteers was eyeing me and whispering, as if deliberating whether or not to come over to offer their condolences. I decided it was time to clear things up.

"Tom and I were not dating," I told Becky in ringing tones that carried.

"I know that. Why are you telling me? Unless…" Her eyebrows wiggled under the spiky green fringe of her bangs. "'He who doth protest too much'…"

My voice rose in real irritation. "Stop that. It was a fix-up. A bad one. All Tom did was talk about his stupid garage sale finds and then filch my dessert. I—"

I realized the parking lot had gone silent. Becky finally noticed all the people staring at us. It was hard not to, with the temperature dropping ten degrees from the icy looks sent my way.

"There's a time and a place," she said, trying not to laugh.

"Shut up."

I dragged her with me to the trucks. Dan and Ian, the tour guide who'd been dressed as Igor, had taken charge, directing the helpers to arrange sets along the chalked path. I didn't realize how heavy the sets were until I helped Ian carry one well into the middle of the horseshoe.

"Man, this is heavier than I thought it would be," I dropped my end with a loud thump and rubbed my sore shoulders.

"I could tell you it's functional, so they don't fall over in the middle of a performance when someone walks by, but the truth is, most theaters can't afford anything lighter. Can't afford to give us, anyway. Most of what we have here has been hanging around in theater basements for decades."

He pulled a ropy cobweb off his shirt. I was about to suggest we upgrade to a less cheesy brand of fake spider webs when I realized it was real. I spun around a few times to make sure a spider the size of Shelob wasn't piggybacking on my clothes.

Ian laughed. "You might have a career on the stage. Not everyone can do the 'help there's a spider on me' fear as convincingly as that."

I picked a microscopic fragment of web off my left sleeve. "I wasn't faking. But hey, I'll keep it in mind. It can't pay worse than teaching."

"Oh, it can." He shrugged. "But that's a vocation for you. Something gets in your blood. You do it because you have to, not for the money."

His face had lit with an inner fire. It was a little humbling, being around people like Ian and Dan, who truly loved what they were doing. I didn't have the heart to tell him my definition of "have to" was a little different than his. I certainly worked for the money, as little as it was.

He stepped back to get a read on how well the haunted house's skeleton was progressing.

"I think a first grader can make a better U-shape than that," I said.

"Agreed, but it's not so bad for our purposes. Having it twist and turn unexpectedly adds to the confusion for the people going through. And if the whole thing's snaky, you don't notice the gaps we deliberately make for people to jump out of."

I took a closer look at the set we'd carried. "And the palm trees and fish?"

"Adds to the confusion."

"Makes me feel like I should ditch my vampire costume and go home and get a snorkel and mask."

His grin widened and he leaned in. "So long as you wear a bikini with it, I won't mind the switch."

I took a step back. "We'd better get moving. Lots more to unload."

"Okey dokey." He flexed his biceps he-man style and led the way back to the trucks.

In no mood to flirt, I stepped back and let one of the prop guys take the other end when Ian picked up the next set. My next partner was a Bayshore high school girl. A confirmed Dan groupie, she was one of the handful of students who'd been with the haunted house from the beginning. I remembered from the walk-through that she had a minor role running across a passage carrying a heavy axe and had high hopes for her as a partner in drudgery.

The axe must have been hollow plastic. By the time she and I had dragged the set into place, I decided to let her get ahead too.

The haunted house progressed surprisingly quickly. Most of the tall sets that formed the walls of the haunted house were in place, and people were already stringing black sheets across the tops to form the ceiling. As I walked along the outer curve, I could hear volunteers inside chatting away.

I ignored the conversations, which were mostly on the order of "a little higher" and "pass the staple gun", until I heard someone say, "I heard he died eating cookies. What a way to go."

I slowed to listen.

"Best way…for him." There was a sound of protest, which the speaker ignored. "For him it was like dying while having sex. I've never met anyone who liked dessert more than Tom. That redhead he was dating—"

"Great," I muttered.

"She was totally right. You could be completely alone in the theater and then open a package of M&Ms and boom, a second later, Tom would be there with his hand in the bag."

I racked my brains. Did I recognize the voices? No. At least I didn't think so.

"We had someone in my dorm who would eat any junk food not nailed down, only they were sneakier about it. The midnight fridge raider."

"We had one of those. You'd put a pint of ice cream in the freezer, duct-taped shut, with your name plastered all over it, and the next day it would be empty."

"Exactly. Someone got so pissed once they made a tray of Ex-Lax brownies and left them as bait. Trust me, after that day in the bathroom, the midnight raider never raided again."

There was an indrawn gasp and a giggle. "Classic."

"Hey, can you pull that end taut?"

I heard the sound of a staple gun being put to use. Feeling guilty about eavesdropping, I started to walk away.

"I wonder if Dan did something like that," one of the speakers mused.

I stopped and silently walked back.

"Dan wouldn't poison his own cookies."

"Maybe not on purpose. But what if he didn't realize it was poison? Isn't he dating a chemistry teacher? If she's anything like the ones I had in high school, she can't tell Ex-Lax from arsenic."

Before I could do something stupid like scale the barrier and punch the speaker in the mouth, the conversation tapered off and I realized they were heading back to the supply trucks.

I remained rooted to my spot on the other side of the plywood sets. They say eavesdroppers hear nothing good about themselves, but aside from confirmation that my public attempt to unlink myself from Tom hadn't worked, it wasn't my integrity that had been questioned, but Dan's.

My thoughts spiraled in unpleasant directions. I didn't know of any reason why Dan might have wanted to kill Tom, but that didn't mean there wasn't one. How easy would it have been for him to poison the cookies? Dead easy. And if he'd "hidden" the cookies just as Tom walked by? I couldn't think of a better way to lure Tom into taking some. Tom dies, Dan's in the clear and all the females fawn over him in concern that he was the real target. It held up disappointingly well.

I knew better than to say anything to Becky. That was a "kill the messenger" scenario if I ever saw one.

It seemed I was going to do a little sleuthing, after all. Only my target was a little different than Becky's. And speak of the devil—look who was crossing the parking lot in my direction.

As he reached my side, Dan said, "Hey, Jo, I wondered if you could—" He jerked his head suddenly toward the tall set next to us. "What the—"

There was a loud crash and darkness.

# Chapter Nine

S omewhere in my world of pain and darkness, I smelled a faint, musky perfume. Something about it made me close my eyes tighter and try to blend into the pavement. I heard a groan nearby and was surprised to realize it wasn't mine.

There was a shout and a cacophony of footsteps ringing across pavement. The darkness lifted.

"Are you okay?" I barely recognized Becky's voice. It sounded funny. Harsh. "Dammit, say something!"

"Ouch," I said, squinting open my eyes and blinking against the floodlights.

Next to me, Dan's voice said, "Double ouch."

Becky let out a loud whoosh of air. "Oh thank God. I saw that set come down on you and…" She didn't finish the sentence.

I did a quick mental inventory of my body. Everything seemed to be intact. Moving slowly, in case I was wrong, I rolled to my side and started to get up. Hands reached down and gently helped me to my feet.

Dan waved off assistance as he struggled to a standing position. He realized his right arm was scraped from elbow to wrist and dripping blood, and swore.

"Move away, people. Give them room." Marty pushed his way through the crowd. "You two all right?"

Dan and I looked at each other and shrugged. "Guess so."

"You're sure now? I don't want to wake up tomorrow morning with a lawsuit on my desk." He said it jokingly, but his gaze was intense.

"I just got the wind knocked out of me," Dan said, bristling at the idea that he'd sue his own theater.

"Maybe you two should see a doctor, just in case," Marty said, clearly hoping we wouldn't.

Ian regarded Marty sourly and said to me, "I can take you to the emergency room, if you like."

"That's not a bad idea." Becky's face was stripped of color. Her eyes were huge and worried.

"We're fine," I assured her.

"You're bleeding," Becky said, unconvinced.

Dan looked dismissively at his arm. "Eh. Nothing a little ointment can't fix."

Becky pointed at the scrapes on my hands. Now that I noticed them, my hands started to sting like mad. But they were superficial scrapes.

"Ointment," I agreed.

Becky raised her voice and called out sharply, "Does anyone have a first-aid kit?"

"I've got one in my car," one of the parent volunteers said, hurrying off to get it.

"You sure you're okay? Both of you?" Marty regarded Dan and me steadily for a moment and then turned away. "You!" he barked at a burly guy I recognized as a stagehand. "You guys are supposed to be double checking the volunteers' work. What if this had happened to a customer? And the rest of you. What are you standing around for? Get back to work." He clapped his hands together and herded everyone back to the supply trucks. Dan, Becky and I remained where we were.

Dan turned me. "Don't let him guilt you out of the care you need. If you're hurt, say so, even if you don't realize it until you wake up tomorrow morning. And having said that, I strongly advise taking a couple of ibuprofen before you go to bed tonight or you're going to wake up stiff as a board."

"Don't worry. I've no plans to be a martyr," I assured him.

There was a grunt and a clatter behind us as a couple of stagehands righted the set. Becky froze, staring at it.

"Are you okay?" I asked her.

She raised a shaking hand and pointed at a jagged line of nails along the top where someone must have ripped away a board.

Dan let out a low whistle. "Better fix that. I'll get a hammer and bend those nails around." He reached up a hand to finger the sharp nail ends and winced. "I think I landed a little hard on my shoulder."

Becky said, "If either of you had been a foot or two to the right…"

"We weren't. We're fine," Dan said.

He reached out his other arm to draw Becky close, but she pulled impatiently away.

"You don't get it. That set didn't just tip over on its own. And it wasn't knocked over by accident or there would have been someone on the other side trying to catch it as it fell. There wasn't anyone. I told you, I *saw*. Someone pushed it."

All three of us were silent for a long moment. Then Dan forced a laugh. "Maybe someone is trying to kill me after all. Not to detract from your importance, Jo, of course."

"Damn straight." I hammed it up a little, for all our sakes. "I'm sure I've got a few students who wouldn't mind seeing me out of the way before I grade their chemistry tests."

"I don't know how you two can make cracks about this. It's pure luck you weren't maimed. Whoever's trying to kill Dan is obviously going to keep trying until they get it right and they don't care who they take with him. We can't even protect ourselves because we don't know who's doing it." She rounded on Dan. "And your solution is to pound the nails back in!"

Dan threw his arms around her and hugged her tightly. "Shh. All right. We'll call it a night. We've got enough people here that the haunted house will get finished in time, whether we're here or not."

Becky pushed him away. "That's it? Someone tries to kill you and you're just going to go home?"

"No," Dan said, frowning at the mess that was his arm. "I'm going to clean this up and then I'm going to go have a drink. A big one."

~*~

A half-hour later, Becky, Dan and I were huddled around a small table at the back of a bar in one of those neighborhood strip malls that crop up every few blocks throughout Long Beach. We had chosen the place because none of us had ever been there before, on the assumption that it was unlikely any of us would run into anyone we knew.

A handful of regulars nursed drinks on stools around the bar and a couple of guys played a friendly game of pool as they worked their way through a pitcher of lager. A constant stream of Eighties songs crackled out through cheap speakers, keeping our conversation private.

Dan took a long pull of lager. "Shit," he said.

"That about sums up my opinion," I said, wondering how much I could drink and still drive home. My conclusion was, not nearly enough.

I was suffering a little from delayed shock. Every time I blinked, I saw that sharp, jagged line of nails.

Becky scowled at both of us. "I've heard of let-down after a shock, but you two are practically rolling over." She pulled a small notebook out of her purse and clicked open a pen. "Let's go through this methodically. First of all, who was at the haunted house the night Tom died?"

"Was murdered," Dan corrected. He took another gulp of his beer.

Becky ignored the comment and began listing names. "The three of us. Marty, of course."

"Half of Long Beach was there, Becky," Dan protested.

Becky retorted, "I don't care about the general public. I'm talking about people connected with the Milverne. People who know their way around the place well enough to have gotten back to the dressing room area unseen or at least unnoticed in the sense that anyone who might have seen them took it for granted that they had reason to be there. People who knew Tom. Who know *you*."

Exasperation flushed Dan's handsome face at Becky's insinuation that he was the real target. Becky stubbornly tilted up her chin, black eyes defiant.

"Ian and Angelina were doing the tour-guide thing, along with Tom," I said mildly. "Other than that, I didn't really see anyone." *Except a couple of vampires. One of whom Jedi-mind-tricked her way into the haunted house, taking some guy with her.*

My words had their intended effect of cutting the tension, or least reminding them they weren't alone and could argue later. Becky bent her attention back to her notebook and added Ian, Angelina and Tom to the list.

In a softer voice that belied her underlying anxiety, she asked Dan, "All the Long Beach Player principals were there, weren't they?"

Dan regarded Becky in taut silence. Then, as if a knot untied inside him, his body relaxed. He blew out a breath. "Marty made sure of it. We all had roles in the haunted house. Joseph was the suicidal mummy, Shandra was the homicidal witch…"

I recognized the costumes, if not the people inhabiting them.

"We had other volunteers too, right?" Becky's pen scratched out more names. "Including your fan club."

"You have a fan club?" I asked Dan.

He rubbed a weary hand across his jaw. "Yeah. Part of the blatant self-promotion we have to do."

"It's not as if you set it up," Becky grumbled. "You can't help it if some people find you attractive."

Dan looked up from his beer and met her eyes. The look he gave her made her blush.

I busied myself reading the names on Becky's lists. "You've narrowed it down to…no one. Everyone who was working the haunted house the night Tom died was also there tonight."

Becky wrenched her gaze away from Dan. "We have to make sure we aren't overlooking anything obvious."

"Such as the fact that we don't know what we're doing?" I muttered.

Becky ignored the remark. "The next step is a little harder. For you, anyway," she told Dan. "We need to make a list of all the people who might benefit from your death."

"Ah." He dropped the level of his beer a little lower. "You mean all my friends and coworkers who might want to kill me."

"You're too good an actor not to have inspired some jealousy along the way," I said. "Which reminds me. Becky, you'd better add the entire Bayshore High School boy population to the list, since their girlfriends all had crushes on Dan."

"That's only about a hundred jealous boyfriends. I was sure I cut a wider swath than that." Dan's smile collapsed almost immediately into a thoughtful frown. He put out a hand. "Give me the pen."

Becky handed it over and pushed the pad in his direction.

"I'm not saying any of these people would have committed a felony over it, but I did come in as the lead in the company over other actors who'd been there longer," Dan said.

"Just make the list." Becky took her first sip of beer.

"Who was there when you came?" I asked.

"Tom. Ian, though he still gets all the funny roles, which he likes. Another guy who left after Marty made the announcement."

"Don't suppose you've seen this guy hanging around lately?"

"Doubt it. He got Kinickie in a revival of *Grease* that is playing down in San Diego."

"Easy enough to check," Becky said. "Anyone else?"

Dan finished his beer. "Angelina and I dated briefly. Didn't end well."

"You dated that Barbie doll?" Becky asked, incredulous.

"You dated tattoo guy from the firehouse," Dan replied.

"You did?" I said to Becky.

She narrowed her eyes at me. "Tell anyone and I'm resurrecting the pregnancy rumor."

Dan perked up interestedly, "What pregnancy?"

Two of the guys at the bar had turned to look at us. "Maybe we should all spit on our hands and shake," I suggested, dropping my voice to a harsh whisper.

Dan laughed, but I could tell Becky wasn't quite ready to let the "dating Angelina" tidbit go.

"You mentioned a fan club. Any of them wacko?" I asked.

"The president's a little..." Becky spun a finger at her temple in a crazy sign.

"Shelly Newman's all right, she's just a little... Okay, she's wacko." Dan wrote her name on the list and threw down the pen. "I really don't see how this helps."

The little hairs on the back of my neck stood up and the outside door pushed open.

The bartender glanced up and waved someone in. I turned and my mouth went dry as Will entered the room. From his leather boots to his long inky hair, he was a symphony in black, but his eyes glittered like hot sapphires. And they were fixed on me, as though no one else were in the room.

Becky stared. Her mouth hung open a little, as if she'd forgotten to shut it. Even Dan couldn't seem to look away.

Will came to stand at our table.

"Hello, beautiful."

"Will." It came out as a squeak.

Becky blinked, as if coming out of a trance. Her voice was so soft I barely heard the words. "*Such* a shame."

I got up so quickly my chair hovered a second on two legs before righting itself. How had Will found me? Vadar? My gaze flicked nervously around the room, assessing all the regulars. Had we stumbled on a vampire den of some sort? If only real life were like the movies, where the vampire's faces abruptly took on an alien cast for convenient identification.

I shook my thoughts back to the present. I needed to get Becky and Dan out of there right away, before anything happened to them. Father Stevens wasn't exactly set up to forgive that sort of sin in the confessional.

"How, er, nice run into you," I told Will. "We were just leaving."

I kicked Becky sharply under the table. She got to her feet and, with a regretful glance at his unfinished beer, Dan followed suit. He slung an arm around Becky and headed out.

Will shot me a lazy, wicked grin that made me tingle all the way down to my toes. "Alone are we? I'll walk you to your car."

Dan and Becky had driven over together in Becky's car. I had followed in mine. And parked in a different row. Stupid.

Will chivalrously let me exit through the door first. I bolted for my car. If I could get inside before Dan and Becky drove off, I would be safe. Assuming that "no entry unless invited" thing worked on cars as well as dwellings.

Will followed unhurriedly, but his slow, gorgeous stride covered a remarkable amount of ground.

Becky and Dan reached the Mustang. She called out, "You want me to stay to make sure your car starts?"

"That would be great." I didn't look up. I was fumbling with my keys.

I found them as Will rounded the back of my car, lithe and powerful as a jungle cat on the prowl. I stuck the key in the lock and turned it. It was too late.

Without breaking stride, Will turned me around and pulled me tight against him. And he backed me against the car and kissed me. The whole of my body was pressed up against his and I nearly passed out from the hormone rush when our tongues touched.

I barely heard Becky laughingly say, "I guess not," before she got in her car and drove off.

If it were a movie, this would be the scene where the audience yells, "Run, you fool! Run!" But I wasn't running. Far from it. My hands were twisted in the silky-crisp cotton of his shirt, pulling him closer. *His* hands were…

"Hey!" I said. "We're in public."

"I wanted to make sure you are still in one piece." His lips brushed, whisper-soft, against my ear. "You had an accident this evening."

"I'm fine."

In reply, he poked a finger through a hole in the shoulder of my sweater, from where I'd hit the ground so hard the rough pavement had torn right through. His somber gaze took slow, silent inventory of all my scrapes and bruises.

"Well, maybe I need a little Bactine. Wait. How did you know about the set falling?"

Just then the door of the bar opened and a woman's laughter danced through the cool October air. A memory I'd suppressed washed back over me like a flash flood. I hadn't seen anything when the set fell, but I had smelled something. A cloying, musky perfume. Only one woman of my acquaintance wore a scent that trashy. Natasha.

I knew the vampiress wanted me dead and out of the way. Was tonight's "accident" her way of reminding me? The line of sharp nails a subtle sign that pointy things can be dangerous?

I opened my mouth to complain to Will and then hesitated. The reality was, no matter what my gut told me, I had suspicions but no proof. And that wasn't enough. Not with him.

Will tolerated my dislike and distrust of Natasha, even found it a little amusing. Because he just thought it was me being nervy.

He didn't have a weakness for Natasha so much as a convenient blind spot. He bought her well-honed "sweet little me" act because it suited him. He liked the idea that they were all a "big happy family" with him as its genial leader. It sort of made sense, when you considered how long vampires had to live with one another. They weren't like a regular family who could count on death giving the family tree a thorough pruning every so often.

If Will realized that I was the cause of real trouble in the ranks? The simplest solution was to finish turning me. I would be brought into the undead "family" on equal footing and it would be really hard to kill me.

I clamped my mouth tightly shut before any feeble accusations could make their way out. Sharing my theories about Natasha with Will was a *very bad* idea. My problems with Natasha were something I was going to have to work out for myself.

As if he'd read my thoughts, Will said suddenly, "You need to be more careful."

His jaw was set tight and the way he said it was odd. As if there were an unspoken "or else" hanging off the end of it. Before I could ask what he meant, he shifted his attention from my cuts and bruises and reached a hand to my neck. His fingertips softly traced the small twin scars he'd put there. A strange longing rose up inside me.

It scared me so much that I shoved Will away and clambered into the car, barking my shin painfully on the door.

He had plenty of time to stop me. But he didn't. He stood aside, radiating power and iron control. His voice was low and, as it did sometimes, vibrated with a faint European accent. "Free will has a way of bending to destiny."

"Then it's not really free, is it?"

I punched the door lock. When I looked up, he was gone.

I drove home slowly, feeling as if I'd downed a handful of tequila shots instead of half a beer. As usual, Will had managed to discombobulate me beyond rational thought.

But then, Will's whole existence was irrational. Everyone knows vampires don't really exist outside of movies, books and TV shows. Except they do.

Will was irrefutably real, only he wasn't acting at all like a vampire was supposed to act. Why? Why hadn't he bitten me again? Completed my transformation? It certainly wasn't for lack of interest.

As I waited at an intersection for the light to turn green, I thought about Ralph Winkerstein who had lived down the hall from me in college. Ralph had a large, ravenous pet boa constrictor. You always knew when it was feeding day by the steady stream of beer-holding guys ambling into Ralph's room to watch. After about twenty raucous minutes of shouting and dollar bills changing hands, there'd be a loud cheer and everyone would file back out.

One time, a couple of hours passed and the mouse was still in the cage. Alive. It was still there the next day. And the next. After a week, Ralph named the mouse Lunch and the snake had a new roommate. We all—including, apparently, the snake—became rather fond of sweet little Lunch.

A few months later, Ralph came home from class, whistling and rattling in his hand a crumbled cookie he'd saved for the little mouse. Lunch was gone and the snake's abdomen bulged suspiciously.

That, I thought, accelerating through the intersection, was my relationship with Will. He was the pointy-fanged predator and I was Lunch, running free in the cage.

How long until Will remembered the natural order of things?

# Chapter Ten

T hought you could use this." Becky came into my classroom and held out a cup of coffee.

"They have the criteria for sainthood all wrong," I said, reaching for it gratefully.

"Don't get too excited. It's only from the cafeteria. How are you feeling? Did the gorgeous, *not*-gay man's kisses make you all better?" She fanned herself with a *What is a Red Shift?* handout from the counter. "Lord, that man is smokin' hot! And the way he just strode over and kissed you..." She sighed dreamily.

"I never said he was gay. I said he wasn't my type."

"Right. And you were kissing him back because...? Never mind. We'll have to deal with your denial later. Come downstairs. I've something to show you."

She darted back in to the hallway.

"Come *on*," she urged when she realized I wasn't right on her heels.

"Oh all right," I grumbled. "Hold your horses." I grabbed my sun-protection gear off the hook by the door and followed her out, trying to sip my coffee without spilling it down my front.

"Let's go, pokey. I thought you were a runner."

"I'd like to see how fast you move after a set falls on you. Where are we going? It better be good. Here, hold my coffee while I get this stuff on."

Becky took my cup and waited impatiently while I tugged on gloves and wound my scarf around my face and neck. As soon as my sunglasses were on, she handed me back my coffee and strode ahead.

"Trust me, it's worth it. Assuming we can ever get there." She trotted nimbly downstairs, as if trying to hurry me along by example. I limped along after her as best I could and caught up to her at the door to the bottom floor of our department.

She whispered, "We'll pretend to be having a conversation on the way to my classroom. When I stop, look to your left."

"Okaaay. What are we pretending to talk about?"

"Never mind that! Leave it to me. Now shush."

We were about halfway to the chemistry lab when Becky suddenly stopped and turned toward me.

"You think so?" she said conversationally. "Hmm. Now, I'm of the opinion that middle schoolers should take finals, so they don't freak out when they get to high school."

She jerked her head a fraction toward a ponytailed high school girl rooting around in her locker. I looked back at Becky in confusion and she widened her eyes meaningfully and jerked her head again.

Becky droned on, "But I do agree that it puts a lot of pressure on them. Maybe if finals counted for a smaller fraction of their semester grade? No, I see your point that if it's too low, they won't take them seriously…"

Becky's monologue faded into the background. I had caught sight of the girl's locker door.

It was a Dan shrine. The actual door of the locker was invisible behind its thick papering of playbills featuring Dan on the cover, in various roles.

Becky nudged me and surreptitiously pointed at the row of photos. Dan in doublets. Dan as a pirate. Dan's headshot.

Most of them I'd seen before, when Becky had made me look at Dan's page on the LBP website. It was the other, unofficial photos that caught my attention. Dan leaving the theater from a play. Dan grinning, his arm around… I leaned closer and jumped back as the locker door clanged shut.

Becky pulled me toward her classroom. "I think you're right that the middle school final schedule merits serious study by the faculty and…" She shut and locked her classroom door behind us.

"Wow," I said.

"Did you see the picture where she photo shopped out *my* head and put hers in?"

"*That's* what was wrong with that picture. I thought I recognized your lab coat."

I also recognized the girl. She was the fake-axe-wielding student volunteer who had helped me carry sets last night.

"Who is she?"

"Surely you can guess."

"How would I know? Oh…"

Becky nodded. "Shelley Stevens. The president of Dan's fan club."

~*~

I arrived in the parking lot a good thirty minutes before the haunted house's grand reopening and already the line stretched around the corner. Apparently, the murder coverage in the papers had indeed been excellent advertising for the haunted house.

Marty had sent a few costumed actors out to the sidewalk to work the line. They had gone for campy rather than serious. A good idea for the mostly teenage line, in my opinion. Marty had parked himself at the front of the line and was deflecting questions with good-humored non-answers such as "Thank you for your concern", "Enjoy the haunted house" and "The show must go on."

One kid in line, egged on by his friends, called out, "Is the dude who got murdered still in there?"

"Ghouls," Angelina said, flouncing off. As she disappeared through a gap in the black sheets that were strung over the parking lot gates, I caught Marty doing a "why me" eye roll at her retreating back.

I tried to follow Angelina into the haunted house area, but Marty caught sight of me and motioned me over. "You're doing tickets again, aren't you?"

"Sure."

"Good. We can use someone with a little experience dealing with kids. This crowd is going to get a little rowdy tonight."

The line surged forward. Marty raised his voice and told them to knock it off. It seemed to work. For the moment.

I didn't want to burst Marty's bubble, but I wasn't exactly the "go-to" person for managing teens. Threatening to send the entire line to the principal's office wasn't going to work on a crowd this large.

I merely nodded, trying to look as much a responsible adult as I could in a bustier and cape. His critical gaze fastened on my mouth and before he could produce yet another set of plastic vampire teeth, I ducked behind the black sheet "door" someone had strung over the gate entrance to the parking lot.

"Holy cow."

I stopped and stared in amazement. What had been an ungainly stretch of mismatched sets and black sheets had been transformed into a huge black serpent with glowing yellow eyes and sharp white fangs. Its cavernous mouth—the haunted house's entrance—yawned black and ominous. Last night's cheery yellow floodlights had been covered with red filters that cast the dark parking lot with a hellish glow.

"Want to take a walk through?"

I was so caught up in the illusion that I jumped at the sound of a voice at my left shoulder. I twisted my head to find Ian hunched in his Igor outfit, grinning at me.

"Pretty effective, huh?"

"I'd say so," I said, stepping into the yawning maw and fingering a fang as big around as my waist. "Is everything the same as before? I mean, inside—the homicidal mummy, Frankenstein and his monster, a hungry witch with a giant cauldron?"

"More or less." Ian shrugged in a comical rise and fall of hump. "I think the innocent victim getting sucked into the giant spider web is a lot better this time round. C'mon, I'll take you through. You have to use your imagination a bit. Not everybody's in place yet." He hunched over and listed toward the snake's black mouth. "Walk this way."

His Marty Feldman impression was dead-on. I told him as much and he broke character to grin at the compliment.

"Jo! There you are." Marty, followed by actors who'd been working the crowd, came through the black sheet and shut the gate with a clang. He motioned for a couple of them to guard the entrance so no enterprising teens could sneak through. "Where's your ticket basket?"

"Um…" I was pretty sure it was behind the crime scene taped doors in the out-of-bounds part of the theater.

"Never mind," Marty said, as if reading my mind. "I'm sure you can find another one in the rehearsal room."

I guess I was on my way to the rehearsal room. "I'll take a rain check on that walk-through," I told Ian. "Maybe I'll tag along on one of your tours so I can get the full effect."

"As you wish," he said, lifting his shoulders and hump in an exaggerated shrug. I was halfway to the rehearsal room before I realized Ian's hump had moved to his other shoulder.

The door to the rehearsal room was open. In the light spilling into the parking lot, I caught sight of two people, one wearing a familiar fright wig, standing outside the actor's back entrance to the haunted house. Dan and Becky. I headed over to say hi and realized I was wrong. It wasn't Becky caressing Dan's chest, but Angelina.

I felt as if I had a tiny version of my mother on one shoulder and a tiny Becky on the other. Mom was reminding me it was rude to eavesdrop and Becky was threatening vile things if I didn't find out whether Angelina had designs on Dan.

I refused to consider the possibility that Dan might also have designs on her.

Angelina's voice was husky with worry. "Are you sure you're okay?" Her hand shifted to his shoulder. "That set came down really hard on you last night."

I guess she hadn't lost any sleep over *my* cuts and bruises.

"I'm fine," Dan told her. He patted her upper arm.

A pat. What the heck did *that* signify?

I must have made some sort of noise, for Dan turned toward me. He let out a breath and his shoulders dropped. "Hey, Jo." He smiled and looked expectantly past me. "Becky with you?"

Angelina muttered something I couldn't hear and stalked through one of the side openings into the haunted house.

I shook my head. "We took separate cars. Becky's probably in the rehearsal room getting ready. If I see her, I'll tell her you're looking for her."

"Thanks, I— Hold on. No need. There she is."

He jogged off toward the entrance in an encouraging display of Becky interest. I was almost a hundred percent positive he wasn't putting it on for my benefit.

The rehearsal room had a row of storage closets along one long wall. As I hunted through them for something I could use for tickets, I couldn't help but compare Angelina's quiet concern over Dan's bruises with her histrionics the night of Tom's death.

She had most certainly amped up her response to Tom's death to get attention. But exactly whose attention was she trying to get? Dan's? To show him she was over him?

That might have been the plan then, but it was pretty obvious that Angelina still wanted him.

Killing Tom to get Dan back was a little excessive, even for my imagination, but what if she'd merely tried to make Tom sick? All that comforting in times of grief had brought exes together before. Were we overlooking the simple explanation?

Someone outside shouted the "fifteen minutes to opening" warning. I realized I was standing in the rehearsal room staring at an open locker of plastic Grecian army breast plates. If I didn't get back to the snake's head with a basket soon, Marty would spend the rest of the night complaining.

Stowing my purse under a pile of yellowing crinoline, I grabbed a small, empty plastic trash can for the tickets and headed out at a slow jog. As I rounded the serpent's head, I saw a small crowd of new volunteers ready to be put to work, but no Marty.

It was cowardly of me, but the last thing I wanted to do was make small talk dressed as a sexy vampire with high school students and their parents. I spun away before they could see me and went to look for Marty.

I hadn't searched long when I heard his voice coming from up around the front of theater. What was he doing *there*? I took the stairs from the parking lot up the hillside and followed the tree-lined path around toward the front of the theater. I was about to round the corner, when the tenor of Marty's voice made me stop and shrink back into the shadows. Marty wasn't just somewhere he wasn't supposed to be, he was having an argument. Positioned myself behind a shrub, I peered cautiously around the corner.

Marty stood before the front door, talking to the paunchy unibrowed LBPD detective in charge of Tom's case. I use "talking" loosely. Marty's voice was just shy of a shout and his arms were flapping in anger.

"How much longer is this going to go on, Detective? I have a business to run."

The detective made a show of looking down at the haunted house, snaking through the parking lot. "Looks to me like you guys are doing a fine job." His voice was so calm he almost sounded bored.

Marty's arms flapped faster. "This is ridiculous! You can't shut me down indefinitely. I demand to have access to my own theater. I will take this higher, don't think I won't!"

Without warning, he turned and stalked away from the detective. If I didn't move quickly, he was going to bump into me. I jogged a dozen feet back the way I'd come, then turned around and pretended I was just coming up the path.

"There you are," I said, flattening myself against the side of the building as Marty nearly mowed me down. "Hey, is everything okay?

"Fools!" Marty took a breath so deep I drew back, fearing he'd pop like a balloon.

On the exhale, his whole body relaxed and he flashed me his "benevolent uncle" smile. "Everything's fine," he assured me absently.

Then his gaze grew sharp and his smile faltered. "What are you doing up here?"

"Looking for you. The parents sent me to fetch you. They wanted to clear up a few minor things before the haunted house opened."

He relaxed again. "Of course, of course. Never underestimate the value of a good pep talk before an event. Now." He clapped his hands together. "Let's go scare some teens!"

He started back down the path, stopping again as I moved to follow.

"Where do you think you're going? Back to the front. You're our ticket-taker. I'm counting on you to hold down the fort until I get there. Take the stairs. It's faster."

He turned away and hustled down the path. Marty really moved quite fast for a man shaped like a barrel.

"Hey, get in position!" he bellowed to a mummy as it ambled out of the rehearsal room, zipping up its costume. "We'll be letting the crowds in any minute."

I turned and began to make my own way back to the front end of the parking lot. I was at the top of the stairs about to head down when I felt a pinch on my shins and the ground suddenly tilted up to meet me. My feet wouldn't move properly. I barely registered a shadowy human form where a tree should have been as gloved hands whipped a dark plastic bag over my head and shoulders. A little shove between my shoulder blades sent me plummeting down the staircase in darkness.

# Chapter Eleven

F alling blindly, I swung out instinctively with both arms. My left hand connected with the railing in a bone-jarring move, but I held on, nearly twisting my arm out of its socket as it bore my weight. My head didn't hit the stairs, but every other part of me seemed to. The collision knocked the wind out of me. Sharp pains shot through my thighs, hips and back.

The plastic bag tightened over my mouth and nose as I gasped desperately for air. Letting go the railing, I frantically ripped a hole in the bag near my mouth, but it wasn't enough. Not for my panicked breath, my oxygen-starved lungs. I needed it off me. The bag seemed enormous, endless. I tore futilely at it for precious moments before I realized it was pinned under my hip. Twisting, ignoring the sharp protests of my abused limbs, I struggled to my feet and cool fresh air billowed under the bag. Bliss.

I was so caught up in unwrapping myself that I didn't consider that whoever had done this might still be around.

Until I heard a shoe scratch on a stair behind me.

The hairs on the back of my neck went up. Through the holes I'd made in the bag, I smelled a familiar sweet, musky perfume. It was faint, barely there. But I noticed it. I knew what it meant.

Natasha.

The panic that had consumed me only moments ago was nothing compared to the terror that filled me now, pouring through my every cell like a sick poison. The bag was still over my head. I couldn't see. I grabbed at the plastic in earnest, trying to desperately to get it off me. I refused to die like a blind, trussed rat.

Hands grabbed me from behind, pulling at the bag, fighting my efforts. I tried to suck in a breath but the bag had shifted and my air holes had disappeared. The plastic tightened over my mouth, cutting off my cries like a gag.

The hands tugged harder at the plastic, pulling me off balance. I stumbled backward and cracked the back of my head against what felt like a rock.

"Ow!" The curse that followed was short, heartfelt and male. I was released.

I grasped handfuls of plastic bag and pulled myself free of it as my assailant disappeared around the corner. I had the impression of light colored hair, but little else, and I wasn't even sure about the hair.

And Natasha? Had I imagined she was there? Confused, I forced my aching, trembling legs to take me back up to the top of the staircase for a better look around. Natasha was nowhere to be seen. I was as alone as someone could be in a parking lot full of people. Marty, who hadn't noticed that I'd nearly met my death on the stairs, was twenty yards away, chatting with the volunteers at the gate.

Just then, something made me look to my left. Way at the other end of the parking lot, nearly invisible in the shadow of the tree he leaned against, was Will. He was looking straight at me. The moment our gazes crossed, I felt a rush of fire and ice slide through my body. My legs seemed to move on their own accord, and I took a step toward him.

And nearly tripped again. I glanced down. A thin gleam of plastic flashed in the faint red glow of the parking lot lights and disappeared. I bent down. Fishing line. I tugged my laces free. The line was looped around a tree trunk on one side of the path and tied off the other. Quick but effective.

All my demise had nearly required was fishing line, a trash bag and opportunity. If I'd been moving at my usual brisk pace, the fall might have broken my neck.

Fury filled me. Driven by pure anger, I stood back up and started toward Will. I was done playing Natasha's little game of cat and mouse. If Will wanted to finish me off, fine. Let him try it. But I was damned if I was going to let his taffy-haired sybarite do me in.

What I'd taken to be a second slender tree trunk by Will's side swayed and Natasha appeared in a patch of moonlight.

I stopped in surprise.

Even a vampire can't be in two places at once.

Natasha hadn't done it.

It didn't make sense. If Natasha wasn't behind these "accidents", who was?

Maybe Dan was the real target, after all. But then why would someone trip me? Was it a mistake? A diversion to put Dan off his guard?

The sound of someone bellowing my name caught my attention. Marty was waving me to the front gate. Limping with pain, I headed over to join him in the parking lot. I could feel Will watching me.

A small group of new volunteers awaited me at the front of the snake. Four people taking tickets was really three too many but I couldn't have been happier to have them there. They were charming and chatty and couldn't possibly have had anything to do with Tom's death.

Nonetheless, after an hour, I'd had enough. I was tired and anything that didn't sting ached deep in my bones. But I would have gladly suffered twice the pain if I could stop the chaotic thoughts running laps in my head.

I knew I had to face the elephant in the room. I had to decide once and for all whether Dan was a target, an innocent bystander or a murderer.

What I decided was that it could wait until tomorrow. It was still early and I was going to go home and do something *I* wanted to do on a Friday night. Eat as much as I could hold, take a long bubble bath and crawl into bed with a good book.

I said goodnight to the other volunteers and headed wearily over to the rehearsal room to get my purse. As I dug it out from under the crinoline pile, Dan came out of the bathroom and headed for the door. Before I knew what I was doing, I called out to him. He stopped, as I knew he would.

"The haunted house turned out pretty good, huh? You get a gold star for helping me round up all our new Bayshore volunteers."

He was grinning, happy. I felt like an idiot. Did I really think Dan was a murderer? No. And yet…

"May I ask you something?" I said.

"Sure."

"Where did you put the gingersnaps after Becky gave them to you?"

From the expression on his face, I'd clearly overstepped myself.

I put a hand on his arm. "Sorry, that didn't quite come out right. It's just that I'm worried about Becky. Whoever doctored the cookies must have either seen her give them to you or watched you stow them away."

His face smoothed out, only to fall back into a frown of a different sort. "I know. But I didn't see anyone."

"Are you sure? I bet people pass back and forth by your dressing area all the time. Maybe you're just so used to it, it didn't register. I thought that if you walked through it again, maybe it would jog your memory."

He shook his head. "Really, I've tried. Believe me. But I don't remember anyone." Frustration limned his voice.

"I mean, walk through it literally. Act it out."

The hunted look left his face and his sky blue eyes lit with interest. "Actually, that's not a bad idea. It might just work. Let's see. So you're Becky." He put his hands on my shoulders and shifted me so I stood facing him, a couple of feet away. "We're talking...I'm putting on my lab coat...Becky takes the cookie tin out of her bag and hands it to me..."

He looked expectantly at me and I pantomimed Becky's actions.

"I was going to open the tin and have one but..." His voice suddenly grew excited. "I heard someone in the hall. Jo, that's amazing, I—"

"Did you see anyone?"

His eyes fixed on the ceiling as he thought. He returned his gaze to me and his shoulders sagged. "No."

"What next?"

"I said something about not wanting to share. They really are my favorite cookies. Or were..." His look grew distant and sad. He shook his head as if to forcibly change the direction of his thoughts and the actor replaced the person again. "I wrapped the tin in my sweatshirt and put it on the bench. And then I thanked her..." Dan turned back toward Becky-me and moved in closer. He had his eyes open and he looked thoughtful, as if trying to remember if he'd seen someone pass by in the hallway as he'd put the move on Becky. And then his gaze shifted to me and he *leaned* in.

"There you are, Jo! I've been looking for you." Gavin barked the words like a disapproving parent who'd caught his only daughter necking on the front porch. I winced and Dan jumped back as if stung.

Gavin came to a stop between us, arms crossed, face hard and judging. I resisted the urge to insist that it wasn't what it looked like.

I glanced at Dan. He blinked a few times, looked at his watch and blew out an expletive.

"I gotta go. Becky's alone in the haunted house and what's Frankenstein's monster without Frankenstein?" He grinned at me, a happy guy who couldn't quite believe his luck at having captured the interest of Becky. He didn't seem to feel any of my awkwardness. In fact, he didn't seem to think anything strange had happened at all.

Of course he didn't. Because he hadn't been hitting on me. He'd been acting a part. It was just Gavin's timing that had made it seem so sordid.

I turned on my heel and followed Dan out the door. Dan ducked back into the haunted house from one of the hidden side doors and I continued out of the parking lot through the main gate. The line for the haunted house still wrapped around the block. I was glad of a crowd, raucous as it was, as I strode to my car. I wasn't particularly worried about vampires, not with

Gavin ten steps behind me. It was Gavin's safety I was afraid for. Right now, I wanted to kill him.

Gavin's Jetta was in my rearview mirror the whole way home. At the first stoplight, I called a local restaurant that delivered and ordered a very rare steak. I hoped Gavin was hungry as well, for I hadn't ordered him a thing.

Parking was abysmal, as it always was on Friday night. I finally got a spot two streets over, where the McMansions had so much closet space, owners actually used their garages for parking. I didn't think there was anywhere left for Gavin to park, but when I got out of the Volvo, he was waiting for me. I ignored him on the walk to my apartment. I ignored him as I got my mail. I ignored him hovering over my shoulder as I unlocked the dead bolt. I tried to shut the door before he could follow but he stuck his foot in the doorway.

"Ow!"

"You should know better than to stick your foot in a closing door," I said.

He ruthlessly shoved the door open, stepped inside and locked it behind him. Almost immediately, there was a knock on the door.

"Excuse me," I told Gavin. "That's for me."

"Do you know who it is?"

"I doubt it."

Gavin blocked my way. "You open your door to strangers, at night?"

"Not normally, no. But if it's a delivery guy bringing me dinner, you bet I do." I pushed past him and opened the door.

A small, wiry guy in a red polyester shirt with a spatula stitched on the breast regarded us curiously from behind plastic-rimmed glasses. I gathered my door wasn't sound proof. He looked from me to Gavin, who was breathing over my left shoulder like a baleful dragon, and held up the bag. "Delivery?"

"That was fast." I took the bag and gave him my most brilliant smile and a wad of cash. "Thank you so much."

He didn't look at the money. He was too busy looking at me. Up at me, to be precise. I had a good five inches on him. And about twenty pounds. And at least a year or two.

Gavin said pointedly, "Don't you have another delivery to make?"

"Yeah." The delivery guy remained on my doorstep as if his feet were glued to the cracked cement. His eyes were glued on my face. His mouth opened and words poured out. "I'm Davy Peter Smith. You're really hot.

You-wanna-go-out-sometime?"

I gaped at him.

"No, she doesn't," Gavin answered for me. He flipped open his wallet to display his police badge. "If you don't leave right now, I'm going to ticket you for double parking."

"Hey!" I barked at Gavin, pushing the badge away. "I can handle this myself, thanks."

The delivery guy took this as an invitation and stepped eagerly toward the door.

Gavin moved in front of me to block the way. He was twice the width and had four times the muscle of my would-be swain. "Leave," Gavin told him. "Now."

The delivery guy watched me as he walked away, head affixed to his left shoulder. As he rounded the corner, he stumbled and nearly took the stairs face first.

"That is the *last* time I'm wearing this costume in public," I muttered. "He probably thought I was a hooker."

Gavin locked the door behind him and plucked the delivery bag out of my hands.

"Hey!"

He put it on the side table. "You can eat whatever disgusting thing you have in there later." Planting his feet shoulder-width apart, he demanded, "Back there in the rehearsal theater... What the hell did you think you were doing?"

I was too annoyed to bother prevaricating. "I was helping investigate."

"Helping? How? By hitting on your best friend's boyfriend?"

"How dare you! I was *not* hitting on Dan! I—"

"Maybe you didn't realize it, but you were."

"That's total—"

"Jesus, Jo. Ever hear of vampire magnetism? You have it and it's getting worse. You get this smoldering look in your eyes and then you smile. Don't you realize the effect it can have on men? That delivery boy almost broke his neck on the stairs getting a look at you."

"Maybe he thinks I'm cute!"

"I'm sure he thinks that. He'd think you're the hottest female on this planet if you were eighty-five, bald as a bat and had lost all your teeth."

"That's a terrible thing to say. You act as if this is my fault."

"Isn't it? That's two men you've lured in tonight. You're a damn vampire. Have some sense of responsibility."

He couldn't have been crueler if he'd tried. I felt the hot sting of tears pressing against the back of my throat. I closed my eyes tightly, refusing to let them fall.

"There! Is that better, Detective? Maybe I can fashion some sort of blindfold to wear around so I don't insult any more men with false attraction."

"Dammit, Jo!" Gavin grabbed me by the shoulders. His strong fingers dug into my flesh.

Then he pulled me to him and his lips came down on mine in a bruising kiss. For a long, dizzying moment I didn't know where he ended and I began. His hands gentled and slid down my back to wrap around my waist, pulling me closer. My own hands crept up to touch his hair. The short hairs were soft under my fingers, like rough velvet.

It ended as suddenly as it had begun. He shoved me away.

I stumbled back against the wall to catch my balance. My eyes opened and his gaze poured into me like liquid silver. Broad chest heaving as if he'd sprinted a dozen miles, he reached out a hand as if to steady me but snatched it back before he made contact. As if I were poison.

"Damn it all to hell," he said. And left.

# Chapter Twelve

*I* stood there a long time, staring at my front door. I heard the soft scuff of a shoe on the other side. Gavin hadn't left.

"Bolt the door," he said wearily.

In two brisk strides, I reached the deadbolt and gave it a savage turn. Grabbing the bag with my steak dinner off the little entrance table where Gavin had stowed it, I marched into the kitchen.

My steak was lukewarm and very, very rare. Perfect, I thought, sticking a finger into the juice puddling around the meat. It was right about body temperature, I'd guess. Just the way I was going to learn to love it.

Ignoring the ick factor that instantly tightened my throat, I grabbed a fork and a steak knife, shutting the silverware drawer with my hip as I reached for a plate. I was starving and there was no one to see. I could have eaten with my fingers out of the Styrofoam packaging if I'd wanted to, but I didn't. I told myself it had nothing to do with Gavin's cruel accusation that I was becoming more like a vampire.

Gavin. He hated vampires, went after them with a singular drive. All too soon, that would include me, if it didn't already. Why had he kissed me? He couldn't blame it on my purported vampire allure because my eyes had been closed when he'd pulled me into his arms. Unwanted heat surged through me as I remembered the feel of his lips on mine. I felt again the barely restrained passion as the kiss gentled and he'd pulled me even closer. Brushed his soft, firm lips across mine. He hadn't been lured by anything vampire. He'd kissed *me*.

And it was me he'd pushed away. I'd been rejected. Simple as that.

I concentrated on my dinner. The steak came with sautéed vegetables and mashed potatoes, which I made myself eat. *See? I'm perfectly normal. Lots of people like their steak really rare. Lots of people don't care for vegetables.* My only problem being that I lived in California where everybody had a weird fascination with roots and berries.

I was about halfway through the meal, which I was eating with military precision—steak, potato, veggie, steak, potato—when my cell phone rang. I checked the screen. Gavin.

Calling why? To apologize? I turned the phone off and pushed it away.

My appetite left me. I scraped the remains back into the Styrofoam box and shoved it in the fridge for tomorrow.

What I needed was a good book, some chocolate and a purring cat on my lap. That's what rejected single women were supposed to do, right? I went into my bedroom and dragged out my shitty-day drawer. I selected a promising romance and a mystery I'd been hoarding and went back into the living room to flop on the couch.

I called to the cat and patted the couch cushion next to me, but Fluffy remained holed up in her kitty condo. Clearly, I was so repulsive that even the cat refused my company. "Fine. I don't like you either," I told her fuzzy back.

After a page and a half, I tossed the romance and picked up the mystery. I lasted three pages. I couldn't focus on the words. Every time I tried, they swam into a black-and-white pattern of thoughts that I was trying to avoid. I got up and paced. Exercise would help. Blow off steam, get some endorphins going.

After five minutes of pacing, all I'd managed was to work myself up to a good, old-fashioned pique of righteous anger. I was ready to call Gavin and give him a piece of my mind when a sharp knock sounded on my door. Hah! Gavin was back, no doubt to drive a stake through my heart. Or throw me in jail. He could do his worst, but first I was going to have the satisfaction of having my say.

I stomped over to the door and yanked it open. It wasn't Gavin standing there. It was Will.

He took a half step back.

"Something's wrong," he said.

"Yes."

He regarded me thoughtfully in silence. "Why don't we go out somewhere? You can tell me all about it."

My initial thought was *nice try*. But then I wondered, why not? So he was a vampire. So was I. Near enough, anyway.

"Give me a minute to change. Uh…"

I didn't want to invite him in. I had a feeling once I did, it would be for good. Besides, my mother and my aunts and my grandmothers on both sides had drilled it into me that one didn't invite someone like Will inside without a chaperone. Several chaperones.

A knowing glint of humor lit his blue eyes. "I'll wait here, shall I?"

I hurried back to my bedroom and swapped my black hot pants for black straight-legged slacks. I unhitched my bustier, selected a soft black turtleneck sweater from my closet and went into to the bathroom. When I held up the sweater for a quick "outfit check" in the mirror, my face reflected so clearly it was nearly opaque.

I perked up until I realized I was still wearing my Hollywood-vampire-slut makeup. I washed it off and turned back into a ghost. Sure I was a more opaque ghost than earlier in the week, thanks to the holy water. But I was hardly back to normal.

*What's normal?* I thought defiantly, tugging the turtleneck sweater over my head. As I stood in front of the mirror, I realized I'd automatically dressed as if I were going to a work function. How long had it been since I'd done anything else?

I yanked off the sweater and replaced it with a deep green v-neck silk blouse. I pulled my hair out of its usual twist and brushed the heavy mass until it shone a coppery-gold. I dabbed on a little shadow that my mother insisted turned my hazel eyes green, brushed a coat of mascara on my lashes, did the blush thing and finished with a little translucent powder.

Unfortunately, I couldn't really tell if it looked okay. But it was Will's fault if my eyeliner was drawn on crooked, and he would have to deal.

I opened the door and Will was leaning comfortably against one of the banister posts as if he had all the time in the world. I guessed he did. The look of male appreciation on his face when he saw me said that he *did* have all the time in the world, as long as I was the result.

With a rush of power and defiance, I stepped outside and locked the door behind me.

"What's next? Do we turn into bats and fly somewhere?"

"That's a bit of a misunderstanding." He leaned in and brushed a slow kiss across my lips that made every nerve ending jump up and take note. "You look lovely." With a simple chivalrous movement of his hand, he directed me to precede him down the stairs. "I thought, tonight, we could drive."

When we got to street level, Will beeped open the gleaming black car at the curb. An Aston Martin. I knew what it was because that's what they had James Bond drive in the movies when they wanted him to look cool. It was out of place on my street.

The car smelled wonderful. Leather and a trace of that scent Will always wore. Probably pure pheromone.

A rustle of clothing against leather and Will was in the driver's seat. We pulled away from the curb with an elegant roar of the engine.

He touched a button on the dash and a full orchestra, tucked somewhere in the back, played Samuel Barber's *Adagio for Strings*. At the end of the block, the achingly beautiful music gave way to a polite plea for contributions to a public radio station's pledge drive.

I realized I didn't understand Will at all. I didn't understand any of this.

"I have duct tape on my phone," I said.

We passed under a streetlight and Will turned to look at me with raised brows.

"My car is sixteen years old and secondhand. But even if I could afford a better car, I like the one I have because it's just the right shade of gray, so you can't tell when I don't wash it, and I almost never do. The most expensive things in my closet, aside from the hideous yellow bridesmaid dress I wore in my friend Sarah's wedding two summers ago, and my long wool pea coat from college, are my running shoes. I teach earth science to twelve-year-olds, who most days manage to make me feel completely inadequate to the task."

I had turned in my seat, the better to impress my words on him.

"What could you possibly want with me?" I demanded. I wasn't speaking to the obvious income gap between us but something more intrinsic. We were just so different. He was Godiva and champagne, I was a s'more, eaten on the beach next to a crackling campfire. I wasn't being coy or fishing for compliments. I really wanted to know. Why *me*?

He was silent. I swept my gaze from the instrument panel that could have run a jet to his beautifully soft, black button-down shirt that probably cost more than I made in a week, and settled on the lean planes of his face. But I couldn't find answers there. If anything, it made me more confused. Will had a vampire allure that could pull a girl in like a tractor beam. I'd experienced it. But he didn't need it. He was the sort of man women dreamed about but only saw in movies.

"You could have anyone."

"I could," he agreed. There was an off note in his voice that I couldn't place.

I waited for him to elaborate. He didn't.

I shifted in my seat so I faced forward again. We had turned off Ocean Boulevard, which—no surprise—runs along the ocean in Long Beach, and were heading inland.

"Where are we going?" I asked.

"That's up to you."

The anger that had propelled me out the door was cooling by the minute and that statement put ice blocks around my feet. Was he speaking metaphorically? Asking if I wanted to complete the transformation? What had I been thinking, getting into a car with him?

"Perhaps you'd like to dine? There's a restaurant I think you'll like a few blocks from here."

I was so relieved I nearly laughed aloud. I had a feeling that if I started, I would never stop. I wasn't remotely hungry, but I latched onto the idea of a nice crowded restaurant like a lifeline. "Sounds great."

Will pulled up to a restaurant I'd seen before but never been in and parked right in front. A uniformed man rushed over to open my door. Will led me inside with a hand on the small of my back. We didn't have to do anything so plebeian as stop at the hostess stand and ask about a table or a reservation. We went straight to a quiet, private table in the back.

My chair was pulled out for me and pushed smoothly back into position as I sat. Menus appeared before us and we were left alone.

"I always wondered what it would be like to be queen," I muttered.

Will barked out a laugh, catching my meaning at once. "I always felt sorry for the servant who didn't procure a chair in time to seat the royal bottom."

"Was there one? Someone who didn't push the chair back in time?"

"There must have been, once. Can't be sure about twice."

"Probably how the Tower of London got its start."

My nerves stopped jangling and shooting warnings at me. As I relaxed and settled into my chair, I realized it was actually quite comfortable.

"Do you want something to eat?" Will asked.

"Honestly? I'm not really hungry. Mostly I wanted to know if you ate real food."

Will's quick grin broadened, completing the transformation from scary lord of the night to nice guy.

"We'll just have drinks then. Maybe dessert? They do an excellent chocolate soufflé. I'll take that look on your face as a yes."

The waiter reappeared as if by magic. I ordered the soufflé and coffee.

"Decaf?" the waiter asked smoothly.

"Sure." *Not decaf*, cautioned a thin voice inside me. Keep your wits about you. "No, regular!"

Will's mouth twitched slightly, as if he knew what prompted the change. He ordered a brandy.

"Tell me..." Will said, as the waiter disappeared. He reached a hand across the table to cover mine. His touch was warm and unexpectedly soothing. "What was it that had you so upset earlier?"

Gavin's kiss flashed into my consciousness, but I locked it back away.

"Just something to do with Tom's murder...um, that was the guy—"

"I know."

"You do?"

In the beat of silence, any number of terrible reasons why he might know that crowded into my head.

"His name was in the newspaper," Will said.

"You did that on purpose."

"I couldn't resist. Your every emotion plays across your face." He watched me a moment and said, "You were saying...about Tom?"

"He died after eating cookies I made. Someone put cyanide on them."

Will absorbed that. "Did you know Tom well?"

"Not really. We had dinner together once, as tagalongs on a double date between two of our friends." I decided not to mention Becky's name. In my experience, once you put a name to a face, it moved from the random jumble at the back your mind to the front. I wanted Becky to remain as far to the back of Will's radar as possible.

"You liked this man?"

I hesitated, torn between two maxims I'd grown up with—"only say good of the dead" and "begin as you mean to go on"—and decided to go with the latter. If Will found me uncouth, he was welcome to drop me at home and forget about me.

"No. He talked *at* me the entire evening. I don't think there's a single corner of his entire existence that he didn't share with me."

Our drinks came.

"He told you his secrets?" Face inscrutable, Will leaned forward slightly as he waited for my response.

"Hardly. He regaled me with his life story. Every boring minute of it. Then he bragged about his thievery. Apparently he 'found' some papers mixed in with a box of useless desk supplies at the garage sale of a grieving son. Tom basically stole what he insisted was the final unpublished work of the guy's grandfather, a local playwright who was popular back in the Twenties. Soler? Solera?"

The intent, searching expression on Will's face mellowed suddenly into something thoughtful. He sat back in his chair and tented his fingers against his lips. "Sydney Solaire."

"You've heard of him?"

"I knew him." Will's eyes got a faraway look. "Shortly before his death, he was working on an intriguing play on the nature of man." His attention came back to fix on me. "You say this...Tom...found the manuscript? No wonder he was murdered."

He said the last so matter-of-factly that I wondered if I'd imagined the intellectually curious dreamer I'd seen sitting across from me seconds before.

"I don't know about that. There is a good chance Tom's death was an accident, that the poison was meant for someone else."

Will shook his head. His brandy remained untouched. "No. The play would have been a masterpiece." His face seemed lit by an internal fire. "Solaire's treatment of destiny and our roles choosing our own fate was brilliant, a work of philosophy rivaling any of the greats. An unpublished play of that caliber, its author dead, his progeny unaware of its existence... For such things, men kill."

Kill. The word lingered in the air, buoyed by a sweet, musky perfume that choked the response in my throat. I turned to find Natasha approaching our table. Her curves were barely contained by a slinky dress in a shade of come-hither red that I was embarrassed to use on my toenails. I could practically see the air currents formed by the swiveling of her hips. Boom-shiska-boom-shiska-boom.

Her eyes were hard as daggers as they slid over me, sending a familiar icy chill down my spine. Once again I had gotten so caught up talking to Will that I had forgotten he was a bomb ready to go off. I never made that mistake with Natasha. For the first time that evening, I was painfully aware how very, very stupid I had been to leave my apartment.

Her attention didn't linger on me and I drew in a shaky breath as her face softened with sweetness as cloying as her perfume. All for Will's benefit.

It was then that I noticed she wasn't alone. One slim hand curled around the steely forearm of a blond demigod. He wore jeans slung low on lean hips, giving us a peek at abs so ripped they'd make a Calvin Klein underwear model hustle self-consciously to the gym. His gorgeously muscled, V-shaped torso was shown off by a thin cotton shirt that molded to his body like a second skin.

My first thought was *Wow*. My second thought was that he seemed familiar. I figured I'd probably seen a model who looked like him pasted on the girls' binders at school. But then he shifted his doglike attention from Natasha to look at me and I saw the same flicker of recognition in his eyes.

I remembered where I'd seen him and choked. Will passed me a glass of water, which I took with shaking hands and pretended to drink to buy myself time to recover.

The blond stud was the guy Natasha had disappeared with into the haunted house the night Tom died. My eyes moved automatically to his neck. Unlike mine, which still bore twin scars from Will's incisors, his was unblemished. He noticed what I was doing and flashed me a self-satisfied smile. Natasha had already turned him, of course, and that curious power of regeneration had healed the wounds as if they'd never been.

It was only the bodies left for dead that retained the teeth marks. The dead and me.

Natasha presented the newcomer to Will as if she were showing off her new Porsche, and then begrudgingly, and only because Will expected the courtesy, introduced him to me.

Natasha's vampire arm candy had a name. "This," she said, "is Leonardo." She drew out the name in an affected way, as if he were famous and we should immediately throw ourselves to the floor and start bowing and scraping.

"Hi! You can call me Lenny," he said brightly.

I coughed. "Lenny?"

Lenny's face lit with pleasure at being mentioned, the way a puppy's does. The sexy veneer disappeared, leaving a guy who would've been at home chewing straw and driving a tractor on a small farm in the Midwest.

"Heya, Will."

Lenny's accent was pure Minnesota. His mother was probably back home dreaming about ways to tweak her blue-ribbon jam recipe for the local fair.

Will's expression was unreadable.

Lenny reached for my hand and pumped energetically. "Jo, it's real nice to finally meet ya. I—"

Natasha pinched Lenny's biceps sharply. He shifted immediately back into cool mode, turning his head and tilting his jaw in a pose of calculated boredom.

That's when I noticed the fading bruise under his chin. As if in recognition, the back of my head throbbed from where it had collided with my attacker's jaw a couple of hours ago.

I'd been right. Natasha was behind the "accidents". Only, she was using her new stooge to do the dirty work, in case Will asked any pesky questions. The way she kept Lenny pasted to her side explained why I had kept smelling *her* perfume.

My teeth started to chatter. I clamped my them together to make it stop, and sneaked a glance at Will, to see if he noticed. He hadn't. He was doing the small-talk thing with Lenny and Natasha. As if this were normal. Just two people out on a date, running into friends. I realized that's what they were to him. Friends. Family, even.

But Natasha and Lenny weren't my friends—not even close—and nothing about this was normal. However gorgeous and charming, Will was a powerful and deadly vampire. Natasha was a psycho-vampette and Lenny, Natasha's vampire arm candy, had been recruited like a piece of meat. Probably with less thought. He'd been in the wrong place at the wrong time and in a snap of Natasha's pointed teeth, the sweet young man from the farm was gone forever. Now, Natasha said "kill" and Lenny said "when and how?" She probably had enough vampire allure to turn an army of men into murderous robots.

I blinked a few times, trying to keep my head, as a surreal mist settled around my brain like a stupefying fog. This was turning into a bad dream I couldn't quite wake from.

As I scanned the restaurant for a back exit, I couldn't help but notice the people at the other tables were carefully not watching us. The couple seated closest to us, whose space Natasha and Lenny were clearly invading, looked as if they were thrilled to tilt awkwardly in their chairs to keep out of the way.

What was this? Vampire Central? Was I next on the menu?

I let out a faint whimper.

Will turned to me in concern and motioned for Natasha and Lenny to leave us. A look of fury flashed on Natasha's lovely face, but she followed his command. As she turned to leave, she sent me a look that clearly said, "it's only a matter of time".

My hands and feet turned to ice as she walked slowly away. Boom-shiska-boom-shiska-boom.

"How is your dessert?" Will asked.

"What?" I wrenched my attention from Natasha.

He was pointing at the table in front of me. I looked down and saw not only had the waiter delivered my chocolate pot, but I'd taken a bite. I put the spoon down, unable to take another.

"I'm sure it's delicious." More words tumbled out. I was unable to stop them. "Don't you see that Natasha *really* does not like me?"

"Are you jealous?"

The look he sent me swung my internal thermometer in the other direction. He threw a couple of bills on the table, stood and held a hand out to me. "Come."

We left the restaurant. The cool night air felt good on my flushed skin. I suppose I could have tried to make a run for it, but it seemed futile. I got back in the car without a fight.

We were halfway back to my apartment, or, for all I knew, on the way to a moldy castle, a bat cave or the coffin Will called home, when he broke the silence.

"Did Tom share details about the Solaire play or did he mostly bore you senseless with his own life story?"

The mundanity of Will's question shocked me into a brief laugh. "No. You have it in one. Tom didn't talk about the play so much as his delight in stealing it from Solaire's grandson."

"Tom bought it at a garage sale. That's hardly stealing."

"Solaire's grandson thought he was selling a box of gently used office supplies!"

"It was his responsibility, don't you think, to have checked it for valuables before putting it for sale?"

I shifted in my seat to face him. "Of course it was his responsibility. But before you start quoting the Latin companion phrase to caveat emptor that implores the seller to beware, let me remind you that what Tom did was unconscionably sneaky. It's one thing to pay a nickel for something that turns out to be a Ming vase, but quite another to pay a nickel for a cheap knockoff because you've noticed it has a diamond ring rolling around the bottom of it."

For a moment, Will was silent.

"Fairness is important to you." It was a statement, not a question.

"I…" My outrage fizzled as quickly as it had come. I blew out a sigh. "Probably comes with teaching middle schoolers."

Will said softly, "I don't think so."

He got out of the car and I realized we were parked in front of my apartment building. By the time I undid my seat belt, he had opened my door. Usually, I lacked the patience to wait for such old-fashioned chivalry. But Will did it in such a natural, unobtrusive way, that for the first time, I understood how very nice it could be.

We walked slowly past the mailboxes toward the stairs and up to my apartment. "I also don't think you dislike middle schoolers quite as much as you profess. Which is a little disturbing."

"Disturbing?"

"I have spent time with thirteen-year-olds," he said darkly. "I can't say I liked it, even when I was thirteen."

And how long ago was that? I wondered.

We were in front of my door. He had brought me home, unmolested. Beyond all expectations, I was safe.

"You're the one who's hard to understand," I said almost peevishly.

The yellowish light from the street light was blocked out as Will bent his head and kissed me.

"I thought you said you were going to bring me back safely."

"I am."

"This isn't safe," I said as Will leaned in for another kiss.

"Nothing in life is really safe, is it?"

A short time later (Or maybe it was a long time, I lost track.) Will left. I collapsed bonelessly against the door, vaguely aware of a dull pain digging into my side. The door key I didn't remember fitting into the lock. I gave it a twist and stumbled inside.

# Chapter Thirteen

The next morning I woke up before sunrise and went for a long run on the beach while dawn slowly turned the sky orange. The scrapes and bruises I'd collected the past few nights made the run more like a rhythmic hobble until my muscles finally loosened up and the endorphins kicked in. By the time I returned home, pleasantly tired and sweating, the exercise had done its job of helping me sort through things. And what it had sorted was that hopping into a car with Will because I'd been pissed at Gavin was stupid. Stupid, stupid, stupid. Never again.

I showered, dressed and was tossing my sock drawer for the mate to a black trouser sock when I heard someone knocking loudly on a neighbor's door. "Self-important idiot," I muttered. Didn't people realize how well sound carried at 6:30 a.m.? After a brief silence, the serious pounding started up again and I realized it was coming from *my* front door.

I ran to unlock it, nearly killing myself maneuvering around the cat condo in my bunny slippers.

"I'm coming, I'm coming."

I opened the tiny eyelevel peephole door. Green spikes. Becky. I flipped the deadbolt and opened the door wide.

"Hey, Becks. What are you doing?"

"You hit on Dan."

She didn't come in. Her voice was cold, condemning, certain. Judge, jury and executioner. Too horrified to respond, I was silent a beat too long.

"No! I—"

"The rehearsal room door was open. I saw it." Her dark eyes were hollow orbs. She started to say something else, but turned and jogged down the stairs. A moment later, she peeled off in her car.

A neighbor across the street yelled, "Shut up!" and slammed his window shut.

I stood there a long time staring after her, seeing only the crumpled ruin of Becky's face as she had turned away.

Clumsily, as if my hands were made of lead, I backed into my apartment and rebolted the door. I forgot about my trouser socks and getting ready for work and sat on the edge of my ugly old couch and put my head in my hands. What had I done?

In truth, I'd done nothing. Dan didn't even remember it. But Becky would never see it that way.

I knew that someday when I fully turned, I would lose my friends and family. For their own safety, it would have to be that way. But I never thought (How could I have?) that I could lose my friends now. Like this.

I managed to pull myself together enough to get to work on time. If I was worried about any uncomfortable confrontations from Becky, I needn't have been. She was little more than a green streak. I entered the faculty room from the back door and Becky left out the front. At morning break, I thought to try talking to her, but her classroom door was locked. I continued on to the terrace, and found her getting coffee. As soon as I stepped out under the ledge, she popped the lid on her stainless steel coffee mug and stepped out into the bright morning sun to chat and giggle with other people. Several of my colleagues, scenting trouble, turned to stare at me.

I was alone, and felt it.

About midway through my class, just before lunch, I wasn't sure I could take any more. Teaching, especially middle schoolers, is not for the thin of skin. If they see you unraveling, they'll pick at the threads until you're naked before them. And today, I was dripping with loose threads. I could practically hear the lip smacking as the more brazen troublemakers mocked my classroom control by talking out of turn and tossing notes in full view.

I could have used my vampire glare to ensnare them into obedience. But I didn't. No matter what anyone thought, I was still human, still their teacher. If I wanted to get them to stop acting out, I would do it as an educator. I would instill in them the fascination that was the Doppler shift.

Right.

There were always those dusty Carl Sagan VHS tapes that had come with my classroom.

Coward.

"Okay." I drew a car on the board and sketched in a road. "Imagine this Porsche…" There were a few giggles. I was possibly the worst artist ever and my sports car looked like a dumpling on wheels. "Is at a stop sign. Not moving. You're nearby on the sidewalk." I added a stick figure on what would be the side of the road. "What do you hear?"

Every boy in the class and some of the girls made rrrmmm sounds.

"Right. That's the sound the *stationary* idling Porsche makes. Now. What does it sound like when it blows by you?"

"Neerww."

"Can someone tell me the difference between the two sounds?"

At the back of the room, Lindsay Park raised her hand. "I don't get it."

Teddy Tomkins swiveled on his stool to face her. "One goes rrmmm, the other goes neerrww."

She nodded. "Oh."

I said diplomatically, "Teddy gave us a good demonstration of the two sounds. Can anyone tell me how one is different from the other?"

Total silence. Maybe that was the real genius of the Socratic method. You ask a hard question and they shut up. "Can anyone give me another example of something that sounds different when it's just sitting there as opposed to when it's moving toward you or away from you?"

A hand shot up in the front. "A train."

"Good example, Dana." It was the one in the textbook. "Can you tell me how the noise changes when the train is moving?"

She glanced at her textbook. "It rises in pitch as it approaches the station."

I'd bet my next paycheck she had no idea what pitch was.

I picked up the desk chime one of my students had given me for Christmas last year and waved my hands toward the door. "All right. Everyone in the hall. Quietly. No, leave your stuff. Qui-etly! Ms. O'Neal's class is in session. Stand by the water fountain. Two lines." I poked my head into the biology classroom. "This will just be a minute," I mouthed. Leah O'Neal nodded without a break in her lecture and I closed the door.

I headed down to my students. Any attempt at being quiet had gone by the wayside and one of the boys had another in a headlock. "We have to do this quietly so we don't disturb the upper-school classes, okay?" They settled down. They were so good that I might have suspected I'd inadvertently brought out the vampire glare, but I knew it wasn't me, even supernatural me, they'd responded to, but the threat of a well-respected high school teacher taking a dislike to them. My good opinion might be expendable on the road to Ivy League collegedom, but the high school teachers' opinions were everything.

I picked up the tiny hammer and whacked the chime. A pure, clear tone sang through the hall. I pressed myself against the wall. "Okay. I'm going to strike the chime again and I want you to run by me. Stop when you get to the door of my classroom. As you run, listen to the chime. Tell me if you hear it change or not."

I whacked the chime and they ran past, giggling and thumping. I jogged the few yards over to them.

"What did you hear?" I asked.

"Everyone running."

"Besides that." I said.

They looked at each other.

"Let's try again. Three at a time. Pay close attention to the sound of the chime as you get close to me and then as you move away from me."

I rang the chime and the first group went. I went through the rest of the class. "Okay. Back in the classroom. Now, write down how the chime sounded. You have thirty seconds. Go."

"How many of you heard the sound change?" About half the hands went up. "How did it change when you were running toward me?"

"It got louder!"

Someone snorted in disgust and corrected, "It got higher!"

"Exactly." I began drawing concentric circles around the Porsche. "Here's why. When the Porsche is at the stop sign, the sound waves travel evenly like waves when you drop a rock in a pond." I flicked on my overhead projector, stuck a fat glass beaker half-full of water on top and dropped a marble in it. Waves rippled in concentric circles from where I'd dumped the marble. "Like this. When the object moves, it still gives out sound in concentric circles, but..."

Ten minutes later, as the bell rang, almost everyone had gotten it. I told them, "Not all of you heard the sound change when I rang the chime, and not all of you have really noticed how a car sounds as it passes you on the freeway. But as you go home today, ask your parents to drive in the slow lane and pay attention. If you take the bus, you don't have to ask the bus drivers. They drive slowly enough already."

They left, chatting and excited. It was a miracle. I was giddy with accomplishment. Humming, I erased my diagrams off the white board.

"What the hell were you doing? It sounded like a herd of elephants running around up here." Roger stomped into my classroom, doing a good imitation of an elephant himself.

"Doppler effect. I had them move around to see how pitch changes."

I wasn't sure if the tone had audibly changed at the speed they were moving, but it had been enough to help them grasp the idea behind it.

"Ridiculous and unnecessary. There's a very good explanation in the text. Unless you're letting them off the hook in their homework? Perhaps if you spent more time on mastering basic skills, you wouldn't need to disrupt others' class time with stupid stunts."

He turned and left, taking my enthusiasm with him. Deflated, I left the board half-erased and went gloomily to lunch. It was a nice warm fall day and almost everybody else was taking advantage of it at the outdoor tables. I caught sight of Carol sitting alone at an inside table. I grabbed a tray of whatever they were serving and went to her like a dumped woman to a box of chocolates.

As I reached the table, she glanced up from her dressingless salad. Her eyes flashed with confusion and there was hesitancy in her greeting that made me stop in the process of putting down my tray.

"Not you too," I said.

She was slow in responding, which made my temper, barely checked after Roger's pigheadedness, soar.

No one was near us, but I lowered my voice anyway. "Oh, for crying out loud. I know Becky's brains are addled, but I thought you at least would have some sense. I didn't do it. I would never hurt Becky like that, especially with someone I'm not remotely interested in."

Her sweet round face pinched with remorse. "Jo, I didn't—"

"You know what? Never mind."

I slapped a benign smile on my face for anyone who was watching and left through the side door. We weren't really supposed to take trays out of the eating area but the cafeteria staff cut the teachers some slack, providing we brought the dishes back when we were done. I carted lunch all the way back to my classroom, slid the tray on a counter then locked the classroom door. I had a terrible, overwhelming urge to put my head down on my desk and cry. Until I saw what lunch was.

The cafeteria staff often made small batches of gourmet "adult" meals for the faculty. For instance, we got grilled shark when the students got fishwiches.

Today was one of the special days. I had a gorgeous plateful of Forty Cloves of Garlic Chicken with a side of garlic bread. I couldn't eat a bite of it. The smell alone was making me nauseous. Instead of crying, I laughed and laughed until the tears streamed down my face.

~*~

A hundred long years later, the school day eventually ended. It had been relentlessly miserable from start to finish. The sort of day that made me want to slink home, crawl under the covers with a family-size bag of mini chocolate bars and not come out until I'd received word that the headmaster had finally opened himself to telepathy and accepted my resignation.

And yet, I lingered. I sat at my desk, working diligently through the "to grade" pile, my classroom door propped open. No one came. At six, after three hours of nonstop grading, my hand was cramped, my eyes swam and my stomach growled with the pain of emptiness. Eleven hours was long enough to spend at work, even if I still had two classes' worth of tests to grade. I stacked them in my book bag and headed out for a burger.

I forcibly stifled the little voice in my head. It was loud, actually, as if my mother and grandmother were in there together chiding me about eating yet another red meat take-out meal.

I'd been eating out a lot lately, but why should I cook? I couldn't eat half the stuff I liked. My famous spaghetti sauce had garlic. My favorite green chili chicken had tons of it.

Sure I could take the evil garlic out. The dishes wouldn't be the same but they would still be good to someone whose taste buds weren't freakishly skewed to raw meat. I didn't understand why everything else (Except sugar and caffeine, it seemed.) tasted like bitter poison to me. But it did.

Anyway, it was a moot point. Regardless of what I had or didn't have in my fridge, I was going to eat out tonight because I didn't want to go home. My apartment held too many uncomfortable memories. And my usual way of dealing with crappy days—baking—held no appeal. I didn't want to be inside. I was tired of *having* to be inside. I wanted to go out. Be outside breathing in the crisp night air instead of huddling inside.

And why not? So there were vampires outside. So what? I'd been out with Will last night and survived, hadn't I? Granted, that outing might have made Natasha and her vampire arm candy even more determined to kill me today. But the mood I was in? After the day I'd had? Just let them try! I dared them!

Full of defiance, I turned into the driveway of a fast-food place within spitting distance of the ocean and parked. I got out of my car and walked inside to the counter to order my burger. No drive-thru tonight, not for me. I was living on the edge. A few minutes later, burger bag in hand, I strode triumphantly back out. And kept going. Tonight, I was having a picnic dinner on the beach.

The sun had gone down, but the beach was far from deserted. Joggers, walkers, and cyclists puffed up and down the cement strip paralleling the shoreline. I hustled across the path through a gap in traffic, pulled off my black flats and trouser socks, and squeaked quickly across the cold sand to the lifeguard tower. At this time of night, I had it all to myself. I climbed up the ladder and sat down on the platform, letting my legs dangle over the side.

I ate my burger slowly, watched by a sharp-eyed night heron who seemed to be of the opinion I was eating his dinner. Despite my insistence that I wasn't sharing and that he didn't want people food anyway, he kept edging closer. I finally tossed him a few lettuce leaves from my side salad so he could decide for himself. He picked at one and drifted away, but not too far, in case I was holding out on him.

I sat there for a long time thinking of nothing, watching the twinkling lights of the offshore oil platforms.

I might have stayed there for hours, except my cell phone rang. I fumbled in my pocket for it, hoping it was Becky. I wanted to say all the things I should have said that morning instead of just standing there like a pole while she reached the wrong conclusion.

It wasn't Becky calling. Of course it wasn't. Becky wasn't one to waffle. I'd been cut out of her life, well and good.

Gavin was trying to reach me. Again. I turned the phone off, fished the lettuce leaves out of the sand and walked back to my car. I got in and headed home.

Will was waiting at the curb in front of my apartment, leaning against his car like something out of a movie.

I thought about driving on. The cat bowl held enough dry food for a week and Aunt Bertha had sprung for one of those filtered-waterfalls, so Fluffy would be fine. It wasn't as if the cranky beast pined for my company. I could crash at my parents' tonight.

And tomorrow?

My best friend would still hate me and Gavin—I didn't know what Gavin was. Not my friend or he'd have shut the door behind him so Becky wouldn't have had to witness her boyfriend responding to a vampire trait I wasn't aware I had.

The past twenty-four hours had been scary, confusing and depressing. But mostly, overwhelmingly, it had been lonely.

There was a space at the end of the block. I parked and got out of my car. A few minutes later, I was driving off again. In Will's car.

# Chapter Fourteen

After a short drive inland, Will pulled into the parking lot in front of a large beige apartment building. Just looking at it made me depressed. It was a no-frills rectangular box covered in thin, gritty stucco that collected grime like it was worth money.

"For you." Will handed me a pair of thin, black leather gloves and drew a larger pair over his own hands.

I fingered the gloves. The leather was sumptuous. "Why are we here?"

Will was getting out of the car and didn't answer. I opened my door and got out, intending to ask again, but the question died on my lips as a skeletally thin man in his mid-twenties pushed himself off the side of the building and sauntered over to us.

It wasn't the best part of town. You wouldn't want to drive through it at night unless you lived there and even then most inhabitants stayed inside, behind locked doors and barred windows.

He wore giant baggy pants that, by some miracle of gravity defiance, remained attached to his colorful boxers by the bottom of his butt. It was jacket weather, or at least long-sleeved shirt weather, but he wore a tank top that showed off wiry muscles and a decided taste for snake tattoos.

"Nice ride," he told Will. "I'd like me to have a sweet ride like that."

What he meant was, "I'll be taking that car off your hands now, chump." His fingers hovered over a deep, bulky pocket as if it contained a weapon that backed up his claim to the car. I wouldn't be surprised if he pulled out a bazooka.

Will was wearing impeccably tailored black pants and the sort of thin black sweater that is made of rare, hand-pulled cashmere from special sheep only found in valleys ten thousand feet above sea level and collected by monks under a full moon. His clothes couldn't have concealed anything more than a pocket knife, and even that was doubtful, as it would have ruined the elegant lines. His gloved hands held nothing more than the car keys on a simple silver ring.

Will tossed his keys as if the scary gang banger were a parking valet. "Excellent. Keep an eye on it while I take care of some business." Placing a warm hand between my shoulder blades, he propelled me forward. We headed into the apartment building without looking back.

That is, Will didn't look back. I couldn't help it. The man stood frozen by the car holding the keys as if they were a bomb about to go off.

Through thin apartment doors placed far too close together, I could hear the blare of televisions and the occasional cadence of real people talking. Smells of cooking—fried chicken, grilled onions, pizza and microwave popcorn—competed with less pleasant smells of urine and alcohol.

"Why are we here?" I asked again in a low voice as we turned a corner and headed deeper into the building. The narrow hallways were brightly lit by harsh overhead fluorescents. Crime deterrent, I thought.

"Tom lived here," Will said.

We passed a girl's bike with a pink seat and a white handlebar basket with daisies on it. I'd had the same one in purple, growing up.

"How do you know where Tom lived?" I asked.

"Phone book," Will said, stopping before a nondescript door marked 18A. He slanted a blue gaze at me.

"And where did you get his apartment keys?"

"I didn't."

I perked up. I should have been appalled to learn we were breaking in, but all I could think was that finally I was going to see Will work his vampire magic.

He pulled a long, oddly shaped key out of his pocket and stuck it in the lock. A few twists and jiggles and something went click and we were inside.

He flicked on a light and turned to look at me. "Disappointed?"

"Confused." About so many things. Will constantly refused to fit the pictures I formed of him. "I thought you couldn't go inside a place unless invited."

"Tom's dead."

Right. I pulled my attention from Will and looked around. The place was a shambles. Everything that could have been searched had been, and messily.

"I don't think we're the first ones here."

"No," he agreed. "But did they find what they came for?"

I held up my hands, clad in the black gloves, and wiggled my fingers. "I take it we're going to conduct our own search?"

My statement didn't come out as cool as I'd planned.

Will was standing close to me, thoughtfully studying the apartment layout and the mess around us as if planning the most efficient mode of attack. He shifted his attention back to me. "You don't have to do anything." He meant it.

"I've already 'broken and entered.'"

"You didn't know where we were going. I brought you here. I picked the lock." He would have made a good lawyer.

"Well then, I guess I can sell you down the river if it comes to that. Now, where do I start?"

This got me a full-blown Will grin. I swayed like a Sixties-era teenybopper at a Beatles concert and he grabbed my arm to keep me upright. His smile widened.

Will began his search methodically at the farthest end of the apartment. I tagged along to get the feel of things. He looked for the manuscript in places I would never have dreamed to look. Inside the toilet tank—in case Tom had gotten creative with the zip top bags—and in tiny places like the garage sale cookie jar collection on the bedroom bookshelves, as manuscripts can be divided. Obviously, Will wasn't leaving finding it to chance.

As he moved on to patting down every item of clothing in the closet, for what I could only assume was secret compartments sewn into linings, I assigned myself the kitchen. I went through everything, including all the cereal boxes. Tom had preferred the ones with cartoon mascots on the boxes and sugar as the primary ingredient, and there were enough boxes in his cupboards that he could have concealed the entire works of William Shakespeare.

All I had left was a sticky set of ugly, patriotic-themed canisters on the counter next to the stove when Will rejoined me. He was holding a thin file folder and there was a keen, almost excited expression on his face.

"Any luck?" I asked, dusting rancid flour off my gloves. Some of the canister gunk had transferred itself to my gloves and the flour was sticking like glue. "Ick. I hope you weren't too attached to these gloves."

"The manuscript is not here. These are some of Solaire's notes."

"So it does exist." His enthusiasm was catching. "What next?"

Intelligence and curiosity danced in Will's blue eyes. I realized he was having fun. I was too. It was an unexpectedly sobering thought.

"What?" he said.

"Sometimes I forget you're—"

In two steps he crossed the tiny kitchen to stand in front of me. Clutching a blue-and-white-striped canister with *sugar* written on it to my chest, I shrank back against the counter.

I was unable to look away. I stared up into Will's eyes and felt a queer, unresisting floating feeling come over me. It was a little like how I felt the year I'd jumped into the freezing ocean on New Year's Eve for a swim. After the initial shock of cold, my body had gone numb and I'd stayed in long enough to swim out to the buoy and back.

"I don't."

The floating feeling disappeared so suddenly that I gasped. Will plucked the container out of my hands, put it gently on the counter, drew me close and kissed me. When he let me go, I had to clutch the countertop to keep from sliding to the floor.

He turned and headed for the door. "Time to go."

With shaking fingers, I picked up the sugar container, but instead of replacing it against the wall as had been my intent, I opened it. Just to be thorough. Or maybe it was to pretend to myself that I wasn't as rattled as I was.

"Of course." Not only was the canister empty of anything related to Solaire, it didn't have so much as a grain of sugar left in it. A brittle laugh came choking out of my dry throat. Tom had probably heaped spoonfuls of sugar on his morning marshmallow puffs and frosted honey bombs.

Will's car was exactly as we'd left it in the parking lot. So was the attendant. Will plucked the keys from the gangbanger's outstretched hand and it no longer seemed funny to me.

By the time we returned to my apartment building, my wildly conflicting thoughts had been reduced to a simple goal—get inside my apartment. The moment the car stopped, I punched my seat belt free and rocketed out of the car.

My mind took a moment to catch up with my fear. And when it did, I realized a five-second head start wasn't nearly enough. Will and I walked up together. I think we chatted about some book we'd both read, but I wouldn't have been completely surprised if someone had told me no, you were talking about lima beans.

I had a bad feeling that Will knew exactly what was going through my head. Every time I hinted that it was time for me to go inside, he found a way to keep me outside. Desperate, I was about to embark upon the world's fakest yawn, when a passing car screeched suddenly to a halt on the street below. A woman bolted out, leaving the car double parked. She sprinted toward us, moving faster than I would ever have imagined was possible in three-inch heels. She was no more than a pinkish-brown smudge in the night as she passed under the fluorescent streetlights.

Will and I were too stunned to move. Which is why my purse-wielding mother made it all the way up the stairs and got in a hard whack to Will's chest before he could defend himself.

He staggered back in surprise. "I beg your—"

My mother hauled back and hit him again. Her purse probably weighed twenty or thirty pounds, and this time something sharp seemed to catch him on the bony part of his forearm. His eyes darkened to black.

"Mom, stop!"

"No!" She was a demon possessed. "Jo, you must hold strong!"

She cocked her arm back and readied her purse for another swing. "I'm sure he told you he's reformed, but don't believe it. Men like him are good at lies. That's how they start. They alienate you from your friends and family and the next thing you know, you're living in a trailer park with a man in a sleeveless undershirt!" Her arm, honed from many dedicated hours at the gym, released like a shot.

This time, Will was ready for it. He grabbed the purse and held it so she couldn't swing again.

My mother pulled hard against the strap. "Let go, you coffee-shop stalker!"

Will dodged a sharp kick to his shin. "Coffee-shop stalker?"

He had directed the question at me, but my mother answered. "Oh, I know all about you, second-rate coffee boy!"

Will's eyes bugged a little. If there was any vampire mind control going on, it was bouncing right off my mother. She was on fire.

"I suggest you go back to your job at the diner and leave my daughter alone, or I'll have a restraining order slapped on you so fast you won't be able to move two feet in this town without the cops breathing down your back!"

Will handed back her purse. "You must have mistaken me for someone else," he said coldly. "I don't work at a coffee shop."

"Don't you patronize me, young man. I—"

I felt it was time I intervened before my mother got thrown over the railing.

"He no longer works there," I said.

Her scathing gaze swept Will in disgust. "It took you five years to get that promotion and you couldn't even keep it?" She turned to me. "Really,

Jo. You can do better than a man who can't even keep a junior manager position at some cheap little restaurant."

It was as if a light had flicked on behind Will's eyes. Comprehension dawned. "Mrs. Gartner." His bland smile held a barely cloaked wickedness that sent the hairs on the back of my neck quivering upright. "I believe I see the misunderstanding. When I met Jo, I *was* in one of my coffee shops." His eyes flicked to me. "On occasion, I liked to get out of my corporate office and do some...research...of my own."

My mother sniffed. "And I suppose you're going to tell me you're not a stalker, either?"

Will crossed his arms over his chest, leaned comfortably back against the wall and raised his eyebrows at me.

He knew. He knew why I had spun her that tale, just as he knew I wanted nothing more than to drag my mother inside the safety of my apartment and lock the door behind us.

I said reluctantly, "That was a bit of a misunderstanding. He's the human resource specialist from an old international firm. And, no, you've never heard of it. It's a private company and they keep a low profile." I stuck out a hand for Will to shake. "Thank you so much for a lovely evening. It was nice to see you again."

"It's always a pleasure to spend time with you, Jo." Will took my hand and kissed me softly on the cheek. His lips landed squarely on a sensitive spot. He murmured in my ear, "We will talk later, you and I."

He shook my mother's hand as if she was an old, dear friend and not a crazy, overprotective mother who had just dented his arm with her purse. "If you'll excuse me, I'll leave you ladies to your evening."

I nearly sagged against the door in relief. It would be okay. He was just going to walk away and leave us.

At the top of the stairs, he stopped.

He turned back, the picture of polite regret. "I'm sorry, Mrs. Gartner, but I believe you've parked me in."

"Oh, I...oh!" Her eyes zeroed in on his two hundred sixty-five thousand dollar car. Will was back in.

"How silly of me." She pulled out her car keys and, flashing him a bright smile, accepted Will's arm as he accompanied her down the stairs.

"Oh, this is just great," I muttered, clattering after them.

My mother had that look again, the one where she was imagining the handsome children Will and I would have. The expression on Will's face was victory itself.

# Chapter Fifteen

---

The next day was Friday, and Halloween, as far as our school was concerned. The rest of the world would celebrate on Sunday.

Not wearing a costume would have been tantamount to announcing I had no school spirit, something Roger would have attacked like an overzealous pep club president. Not that he ever wore a costume. It was beneath his dignity as science department chair.

He was such a troll.

Going as a bustier-wearing vampire vixen was out so I dug my old standby out of the closet. A nun's habit. As I pulled on the shapeless black dress and strung a rosary around my neck, I felt nice and safe for the first time in weeks. It reminded me comfortingly of Sister Gerald Gervaise who ran my high school like a well-oiled machine. If anyone could have stared down a vampire, it was she.

If only I could borrow her for a little bit, everything would go back to normal in no time. Whoever killed Tom wouldn't last a half-hour in her company before he or she was prostrate from guilt and confessed on the spot. It goes without saying that I had spent a lot of quality high school time in her office. Sometimes I couldn't help but wonder if she had used her clout with The Almighty to give me the most ill-behaved possible combination of students in my classes. A little penance for all the trouble I'd put my own teachers through.

As I drove up to campus, a giant pink gorilla was swinging from the front gates. Roger, who was a few cars up from me in the morning traffic line, stopped to give the ape a vehement dressing-down. The ape shrugged and started to walk away but a car full of laughing kids in front of me got him up and swinging again. As I got near the gates, I recognized him as a cheerful, wacky history teacher whom I rather liked, and honked along with the rest of the cars. As I slowly passed by, he jumped off the gates and popped his furry pink head in my passenger window, "Bless me, Sister, for I have annoyed your department chair."

"Not to worry," I told him. "We're having him excommunicated."

He gave me a high five, scratched his underarms and jumped back up on the gates amidst loud hoots from the car behind me. His performance seemed to cheer everyone and cast a lingering good mood over the campus that stretched well into the day.

My students were in rare form, cracking jokes instead of looking for costumes to mock. Which, if I'm being totally honest, was a lucky thing for some of the kids. I mean, I'm all for personal expression, and I don't think parents should helicopter their kids into being carbon copies of the popular group. But when your thirteen-year-old is about to commit social suicide with a My Little Pony costume, maybe it's time to step in with a little guidance.

It was a perfect day for dousing the lights and teaching in a pitch black classroom. The one benefit of having a "sun allergy" was that I had been able to replace the tatty gray plasticky curtains with solid blackout blinds. When I projected the night sky on the ceiling, it looked really cool. Class participation was at an all-time high.

I had planned to spend all the breaks holed up in my classroom so I wouldn't have to spend another terrible day being publicly shunned by my former best friends. But I really was having such a *nice* day that when one of the sweet, slightly geeky girls who had gone all out on her witch costume (She had green skin and black buckle shoes and everything.) shyly asked me if I was coming to watch the costume contest during lunch, I couldn't say no.

I had followed the crowd downstairs and was standing in the covered walkway outside the entrance to the first floor of the science department, unwrapping the scarf from around my face, when I realized my shoelace had come untied. In my mind, that was the best part of Halloween—I could wear my comfortable running shoes and real socks instead of librarian-dress-police-approved flats and those stupid little nylon jobs.

"Excuse me, er, Sister?"

I felt the tap on my shoulder more than I registered the words.

"Yeah?" I peeked around my wimple to see Gavin, dressed in his work clothes of slacks and a nicely ironed button-down. He projected an image of calm authority, but I knew him well enough to see the frustration bubbling underneath. There were faint shadows under his eyes and he had lost enough of the summer tan that the slight crook in his nose stood out.

He wasn't looking at me but was busy scanning the crowd. I got to my feet but kept my knees bent so I was a full head beneath his six-one instead of the usual three inches. I clasped my hands and stood demurely, tilting my head down so the habit hid my features. "Yes, my child?"

"I'm wondering if you can help me find one of the teachers here? Jo Gartner."

"Of course," I murmured. "What does she look like?"

"Tall, red hair, hazel eyes."

"Is she pretty?"

He was thrown by the question. "Very. But, I, er…" His pale gray gaze shifted suddenly from his study of the quad to me. "Jo?" His mouth tightened in a sharp line.

I straightened to my full height and crossed my arms over my chest, careful not to smoosh the rosary. It had belonged to my grandmother. "What do you want, Detective Raines?"

"I— Is there somewhere we can talk?"

My stomach did a flip. Quite against my will I remembered that kiss as if I'd been in his arms only seconds earlier.

"I'm busy. I'm expected at the middle school costume contest in the cafeteria." Which wouldn't take place for at least another twenty minutes. "Perhaps you can call me."

"Your phone seems to be out of order."

The walkway was deserted, but I lowered my voice anyway. That's as far as my discretion went. I couldn't quite keep the anger out of my voice, but at least I controlled the hurt. Letting Gavin know that his rejection had cost me the slightest pain would have been unbearable.

He might want to talk to me, but I didn't want to talk to him. "Out of order, huh? What a shame. I'll be sure to look into that."

We both knew I was lying. A student burst through the door from the first floor of the science wing at a run. Immediately, Gavin and I pasted benign smiles on our faces. As she became a green plaid dot in the distance, Gavin's smile grew brittle.

I said, "This isn't a good time. If you need to talk to me, you can stop by my—"

"I've tried your place. You've had company." His face was carefully blank.

"Can't help it if I'm popular, can I? Look, I'm sorry but—"

"It's either here or I bring you to the station. Which is it going to be?"

I heard brisk footsteps coming up the path behind me.

"Fine." I rewrapped the scarf around my head and shoved on my sunglasses. I tucked my hands back away in the long, full sleeves of my costume, and through the material grabbed up a handful of the skirt to keep myself from tripping over the hem as I jogged back upstairs.

Gavin followed me in as I unlocked my classroom. He shut the door behind us. "Well?" I pulled off my protective sun gear. The veil came off with it. I tossed it on the counter and ran a hand through my hair, which I'd worn loose. The last thing I needed was to have habit-head in front of a man who'd rejected me.

He stood a few feet away, hands on lean hips, watching and waiting. His expression was growing colder by the second. "You went out with Will. Any changes I should know about?" Without warning, he closed the distance between us and reached a hand to my neck to check for fresh vampire bites.

I slapped his hand away. "Don't you dare!"

He and I glared at each other for a long moment and then he stepped back and lowered his hand.

"All right, then. You tell me. What did he want? Start with the first night."

I shrugged and turned toward the window. As usual the view—a drain pipe and the west wall of the theater—was hidden by the curtains. "We went to dinner."

"You had dinner delivered, remember?"

"I had coffee and dessert. A chocolate pot. It had whipped cream and a tiny mint leaf—"

"I don't give a damn what you ate!" He ran a hand down his face and turned away. He wasn't as controlled as he would have liked.

"Natasha was there. She has a new boyfriend. Lenny."

"I'll let missing persons know." A grimace of profound regret skittered across Gavin's profile.

It was so exactly how I had felt when I'd seen Lenny on Natasha's arm that I forgot for the moment that Gavin and I were at odds. I stepped closer and touched a finger to his arm.

"He's the one I saw her with at the haunted house, before she disappeared. About my age, your height, blond, blue eyes, very fit. Could be an underwear model."

Gavin's face grew more inscrutable. He nodded tightly.

"There's something else. Remember that night at the diner? You were with your girlfriend." Until I mentioned it just now, I'd forgotten he had a girlfriend. It made his behavior the other night all the more deplorable.

"Sara is not my girlfriend. And yes, I remember the night at the diner."

*Not his girlfriend? But*— I cut off the line of thought. It didn't matter. Wasn't any of my business. I told him about Tom's excitement over the manuscript he had "bought" at the garage sale.

"I think Tom was the murder target all along. Someone knew about the manuscript, knew how valuable it was."

"How do you know it was valuable?"

"Will told me. He..." My triumph faded under Gavin's wintery gaze. "He knew the author, a local playwright named Solaire."

"Of course."

"The point is, the manuscript was virtually worthless to anyone else as long as Tom was around. They could steal it, but they could never market it. And how better to get everyone off the track than by feeding Tom poisoned cookies belonging to someone else? We all knew he had an insatiable sweet tooth and saw nothing wrong with helping himself to other people's candy stashes. It was all too easy to believe he was 'hoisted by his own petard'."

"If Tom told you, a virtual stranger, about his precious find, he probably told the entire theater troupe."

"Then why isn't the entire theater troupe talking about it?"

Gavin shrugged dismissively. "The latest 'great find' of a garage sale junkie? Why would they?"

"It wasn't like that. It's true Tom was excited, but he was guarding that secret like the entrance to Tut's lost tomb."

"Yet, he told you."

"Yes," I snapped. "Would you like to speculate why?"

"It's an interesting theory," Gavin said after a moment's silence.

"Interesting theory? It's right and you know it."

"I don't know it, and neither do you. And before you go off half-cocked, what makes you think we ever stopped considering Tom as the intended victim?"

"I thought the LBPD had finally accepted that Dan might be the real target."

"That's one of several possibilities being explored. Let the police handle this."

I snorted. "Which police? The branch that can accept that there's a man alive who saw Solaire working on his masterpiece? Or the ones who still think vampires exist only in fiction? And if they're exploring reasons behind Tom's death, why hasn't anyone noticed his apartment has been trashed?"

"Don't tell me you went to that hellhole, in prime gangbanger territory."

"Will was with me. I'm sure I was perfectly safe."

Gavin closed his eyes and pinched the bridge of his nose. "Jesus, Jo." His pale gray gaze lifted bleakly to my face. "I don't know what to do with you."

I felt something tangle deep inside me. The anger and confusion I'd been suppressing the past couple of days poured out.

"Why didn't you warn me? About the vampire allure. You saw it that night at the diner, didn't you? When Tom was pouring his guts out to me like I was his most intimate acquaintance."

His silence was admission enough.

"Why didn't you tell me?" My voice cracked as I thought of all the problems that could have been avoided with just a few words from him.

"I didn't think it was a good idea."

"Why? Did you think I would use it? Run around and mesmerize all the men I could find and led them to their doom like the pied piper?"

"No."

"What was it then?"

Concern flickered across his face. "I hesitated to tell you because I was afraid you'd take it as a bad sign."

"How else could I take it? How else should I take it?" My nails dug into my palms so hard they left marks. "You should have said something. You should have at least shut the door behind you so my best friend didn't have to see her boyfriend inexplicably making a pass at me."

"Becky was there? I didn't realize."

"No, you were too busy watching, waiting for me to fail. Sometimes I think you want me to finish the transformation so I fit into an easy category…"

"That is not true."

"But I'm still alive. I'm still me." My throat was so tight I could barely get breath for the words.

Gavin reached for me then, offering the comfort I so badly needed, but I turned away. After a long silence, one so absolute I could hear the clock over the whiteboard tick the time, he headed for the door.

I heard the doorknob turn, but he didn't leave, not right away. He spoke so softly that I barely heard him.

"Jo?"

"What."

"If you need me, I'm here." He closed the door quietly behind him.

~*~

I tried for lunch a second time. This time, I actually made it through the door of the first floor science wing before someone stopped me.

"Jo!" Dan was heading down the hallway in my direction, a friendly smile on his golden-boy face. "Hey, how come you weren't at the haunted house last night?"

His question flummoxed me. As did his relaxed friendliness. Didn't he remember our near embrace the night before last? I guessed not. Apparently my vampire allure came with a convenient amnesiac aftereffect.

I let out the breath I was holding. But I made sure I didn't keep eye contact too long. Just in case.

Dan held up a hand. "No need to answer that. You deserve a night off and I don't want you to think we don't appreciate all the hours you've given to the LBP."

"I'm sorry, Dan. I guess I assumed you didn't really need me. Not with all the new volunteers."

I noticed the tightness in his body then, as he released it in an exhaled breath. "Of course. I'll bet Becky thought the same."

"Wasn't she there last night?"

His easy smile seemed a smidge forced. "No. Total no-show by the science department. In fact, that's why I'm here. Hoping to get my best people back." His glance flicked betrayingly toward Becky's door. He pulled himself together with an effort. "The temporary volunteer squad from the other night has all but disappeared, and I'm afraid we're going to be even more short-staffed than before."

I found myself saying, "You can count on me. I'll be there."

"Thanks, Jo. I really appreciate it."

The bell rang. Great. I'd missed the costume contest *and* lunch. Dan looked back over his shoulder at Becky's door.

"I gotta go," I said.

"Me too." Dan wrenched his attention back to me. He seemed to take in my outfit for the first time. He grinned. "You should wear that tonight. Great costume."

~*~

I made up for lunch, in every way, by eating tons of Halloween candy. I started coming down off my chocolate high on the way home.

It was tempting to try to bump up my flagging energy levels by ripping into the bag of Hershey's Kisses in my purse, but I knew I'd be better off eating dinner, even if it was hamburgers again.

I sighed aloud as I walked sluggishly up the stairs to my apartment. If I kept up these eating habits, I'd have both feet in the grave before I reached the age of thirty. I'd have to let Will finish turning me into a vampire just so I didn't upset my parents by dying before them.

I was so caught up in my morbid thoughts that I had actually touched my key to the lock before I noticed my front door was ajar. I stood frozen for a long moment, deliberating what to do. I dithered so long that, if someone was inside my apartment, they were either unnaturally quiet, or dead. I know I should have turned around right then and left, but I didn't. I pushed open the door.

# Chapter Sixteen

*I* didn't go in right away. It was dark enough outside that the building's automatic outdoor lights had flicked on, and the inside of my apartment seemed black as pitch. I scrabbled a hand along the wall for the light switch and was momentarily blinded by a beam of light shooting upward from the floor through a broken lampshade.

When my eyes adjusted and I could see again, I gasped. And then I whimpered. My bag slid from my boneless arm to slump in the doorway at my feet. Every piece of furniture was overturned. Couch cushions pulled off, slashed open and tossed. Books pulled from the shelves and scattered, ripped and broken. Papers and clothes were twisted throughout the mess as if by a tornado. My apartment was as quiet as a grave except for an occasional soft squeak.

A squeak? I bolted in, slipsliding over books and papers, nearly turning an ankle on a geode bookend. Climbing over the upside-down couch, I reached the cat condo. It was tipped flat on its side. The door holes were pressed against the carpet and weighed down by a heavy bookcase.

"Fluffy?"

I heard a squeaky meow and a rumbling purr resonated loudly inside the cat cave.

"Oh thank God!" I righted the bookshelf, shoved a mess of books and papers out of the way and rolled the carpeted cylinder around so the entry was free.

"You poor thing. How long have you been like that?" I reached inside and Fluffy bit me. She was fine. I sagged against the nubby-carpet side in relief.

Nursing my hand, I climbed to my feet and looked for some sign of my phone so I could call the police, as I should have the moment I realized my front door was open. I couldn't find any sign of it in the mess. Picking my way to the overturned table where it had been, I decided my best bet was to trace it from the jack. But the jack was gone, ripped from the wall along with a small chunk of drywall.

For some reason, that infuriated me. I slipslided my way back to the front door, where I had left my book bag. I refused to consider the very real possibility that my cell phone might be dead, as I had gotten lax about charging it.

My front door had drifted almost shut. I shoved it open and reached for my bag. My fingers closed over empty air. It was gone.

"What the *hell*?" I stomped outside and that's the last thing I remembered for a long while.

~*~

I was drowning. My chest was tight and I couldn't breathe. Long fingers of seaweed rasped across my face and I was aware of a soft, rhythmic humming. Gasping, I blinked open my eyes and found all fifteen pounds of Fluffy perched on my chest, licking my face and purring.

"You're trying to smother me, aren't you?" I reached a hand to pet her long, soft fur and she skittered away. So much for cat love. I let my hand fall back to my side and closed my eyes again. My head hurt and I didn't want to move. As I started to drift off, there on the concrete walkway in front of my door, a faint, musky scent tickled my nose, teasing me awake. I recognized it. Why?

Natasha's perfume. I sat up. Fluffy hissed at a shadow and a wave of dizziness curled around my head and back down I went.

When I came to again, my head still hurt like crazy, but the dizziness was gone. I carefully rolled onto my side. Encouraged, I pushed slowly to a sitting position. Still no dizziness. I got to my knees and then to my feet.

I propped myself against the side of the building while I took stock. Everything seemed to be in order. I reached a hand up to touch the side of my head. There was a tender spot, but nothing like the lump I'd expected. Was it just my imagination, or was I recovering from a whack to the head with near miraculous speed?

Hearing the metallic rattle of a mailbox opening, I cautiously looked down into the alley to see my next-door neighbor. Sally was a flight attendant and rarely home. She bumped her small suitcase up the stairs, greeted me with her usual cheery hello and then stopped dead.

"Oh my God, what happened? Are you okay?" Her lips parted, revealing pearly, even teeth as her gaze moved from me to the mess in my apartment, lit crazily by the naked bulb of the lamp on the floor.

"I'm fine. But I..." To my dismay, tears welled up in my eyes. I tried to sniff them back, but there was no stopping them.

"Have you called the police?"

"No, I..." I kicked at some broken bits of plastic on the walkway. "They broke all my phones."

"Oh, honey." Sally enveloped me in a hug. She smelled comfortingly of peanuts and a light floral perfume.

The sympathy undid me. Here she was, undoubtedly tired and jet lagged after a long travel stint and hungry enough to have eaten airplane peanuts, but she got out her phone, called the police station and parked herself next to me to wait until they came. She didn't move from my side as they quizzed me and filled out a report. She rounded up Fluffy and put her in the cat carrier. She called my parents, told them what had happened and asked them to come get me. And all the time, she stayed with me, one hand gently rubbing my back as I quietly cried my way through a box of tissues she'd somehow found in the mess.

"It's okay, Jo. It'll all be okay. You'll see. We'll get it all back to rights in no time. Don't you worry."

She sounded so sure of it that I almost believed her.

~*~

I spent the night in my old room, in my old twin bed, snuggled deep under the colorful Andy Warhol-inspired comforter I'd chosen in high school. For the first time in weeks I slept like a log. (Except for my mother waking me up every three hours to be sure I didn't have a concussion.)

The next day, I didn't talk about going home, and my parents gamely went along with the fiction that I was there for no other reason than to visit. It was all going very well until Saturday night.

The beef stew was burbling away in the oven and it was cocktail hour in the Gartner household. I don't know why we called it that. My dad was the only one who ever had a cocktail before dinner. It was very 1950s. I think it was his way of asserting his masculinity in a house where he was outnumbered by females. My mother said it gave Dad time to transition from his job at the bank—a male bastion where he was a figure of unquestioned authority—back to the real world.

As usual, Dad had settled deep into his leather club chair with the newspaper, his fingers wrapped around a stout whiskey and soda. My mother had a wineglass with mineral water and a twist of lime. I grabbed a beer out of the fridge for myself.

My mother plucked the bottle out of my hand and handed me a glass of cranberry juice instead.

"Hey!"

"You might have a concussion."

"I'm fine."

"That remains to be seen." Ignoring my sputtering protest, she turned to Dad and said, "Jo's dating a nice young man."

I nearly dropped my glass on the carpet. The only correct words in that sentence were "Jo" and "a". Will wasn't nice, young, or a man, in the usual sense of the word. And while I couldn't begin to define our relationship. "Dating" was too pedestrian by half.

I hoped my dad was too absorbed in the *Wall Street Journal* to have heard. But then the paper rustled and his hand twitched. I threw my mother a furious look, which she pretended not to see.

When I was in high school, dad had kept a bat beside his chair. He would take it out and show it to my dates while I was in the bathroom doing my last minute primping. I didn't know about this until junior year in high school, when I caught him calmly informing Trent Buckner he'd beat him with it should I come home with so much as a hair out of place.

Furious, I'd made Dad apologize and demanded he get rid of the bat. Which he had, with surprisingly good grace. The next day he'd disappeared after church and returned at dusk with a carload of NRA paraphernalia. My dad, who'd probably never even held a gun in his life, plastered his car with bumper stickers of the "Shoot first, ask questions later" variety and wedged "This house protected by the NRA" signposts in every corner of the lawn. When he sat down for his cocktail that night, he brought with him a thick stack of NRA pamphlets, which he feathered across the side table.

Needless to say, I got no action at all in high school.

"I'm not dating anyone," I said. It came out a little bitter.

"What about Will?"

"Who? Oh, you mean that guy you met on the stairs? He's just a friend."

My father reburied his head in the *Wall Street Journal*, absently patted the place where the pamphlets used to reside, and sipped his nightly glass of whiskey.

Sunday morning, the honeymoon was over. At eight, the locksmith and I were in front of my apartment admiring the shiny new locks on my door. My parents were there too, as was Fluffy, who was spitting mad about being in a cat carrier during what she had clearly designated as morning nap time.

My mother withheld the check—my check—while she grilled the locksmith. "You're *certain* there was no damage to the lock or the door."

"If you're asking if the lock was forced, it wasn't. They probably had a set of keys." The locksmith turned to my dad. "You know how these apartment landlords are. They don't spend good money changing the locks between tenants." He pushed back his Dodgers cap, gave his scalp a scratch and refit the hat low on his forehead. "Probably dozens of keys to this place floating around out there."

My mother's alabaster skin darkened to a shade of red that clashed with her candy-apple red hair. Dad and I unconsciously moved closer together. It was hard to say what had set her off the most. The fact that the landlord had gone all "this is man's talk" in the middle of responding to her question, the assumption that she didn't know everything there was to know about landlords, or the idea that I had been living alone in an apartment where dozens of lowlifes with keys could have popped in at any time.

Under other circumstances, the idea of all those keys "floating around out there" would have freaked me out even more than it did my mother. But I knew my apartment hadn't been ripped apart by a former tenant. The person who had done this to me was the same person who had trashed Tom's apartment, looking for the manuscript.

It wouldn't have been hard to break into my place. Like every other female volunteer at the haunted house, I'd left my purse "hidden" in the rehearsal room. Anyone who wanted to get my address and "borrow" my keys to make duplicates at the hardware store need only to have conducted a half-assed search.

What I didn't understand was why. Why would they think I had it? Why now? And then I remembered. The notes. Will had found Solaire's notes. Someone must have seen us come out of Tom's apartment looking victorious and misunderstood. I closed my eyes and thought back. I'd been carrying my big purse, the one that functions as a book bag. Oh, yeah. They thought I had it.

I opened my eyes to find my mother, my father and Fluffy looking at me. The locksmith was looking at my mother as if she were a volcano about to blow. I plucked the check out of her fist and passed it to the locksmith.

"Thanks so much for coming out here this morning. I really appreciate it."

"No problem." Clearly relieved, he handed me the keys. "Here ya go. Two sets. Comes standard with the new lock."

As the locksmith bulleted out of there, I shoved one set of keys into my mother's hands. Later, I'd make extra copies for myself and one for my landlord.

Her sunset-red mouth pursed as she assessed my door. "Hal, I think—"

"I'll go get my tool kit from the car." Dad started down the stairs.

"Why does he need the tool kit?"

"Your father is going to install a safety latch on your door."

"I'm not sure I'm allowed to put holes in the door without my landlord's permission." The only reason my landlord had allowed me to have my locks changed was because Sally had had the foresight to call and ask him while the police were still here.

"A few dollars out of your deposit is a small price to pay for your safety."

If only safety came that cheap.

The keys turned smoothly in the new locks. I pushed open the door and sucked in a breath. If anything, the damage looked worse in the daytime. My mother, right behind me, didn't make a sound. She picked a path through the books and papers to stand in the middle of the room. After a brief survey, she pulled a fresh two-pack of dishwashing gloves out of her purse and handed a pair to me.

"Put those on. We have work to do."

Four hours later, the three of us had righted all the furniture and returned all my books and knickknacks to their proper places. My mother was walking around, clicking her tongue and making a list. My father had disappeared into my bedroom with his tool kit. At the sound of the whirr of his drill, I left my mother to her muttering and list making and jogged into the bedroom. Dad was making holes in my windowsill so he could install a security bar.

"I'm not sure my landlord allows…"

He shot me a look that told me what he thought of my landlord's rules and continued drilling.

A little before one, we left to get lunch and then made the circuit around the mall. I needed a new futon mattress, sheets and pillows (The burglar hadn't bothered to strip the bed before taking a knife to it.) and a host of other things, from a new cell phone to vacuum bags. My parents kept trying to sneak in upgrades but I drew the line when I sighted my father in the furniture department, sitting on a couch. I thought he was tired and taking a well-deserved break. Until he got up, walked over to the next couch and plunked himself down on it.

My father never gave up a seat on a perfectly decent couch without a good reason.

I strode over and positioned myself between him and the leather ottoman that matched the couch he was presently sitting on, forcing him to look up. His look of irritation changed to guilt when he realized the pair of legs standing between him and the ottoman belonged to me.

"My couch is fine," I said.

"Oh, em..."

"Don't be ridiculous, Jo," said my mother, coming up beside me. "The stuffing is coming out of yours."

She put her fingers around one of the couch cushions and squeezed it thoughtfully.

"Yet another problem duct tape can solve," I said.

"This one's too soft," she informed my father.

He didn't reply. He was relaxed back on the couch, lost in happy visions of duct tape, man's greatest tool, a dreamy smile on his face.

She turned back to me. "You are *not* going to repair that couch with tape."

"No one will see it when I flip over the cushions. I can sew the rips properly, later. It will be a nice, relaxing project for me."

She inhaled a breath and let it out through tight lips. "Let us do this one thing for you."

"No!" I squeezed my mother's arm. "I appreciate the offer, but you've both already done too much." As she started to protest, I added, "Really. I don't know what I would have done without your help, but it's important to me that my apartment still looks like *my* apartment."

As I said the words, I realized how much I meant them. To my mother, it was a loss of a few hundred dollar's worth of cheap, often secondhand, mostly mismatched things. But they were things I'd picked out. I'd bought them with my paychecks.

"As ugly as that couch is, it's mine and I like it."

Dad grunted and got up off the couch. He pulled out his car keys. "Jo's right. It would be impossible to find another couch that ugly. Let's go."

By the time we got back to my apartment, it was after five. Twilight. The early trick-or-treaters, costumed and clasped in their parents' arms, were making a slow circuit of their immediate neighbors. Becky had joked that I lived in Brady Bunch land and it was never more apparent than on nights like this. Soon it would be dark enough for the kindergartners and grade schoolers to come out. Parents would stand around on the wide sidewalks, chatting in groups and watching the kids race from door to door, collecting candy from each other's houses.

My mother was cooing over an infant in a bee costume. I took bags from the trunk and started upstairs. My new key turned like butter. Flicking on the light, I winced from the glare of the naked bulb and stopped dead on the threshold.

For a breathless moment, I thought it had been broken into again…by a gang of scrubbing bubbles. My apartment was cleaner than it had ever been. The carpet had been vacuumed into a paler shade of beige, the books on the bookshelves were aligned by ruler, and every surface sparkled. Even the walls looked as if they'd been scrubbed.

"Oh good. I was hoping they'd be done before we got home."

I dropped my bags, turned to my mother and hugged her tightly. "Thank you, thank you, thank you."

My mother sniffed. "Well, we weren't going to leave you with all that fingerprinting dust everywhere."

Dad, loaded with purchases, pushed his way through the door.

"You guys have been so great, all weekend."

"We're not done yet," Dad said gruffly, planting a kiss on the top of my head. He dropped the bags and headed back down to the car. "Come help me with the futon mattress."

A half-hour later, they left. They tried to take me for dinner, but a relaxing sit-down meal would only make me tired and I still had a lot of settling in I needed to do.

Two hours later, my new sheets were clean and smelling of fabric softener, every bag was unloaded and I'd put away and puttered to my heart's content. I fried up a hamburger, made myself a small salad and threw a few cookies in the toaster oven to reheat, so my apartment smelled like home again, instead of cleaning products.

By eight o'clock, I was bored silly. I'd given up all hope of having any trick-or-treaters (Apparently apartments were still considered dangerous by the neighborhood parents who decided such things.) and was unwrapping mini Krackels for myself. There was nothing on TV because, for some reason, they had aired *It's the Great Pumpkin, Charlie Brown* a week ago.

I could hear party sounds through the open slits of my newly armored windows. I had been invited to a couple of the neighbors' parties, in a casual, "Hey, you should come" sort of way. I suppose I could still go. I could walk over to the gas station on the corner and get a six pack of beer to share. When they asked why I wasn't at the haunted house I'd simply tell them I was no longer volunteering there.

So what if I'd promised Dan I would help out? That was Friday and this was Sunday. Two days away from the place helped me see the Milverne for what it was—a freaking breeding ground of misery. Tom was dead. Nice-boy Lenny had been turned into Natasha's vampire arm candy. I'd been knocked out and my home had been ransacked. And in a nice twist, newly bloodthirsty Lenny now lurked in the shadows for an opportunity to get rid of me.

The only reason I had gotten involved in the first place was because of Becky and now she hated me for something I didn't really do and would never be able to explain to her satisfaction. Not that she was giving me the chance.

Self-pity filled me nearly to bursting and then suddenly gave way to anger. I was tired of being discarded, bullied and intimidated. Even little kids were outside having fun while I cowered, once again, inside my apartment like a mouse. I threw a half-eaten Krackle back in the candy bowl and pushed myself up off the couch. The sound of duct tape squeaking against the divots in my jeans hardened my resolve.

I charged into my now-spotless bedroom, reached into the back of my closet and yanked my vampire costume off its hanger. From my bathroom cupboard, I pulled out my sewing kit and sewed a small pocket into my cape. It might be poor form to take scissors and thread to a borrowed theater costume, but after being skidded along pavement through two falls, another hole was the least of its worries. And I was damned if I was going to be without a cell phone again. Ten minutes later, I threw open my shiny new deadbolt and stepped into the night.

~*~

Walking to the front of the line, I stepped through the black-sheeted gap in the gate to the serpent-headed start of the haunted house.

A heavy hand clamped down on my arm. "Thank God you're here." Marty shoved the ticket basket into my hands. "We're swamped. I've been calling in favors, trying to get people out here."

As usual, he was wearing a suit, but tonight it seemed to hang off his body like loose skin. He was sweating and looked haggard.

"Are you okay?" I asked.

"Fine, fine." He didn't meet my eyes.

The crowd surged against the gate and a dozen people came through the opening, handing me tickets. Marty glanced into the dark mouth of the snake and waved the group through.

That was different. "Where are the tour guides?" I asked.

"They're there, waiting just beyond the fangs. Faster that way."

As my eyes adjusted to the dim light, I saw Angelina standing inside the serpent's mouth, just beyond the long white fangs. As usual, she looked impatient and a little bored.

A volunteer I hadn't met before came in through the gate, breathing heavily. "Animals!" He turned to Marty. "We're going to have to sell tickets here. It's not safe being out there with all that cash."

A second volunteer arrived on his tail. "Jesus!"

Without them out front, the ticketing problem escalated into a raucous bottleneck at the gate. Ian lurched out through the fangs and limped over to my side.

"Need a hand?" he asked.

"Actually, if you'd take this group through…" There were only a half dozen people waiting while we reorganized, but they were in the way.

"No problem." Hunching over into his Igor posture, he beckoned to the group. "Walk this way."

For the next ten minutes we were too busy sorting out a new system to talk much. Which is why I didn't notice at first that Marty had gone.

"Can you guys hold the fort for a while? I have to…" I caught sight of Becky coming out of the rehearsal room. She glanced in our direction, hesitated and then hurried into the haunted house. Fine, I thought. Be that way.

"Nature calls?" The volunteer on my left was dressed as a surfer in long shorts, loose shirt and flip flops. I was pretty sure those were his regular clothes. He was handling ticket sales with a relaxed efficiency that couldn't be faked. He eyed my costume and grinned. "Always wondered if vampires did normal things like that."

"Me too." *You've no idea how much.* Handing him the ticket basket, I made a beeline for the rehearsal room in case anyone was watching. Once I was in the shadows, I stopped and looked around.

I caught sight of Marty's bulky form threading through the shadows along the side of the theater, where no one was supposed to be. The man had practically haunted the place since the LBPD had kicked us out and strung heavy chains through the door handles.

His desire to reopen the theater as quickly as possible was certainly understandable. Theaters were expensive to run. Even old landmarks that had been in one's family for generations had costs. There was the usual upkeep and property taxes, but also remodels mandated by new fire codes and accessibility laws. Working in a school, I had become inured to the sight of administrators wringing their hands over finances. What if I'd underestimated how bad things really were?

What might someone in Marty's position do to keep his family's namesake from disappearing? It hadn't occurred to me to seriously suspect Marty because he'd been in the lobby with me all night. But in truth, once Will and Natasha had showed up, he could have danced naked on the will-call desk and I wouldn't have noticed.

I caught another glimpse of Marty's white dress shirt as he paused by the side door of the theater. With all the craziness of Halloween, everyone would be even more focused than usual on the haunted house. Marty could drive a bulldozer through the theater's front doors and no one would notice.

Marty was going to break in tonight. I could feel it in my bones. By the time anyone noticed a tampered lock or a broken window—probably not until morning—it would be easy to blame it on Halloween revelry. On bored teens who had gotten out of hand after being revved up by the haunted house. Who would tie it to Marty?

Me.

"Gotcha," I said softly.

Pulling my new cell phone out of the pocket I'd made for it in my cape, I started up the path after Marty, taking care to keep to the shadows as best I could.

Marty was on the move again, heading for the front of the theater. And he was moving fast.

Too fast.

I stopped, unsure what to do. After the boisterous noise of the haunted house, the wooded path around the theater seemed awfully quiet. I couldn't continue following him while I was calling for help or he'd hear me. But if I let him get away, I could lose him.

My finger hesitated over the call button on my new cell phone. My new phone that had a built in video camera.

*Right.* I continued up the path without calling the police. All I was going to do was get a picture of the proverbial smoking gun and hand it over. I'd leave it to the police to figure out what Marty did after he got inside. If he destroyed evidence linking him to Tom's murder or found where Tom had hidden the manuscript, that was their problem.

I wasn't stupid enough to do more. And yet I couldn't do less. I had a score to settle.

I had reached the trees at the southern edge of the theater. It was now or never. I started the video recorder, held it in front of me and eased around the corner, careful to try to stay out of sight in the foliage.

A flash of light blinded me. I reeled back and pressed myself against the side of the building, blinking rapidly to regain sight.

Marty's voice rang out. "Our season opens in December with *The Underpants*, a lighthearted play that will be fun for the whole family."

There were some clicking noises and more flashes of light. *Cameras and flashbulbs*, I thought. Marty was talking to a journalist, using the press's interest in the haunted house to drum up some publicity for the theater.

I sank against the wall behind me, feeling like an idiot. My Nancy Drew-like enthusiasm for single-handedly running Tom's murderer to the ground had evaporated.

Realizing the interview was winding up, I pulled myself together and started to creep away. I had an odd feeling of being watched. I whipped around to make sure no one was behind me and my foot crushed a dry branch.

"Who's there?" Marty demanded.

I remained motionless in the shadows, unable to lift my foot off the branch, lest it make more noise. After what seemed like an eternity, they finished the interview and the journalist went on his way with promises to e-mail a copy of the article when it went to print.

Marty, whistling cheerfully, passed within a couple of feet of me as he hurried back down to the front of the haunted house via the staircase. I waited until he reached the giant snake head before I followed.

I had one foot on the stairs when I realized I wasn't alone.

# Chapter Seventeen

here was no way I could make it back down to the haunted house. Natasha's vampire arm candy was standing on the hillside below me, about twenty feet away. He stood perfectly still. Waiting.

I turned and ran. Any lingering thoughts that I was overreacting disappeared as he plunged into the ivy and crashed up the hillside after me.

*Oh God.* I picked up my pace, fighting the burning in my legs and lungs. If I could just make it around the front of the theater, I could pop onto the sidewalk, where about two hundred people waited in line for the haunted house.

I was fast, but Lenny was faster. As I sprinted toward the front of the theater, his footfalls rang hard and fast on the pavement behind me. I knew better than to look back to see how close he was. I knew it would slow me down. I knew I couldn't afford it.

I looked. He was angling toward the street, closing off my escape route.

A noise between a scream and a sob wrenched from my chest. He was trapping me. I doubled back a few times, in ever-decreasing arcs and found myself in front of the theater. The locked theater.

Lenny slowed and walked toward me, arms stretched wide, ready to grab me if I tried to get past him. The outside lights bathed him in a golden glow. I heard my own breathing, harsh in my ears. I knew it was over.

"Don't panic, just let me—"

I panicked. My fingers pushed past the sagging yellow police tape to close over the old-fashioned door handle. I depressed the latch and tugged hard.

The door opened so easily I swung off balance and fell to my knees. Lenny cried out. I didn't stop to ask why the long-barricaded door was unlatched. He was nearly upon me. I pulled myself back to my feet and careened over the threshold.

I smacked right into someone. A strong arm reached out and steadied me.

"Whoa. Easy there, Jo."

I shoved the arm aside. Reaching back with both hands, I yanked the door shut and slid the old-fashioned bar. With a howl, Lenny slammed against the door so hard it strained against its moorings. The bar held.

Relief turned my legs to rubber. I slumped back against the lobby wall and closed my eyes. Safe. I was safe. I nearly laughed aloud.

"You okay?"

I swiped at the tears puddling under my lashes and looked up. Ian, wearing his voluminous black Igor costume, regarded me with a curious smile. I realized I must have looked ridiculous, running away from good ol' Lenny as if he were the devil incarnate.

As I tried to think of a possible lie, the heavy old doors rattled and shook as Lenny grabbed hold of the handles and tried to pull them open. For a heart-stopping moment I thought he might succeed.

All of a sudden he stopped trying to break down the doors. His voice carried through the narrow gap between them, sweetly pleading. "Jo? Let me in."

He didn't sound as if he wanted to kill me. He sounded…worried. As if he were trying to *help* me. Such deception was probably covered on the first day of their training. If there was one thing I'd noticed about vampires, it was that they were all damn good at telling their victims what they needed to hear.

"Jo? Let me in, *now!*"

I curled my fingers around Ian's arm and tugged him into the lobby. Explanations could wait. "C'mon. We can go out the side door."

The lobby had a sour, musty smell from being shut up so long. My eyes slid to the place where Tom had fallen to the ground, dead. I looked away.

"Who was that guy?" Ian opened the connecting door to the theater and chivalrously motioned me through. The minimum of lights had been turned on and there was no heat. To our immediate left, the abandoned entrance to the original haunted house yawned large and black. I shivered and pulled my cape around my shoulders.

"Crazy old boyfriend," I explained.

"Old relationships can be a problem." The bitterness in his voice made me look at him. His face was twisted, his eyes cold, appearing as hard as pebbles. "You start out good, looking out for each other, and then people change. They sell out."

For the first time since I'd stepped into the theater, I stopped worrying about escaping from Lenny and thought to wonder why Ian was inside.

And why he was carrying a crowbar.

He followed my gaze to the long metal tool in his right hand and held it up a little, for my inspection.

"Is that a prop?" I asked hopefully.

"No."

Time to bolt for the side door. I didn't get more than a couple of feet before Ian's fingers fastened around my arm like a vise. I struggled and he hit me on the shoulder with the crowbar.

"Don't make me hurt you."

Pain throbbed down my arm. I stopped struggling. He pried my new cell phone out of my hands, tossed it into a dark corner and shoved me along in front of him, into the haunted house. I blinked, trying to get my eyes to adjust to the darkness. There was barely enough light coming through the gaps to see where we were going, but that didn't slow Ian down.

Ian moved quickly, half pushing, half dragging me. My legs refused to function properly. There were no knife-wielding maniacs, homicidal mummies, or headless bodies rising from caskets, and yet every dark curve of the place terrified me. One good crack on the head from that crowbar and the detectives would find me dead in a pool of my own blood in a dusty corner.

We were rounding the middle of the haunted house's U-shaped path when he abruptly turned and headed straight for a wall. I let out a scream as he rammed me into it. I braced myself and my scream rose to a shriek as a black sheet whispered across my face. He laughed softly, cruelly.

Ian's grip tightened painfully on my arm as he pushed me ahead of him up the stairs into the men's locker area. He shoved me hard, through the doorway. I stumbled into the room and fell to my knees.

"Sit." He pointed to a bench at the rear of the room. I sat.

Ian positioned himself between me and the door, fit the crowbar into the seam of a locker door and gave a sharp downward tug. The door swung open with a wrench of metal.

I looked around for something—anything—to use as a weapon but the room was clean, as if a giant vacuum had sucked out everything that wasn't nailed down.

Reaching inside the locker, Ian pulled out handful after handful of stale-smelling clothes and well-worn sneakers, discarding them with increasingly frustrated grunts of irritation. I recognized the polo shirt Tom had worn the night of our "date" as it fluttered to the ground.

Eventually, Ian ran out of crap to toss. He also ran out of patience. He slid his hand along every seam in the locker and came up empty.

"It's not here!"

He started prying open lockers at random, hurling people's belongings across the room. Panting with anger, he rounded on me. And I was reminded I wasn't entirely weaponless.

"Where is it?" he demanded.

"Where is what?" I tried to make eye contact, but Ian's gaze was everywhere but on me.

"Don't play stupid with me. I know Tom told you about the Solaire play."

Will had been the one with the information. Tom hadn't really told me squat, but I didn't think now was the time to quibble over details.

"We've been acting together since we were kids. Did he tell you?"

I shook my head. *Keep him talking. Eventually he will look at you.*

"We planned to be great. Take the world by storm. He was going to be the next Laurence Olivier, I was going to be another Gene Wilder or Marty Feldman. A king of comedy. Only didn't quite work out that way. Never does, does it? Doesn't matter how talented you are if there's no luck."

Ian reached into a locker, swept another person's belongings onto the floor and cursed when he found no papers hidden in the clothing.

"And then we had it. Finally, we got our break. Tom found that lost play at a garage sale. A garage sale, can you believe it? It's brilliant—a masterpiece."

His face shone with that inner fire that swept through him whenever he talked about acting. "It had roles that would send an actor straight to the top. Everyone would come see it. Would come see *us*. It was our luck. Our big break."

The inner passion disappeared, replaced by a look of bewilderment. "And he wanted to sell out. Auction it off to the highest bidder. Trade the chance of a lifetime for *money*." He spit out the word. "After everything we've worked for."

His gaze swept over me too quickly for me to try anything. His attention returned to the lockers.

"I should have found it by now," he muttered, flipping through someone's dog-eared books, one by one, before hurling them to the floor. "But it's not in Tom's apartment or his car. I thought maybe he gave it to you." His voice rose.

"No, I swear, I barely—"

"I've tried to get you alone every way I know how. I tried being your friend, I tried hitting on you."

That caught me by surprise. I had thought him an early victim of my vampire allure.

"I tried getting you into my car to take you to the hospital after the set fell on you. Nothing worked. You wouldn't even step five feet into the haunted house with me, would you?"

The room rang suddenly with his laughter. "And then I realized you didn't know where it was either. If you had, you and your boyfriend wouldn't have gone to Tom's apartment looking for it. Did you tell Mr. Moneybags the truth or did you spin him some sob story so you could keep it for yourself? Not as if he needs the cash, is it?"

I had a vision of Ian going after Will with a crowbar and thought it was a shame I wouldn't be alive to see it.

Abruptly, I stood.

As I'd hoped, Ian looked at me. But only just long enough to take a powerful swipe at my shoulder with the crowbar.

"What are you doing? Sit back down!"

I sat, rubbing my shoulder, trying to stanch the pain shooting down my arm. Ian fit the crowbar into a gap between the lockers and the wall and yanked down hard. He got a tiny glimpse of drywall for his pains.

"Where is it? Where is it?"

Ian's thoughts were swinging around so rapidly that I could almost see his head rocking with it. "The way you two came out all confident, I thought maybe you had better luck finding his hiding place. Did you? It wasn't in your apartment. I looked in every inch of that place. I thought it must be here, the one place I couldn't look, but it's not!

"It's not anywhere! Why can't I find it?" He pried open another locker with a vicious twist of the crowbar. It was empty. "You gave it to moneybags, didn't you?"

He rounded on me so fast the crowbar came within millimeters of my right eye.

"No." I swallowed. I desperately wanted to dive under the bench but I clasped my hands so he wouldn't see them shaking and made myself stay where I was. "We didn't find it." I slowed my voice, giving our gazes time to lock.

If ever there were a good time for my vampire glare to kick in, this was it. For a second, I thought I was getting somewhere. He stared into my eyes and his gaze grew hazy. Relief flooded through me. With a little luck, I would be able to talk him into letting me go.

All at once, Ian turned away and kicked savagely at the pile of people's belongings he'd thrown on the floor. "If you and moneybags don't have it, it must be here. It must be!"

It hadn't worked. Oh God, why hadn't it worked? I should have practiced.

"Where is it?" He was getting more hysterical by the second.

"I don't know."

"Tom must have told you where he kept it!" he grabbed hold of my shoulders and shook me so hard my head snapped back on my neck. "Where is it?"

"I don't know! I swear!"

All at once, the anger ebbed, and he gave a keening moan and fell back onto one of the benches, clutching his head in his hands. "He's dead, he's dead and I have nothing!" Great racking sobs tore through his body.

I bolted for the door.

He swore, reached for me and tripped on the pile of clothes.

I flew down the stairs and shot into the haunted house. It was black as night. I stretched my arms out in front of me and ran in what I hoped was the right direction.

I made it about twenty feet before I caught Becky's Frankenstein gurney in the gut and pitched to the side. I landed hard on my abused shoulder and slid through the wall.

Through the wall? I blinked against dim lights that seemed too bright and realized I'd blundered through one of the hidden exits. I was outside the haunted house, near the side of the stage. I got to my feet and held my breath as Ian ran past me, not five feet away from where I was standing.

I managed to match my footfalls to his for a few strides until he realized I was no longer racing ahead of him. He stopped and so did I.

The exit sign glowed red near the ceiling, about twenty yards in front of me. If I could somehow get him behind me, I could make a dash for it. All I needed was a few seconds' head start and I would be outside in the cool night air, a stone's throw from the parking lot. I looked around for something to throw behind me for the age-old dodge.

The little hairs on my arms and neck were standing up like antennae. I could feel Ian getting closer on the other side of the thin black wall.

A squeak of the gurney was all the warning I had before he burst through, pulling a black sheet with him. It wrapped around his legs and he crashed to the floor.

I sprinted for the exit and hit the crash bar at a run. Too late, I realized the door was bolted shut. The reverberations shook my arms so bad, I was sure I'd broken a wrist.

Shoving the sheet aside, Ian cried out in victory and came after me at a sprint. I refused to give in. Biting my teeth against the pain, I turned and started running for the front door. But I didn't get very far. Blocking my way was Lenny.

# Chapter Eighteen

*I*an dodged back into the haunted house. I spun around and disappeared into the curtained wing off the right side of the stage.

Back when Becky had dragged me to the very first fundraising meeting, the actors had just come off a production and the backstage area had been crammed with junk.

Some damn anal clean freak had emptied it. There was nowhere to hide. I was trapped. I ran around in fast, tight circles, clutching my aching wrists and sobbing in panic. However hard I wished it to be different, there was nothing there but ropes and scaffolding.

My eyes followed the scaffolding up to a catwalk above the stage. I wouldn't make it.

"Jo?" Lenny was coming up the stairs. "What are you doing?"

I put a foot on the bottom of the scaffolding and reached up to grab a ladder rung near my head. Sharp pain shot through my wrists and my shoulder felt like it was on fire. But my grip held. I moved to the next rung and the next, biting my lip against the pain.

"What the—" Lenny sprinted to the bottom of the ladder and made it up about halfway before he emitted a funny, groaning noise and wrapped his arms tightly around the scaffolding.

I pulled myself up onto the catwalk. Lenny stayed where he was. Not moving. His head was pressed into the crook of his arm.

Natasha's vampire arm candy was afraid of heights. I laughed aloud.

My giggles were reaching a hysterical note when I felt the catwalk shift hard to the right. Ian was coming up the ladder on the other side of the stage. Every step he took made the narrow platform shimmy and shake in the air above the stage.

I wound my arms through the rope railings to keep from falling. "Stop! Stop it!"

The catwalk creaked and swung farther to the right. Ian's head popped over the end of the catwalk. His eyes were dark and fanatic.

"It can't hold you!"

Ignoring my warning, he pulled himself up onto the catwalk.

"You lied to me. You knew where it was all along."

"No!"

"It's here, isn't it?" He scanned the catwalk.

"Ian, you must listen to me. You have to go down now, or we'll both fall. The manuscript isn't here."

"Liar! You want it for yourself." Ian inched closer.

The catwalk made a sudden, stomach-dropping dip. Lenny was moving again. I couldn't tell if he was coming up or going down.

"Ian, please. I swear, I'm telling the truth!"

I looked wildly around. There was nothing up there but lights and the thick metal scaffolding that ran the length of the ceiling. Thick, burly scaffolding, strong enough to hold columns and canoes.

Lenny's voice came from down below. "She doesn't have it. Ian, why don't you come down, and then, Jo, you come next."

Ian peered over the side of the catwalk down at Lenny.

It was now or never. I wrapped my right hand around a metal bar for balance, said a quick prayer to anyone who was listening and stepped off the catwalk.

My foot hovered over empty air. The scaffolding was farther away than I had thought. I was about to pull back when Ian realized what I was doing.

"Oh no you don't!"

Ian lunged for me. With a cry, I let go the catwalk and jumped. My feet connected to the scaffolding and I wrapped my arms around a support bar from the ceiling in time to keep from pitching down to the floor. My stomach lurched sickeningly.

Ian swiped at air. "No!"

I shimmied my hands down the bar. Telling myself not to look down, I wiped my sweat-slicked hands, one by one, across my pants and crawled farther into the maze of metal bars. Ian dropped to his hands and knees and reached a hand across the void to grasp the scaffolding.

"Is it there? Is that where you put it?"

Ian pulled himself across the gap. Something in the ceiling gave way in a sprinkle of white powder.

"Ian, stop! It can't hold both our weights."

"You'll say anything to get it, won't you?" He reached across to the next bar and pulled himself forward another eighteen inches, into the scaffolding.

My stomach lurched sickeningly as the entire right side of the structure groaned and dropped a half inch. I tightened my hands around the bars, unable to move in any direction. "You have to go back!"

Ignoring me, he moved forward, across another set of bars. One of the grommets holding the scaffolding pulled out of the ceiling. I screamed in terror.

"Jump!" Lenny yelled. He was circling under me like a shark, fifty feet below.

"Are you crazy?" I asked.

The scaffolding creaked and jerked and we dropped another inch. A long, narrow box slid across the metal bars and crashed to the floor, scattering plastic swords.

A gap yawned in front of me and I saw it. A ream of yellowing paper wrapped in bubble wrap. Of course. Every other part of the theater had been crawling with actors and volunteers. The only place no one would go was up. No one ever looked up.

I spared a thought that Tom could have done a better job preserving an old masterpiece, before fear pushed all nonessential thoughts out of my mind.

Ian sighted the manuscript. His cackle of victory filled the air.

"Jump!" Lenny sounded panicky. "For heaven's sake, Jo, jump!" I realized what he was trying to tell me. But I couldn't do it.

I shook my head and gripped harder, unable to move another inch. I had levitated, once. Badly. I didn't know how I'd done it, and I wasn't going to step off into air fifty feet above the ground and trust that I'd figure it out again. My vampire stare hadn't exactly worked to plan, had it?

Ian crawled out farther.

"You have to stop!" I sobbed.

The manuscript was only a few feet from him. He pulled himself across another gap and reached for it. There was a loud, metallic groan. The whole front right corner of the scaffolding pulled from the ceiling. The metal bars tilted sharply toward the floor. For moment that seemed like an hour, Ian's grasping hand closed on air. He gave a shrill scream and disappeared in a cloud of gray dust.

I closed my eyes and hung on for dear life. The scaffolding screeched and jerked under me like a living thing.

And then it stopped.

Coughing on dust, I cracked open one eye and then the other. Ian lay unmoving on the floor, far below. Lenny had disappeared.

My section of scaffolding was holding to the ceiling—just. The only reason I had survived was that I had managed to shift my weight close enough to one of the attachment bolts that still held. If I'd been a few inches more to the right, the stress would have levered that bolt the rest of the way out of the wall, and I would have gone down faster than a fat kid on a seesaw.

Who says a science degree isn't worth its weight in gold?

I heard sirens and the sound of footsteps pounding toward me from the lobby. Help had arrived.

~*~

I won't talk about how I got down. Suffice it to say, it involved two ladders and several firemen. I have no doubt a video will show up on the Internet.

Gavin wasn't around. I talked to the actual detectives in charge of the case. The fact that the taller one was a dead ringer for Bert from Sesame Street was actually quite soothing, and both officers were very nice. They didn't mock me in the slightest about how I'd refused to come down. Unlike some detectives I could name.

Ian had managed to land feet first and was alive but in traction. I don't know if it was the pain meds they gave him or guilt from killing Tom, but he opened up like it was last confession.

~*~

I left for work a half hour earlier than usual the next morning in the hopes of avoiding everyone, but I hadn't been in my classroom for more than a few minutes when Roger barreled through the door.

He brandished a handful of newspapers. I hadn't just made the local paper, but the *Los Angeles Times*.

"This is the last straw, Jo. I can no longer give the administration my recommendation that you continue teaching here. You are consistently unable to deport yourself in the manner expected of a representative of the Bayshore Academy. You had better start making plans for teaching elsewhere next year, for I don't believe there will be a position for you here."

"Stick a sock in it, Roger," said Becky, coming through the door.

Carol followed. "You do not have the ability to determine contracts,

Roger. That is the middle school principle and the headmaster's provenance."

They came to stand by me.

Roger turned an odd shade of purple. "The headmaster listens to my recommendation."

Carol crossed her arms and glared at him over the top of her glasses. "Headmaster Huntington also listens to mine."

"We'll see about that!" Roger glared at us and swept from the room.

"Troll," Becky said, locking the door.

Carol put a Peet's bag on my desk and pulled out three giant coffees and an assortment of cookies and pastries. "Can't compare to anything out of your kitchen of course, Jo, but I thought we needed a treat."

I looked at them, confused. "What is all this?"

Becky spoke first. "I owe you an apology, Jo. I've been acting like a pushy, petulant jerk. You did nothing but put yourself out to help me and what did I do but throw it back in your face."

"It's okay," I said awkwardly.

"No it's not. I've wanted to tell you I was sorry so many times in the past couple of days, but I didn't. I thought I saw you heading for the theater last night. Did you know? I decided to wait to apologize until you came back. But you didn't. And then there was that god-awful noise, like a train had crashed inside, and…" She made a gulping noise and looked away. "I called the cops, but—"

"That was you?" I felt warmth spreading through me. She had been looking out for me.

We stared awkwardly at each other for a moment and then hugged tightly.

"It's not your fault," I told her after I blew my nose. "You saw what looked like Dan and me—"

"And that's not the worst of it," Becky said, rubbing the smeared kohl from under her eyes. "I mean, how nutso was I to even think you'd do something like that?" She pointed at me. "Don't answer that." She blew out a dramatic sigh. "If I'd known that really liking a guy was this much trouble, I would have avoided it."

Carol and I looked at each other. "Uh-huh."

Becky didn't respond with her usual smart comeback. She leaned back against the counter and sighed. "The truth is, Jo, I knew he didn't do anything. Dan explained it to me the next day. It's just that…well, I was being an ass."

"It's okay, Becks. I understand. Really, I do."

Carol cleared her throat. "I'm sorry too. I didn't support you like I should have when you needed me and I'm sorry."

I hugged her too and had to blow my nose again. The tissue felt like sandpaper. "Why is it that we get such crap tissue?" I asked, fingering my raw nose.

"Roger probably ordered it," Becky said.

I gave a small choking laugh and reached for my coffee. "This is getting a little maudlin. We need to start celebrating fast or my students are going to know I've been crying." I didn't need to look in the mirror to know my eyes were puffy and my nose was red. I was not a pretty crier. "Er, what are we celebrating?"

"This." Becky produced an armful of newspapers with a crinkly flourish. They were all folded to pictures of me.

Carroll's brown eyes sparkled wickedly. "It's not every day our Jo gets her picture in the paper."

"Because she's stuck on scaffolding and won't come down," Becky said, pointing to a picture I hadn't seen.

"Oh God. I hate you both."

"Well, if that's not reason to celebrate, I don't know what is. Here." Becky shoved a thin, narrow package at me. I unwrapped a set of black hair chopsticks. "I've lost hope of getting you to stop wearing your hair in a bun. But you might at least go for 'sexy' instead of 'schoolmarm'."

The sticks were very cute but obviously made for someone with less hair. I had to supplement with a pencil from the "I heart science" mug one of my students gave me for Christmas last year.

"What do you think?"

Becky groaned and rolled her eyes to the ceiling. "I give up. You're hopeless."

Carol made a twirl sign with her index finger. "Turn around. Let me see." I did a spin for her and she smiled. "Cute."

"You're going to believe someone who wears twin sets over me?" Becky said. And then she sighed. "At least, tell me there aren't chew marks on the pencil."

"Of course not," I said, slapping away Becky's hand when she reached up to check.

# Chapter Nineteen

ecky and Carol stuck like limpets to my side all day, but even so, it was an ordeal. Everyone who could find an excuse to come near me did, bombarding me with questions. Everyone else just talked about me in loud voices. As soon as the school day ended, I locked my classroom door and graded papers until it was nearly dark and I was sure everyone had gone home.

I stopped by the supermarket to stock up on baking supplies. As I filled my cart with chocolate chips, unsweetened chocolate, butter, sugar, cream, and cake flour, I felt my problems start to wash away.

There is such a thing as too much enthusiasm for dessert. I was so preoccupied with plans of a very elaborate devil's food cake with chocolate icing and piped whipped cream that I got out of the car without doing my usual nighttime safety scan. I was trotting upstairs, juggling bags and trying to locate my front door keys by feel, when I realized someone was standing in front of my apartment. A sickening, musky scent teased my nostrils.

Lenny moved to the top of the stairs. The porch light backlit him like a rock star. "Do you need a hand with those?"

"Is that supposed to be funny?" I demanded.

"No. I—"

I put the bags down on the steps. "That is *it*, arm candy. I've had enough of you."

I'm not really sure what I intended as I barreled up the stairs after him. All I know is that I'd reached my limit. Lenny stared at me wide-eyed for a moment, and then turned and ran. I chased him past my front door, past Sara's and around the corner. Lenny reached the dead end a few seconds ahead of me and peered over the railing at the drop.

Suddenly, he looked down the street and then hurtled over the side as if it were a five foot drop instead of twenty-five.

I skidded to a halt and looked over the railing as Lenny hit the ground at a barely controlled run. He disappeared into the dark space between the buildings.

I couldn't believe I'd missed his path down. Had he levitated? Part of me still didn't believe it was possible.

The sprint had taken the edge off my anger-fueled adrenaline and I realized I was damn lucky that Lenny hadn't just pitched me over the railing. Reaching for my new phone, which the firefighters had found while waiting for me to come off the scaffolding last night, I flipped through the numbers until I reached Gavin's.

I was tired of dealing with vampires by myself.

And, I admitted to myself, I missed having him to talk to. But only because he was the one person I could level with. I punched the connect button and jogged back along the walkway to get my groceries.

As I reached the top of the stairs, I heard a car purr up the street. Seconds later, the elegant black Austin Martin stopped in front of my building. Will got out, a tall lean silhouette in black. His gaze fastened on me for a long moment. I punched the end call key without really thinking about it.

Will turned suddenly to his left, toward something out of my range of vision. It didn't take a rocket scientist to realize he could sense that Lenny was in the vicinity, just as Lenny had known Will was coming before he went over the railing. Must be that bat-like hearing.

It got me angry again. I was tired of being in the middle of all this vampire power-play crap. I stomped past the groceries listing on the stairs and intercepted Will at the mailboxes. He pointed at the overhead apartment windows stretched like a row of unblinking eyes and led me a short distance up the street to the large, landscaped front yard of one of the few houses on my street. The owners weren't home. Thick, fragrant Mock Orange hedges and a leafy jacaranda tree reaching well into the street, gave us some privacy.

Will spoke first. "How are you?" He wasn't offering sympathy. His cheekbones looked carved on his face. He was furious.

So was I. "How am I? I'll tell you how I am. I've spent the last week and half pulling myself up off the pavement after all those so-called 'accidents'. I've got cuts and bruises on every inch of my body, my left wrist is sprained and my right shoulder feels like it's on fire when I move my arm. I'm damn lucky I'm not in the hospital or dead. And just when I think I can finally come home and crawl into bed without worrying that someone's going to come out of the closet with a knife, I find Lenny waiting for me on my doorstep."

"Lenny was there to protect you."

"He— What?"

"I asked Lenny to watch over you when I wasn't with you."

"Oh my God. You have no idea what's going on, do you? Natasha—"

"Last spring you asked me not to use Natasha."

"You remember that?" Surprised, I looked up at him.

"Of course."

An odd rush of warmth suffused me, dampening my anger. "Thank you."

He nodded tightly.

I drew in a long breath and marshaled my scattering thoughts. It was a little like gathering dandelion fluff in a wind storm. "Lenny was there the night the set collapsed on Dan and me, and again the night I was nearly killed tripping over that fishing line."

"Of course he was. I sent him. I know he startled you when he went to help pull the plastic bag off you, but he was concerned you had gotten hurt. I have spoken to him about it. He came here Friday night to offer his apologies, and found you lying unconscious in front of your door." Will's voice had an odd note I couldn't place.

"Great," I muttered, putting my head in my hands. I'd been so wrapped up in my conviction that Natasha would do anything to get rid of me that I'd fit the facts to my theory. Running from Arm Candy last night had nearly cost me my life. "I guess I owe Lenny an apology for chasing him over the railing tonight."

Will tipped back his head and laughed.

"It's not funny. I was scared."

With a soft rustle of clothing, Will moved in close and put his arms around me.

"So was I. I nearly lost you last night." He bent his head and brushed his lips across my ear. "Why didn't you levitate?"

He pulled the chopsticks from my hair and let them fall to the ground. The support pencil dug against my scalp against the weight of my hair. I disentangled it and Will buried his fingers in my hair as it cascaded down my back.

I was having a hard time thinking. His light, teasing kisses had my nerve endings on fire. "I don't... I wasn't sure it would work."

He pulled back to look at me. And then he broke away. His hands dropped and he looked to the luminous full moon above us as if it had answers only he could see.

He spoke, his voice so soft I could barely hear it. "I put you between worlds. Unguided. Unprotected."

He turned suddenly to face me. Too many emotions were on his face for me to sort through them all. Sorrow, excitement, regret. And something feral that made me step back a pace. "And I left you there. Because it suited my own needs."

His eyes locked on mine. The street faded away, leaving only the two of us. My body began to shake as if I'd been dipped in icy water and would never get warm again. Will moved closer, blocking even the cold comfort of moonlight.

I was surrounded by black nothingness. His lips descended on mine and I pressed into to his warmth as if I would never feel it again. His arms wrapped around me, holding me as the terrible void closed in. His mouth slid across my cheek over the curve of my jaw to my neck. His tongue tasted the tiny, twin scars on my jugular.

Just as suddenly as it had disappeared, the crisp night air with its faint tang of ocean rushed back with a deafening roar. "No. Will, please, don't do this. I don't want—"

I made the mistake of looking at him. His face was beautiful in its terribleness. His incisors had grown into sharp points. Any trace of the man was gone.

"Please, no. Don't!"

His teeth arced toward my neck. Without thinking, I tightened my fingers around the pencil in my hand and shoved it deep into his chest.

A terrible cry rent the night air. Will released me and I tumbled backward, onto the sidewalk. His hands clutched wildly at the protruding bit of pencil as he collapsed onto the grass. For a terrible moment that lasted forever, he stared at me in hurt and surprise. And then he lay looking at nothing.

"Will?" I fell to my knees beside him. "Will!"

What had I done? I reached out a hand and touched Will's soft black hair. Tears streamed down my face and dripped onto his. I brushed them off, my trembling fingers lingering over his cheekbones, his strong jaw. I barely registered the sound of footsteps running toward me.

"Jo!"

At the sound of my name, I jumped to my feet. Turning, I stepped in front of the hedge and held out my hands.

"No," I cried, as Gavin tried to get by me.

"Jo, stop it!" He grabbed my arms and held me still. He looked around me. "Dammit! Where is he?"

I whirled around. Will was gone. I sank onto the grass and reached a hand to the place where he had lain. Now only a handful of ash, already lost in the wet grass, remained. What had I done?

"No," I said, shaking my head. I had taken away his life, leaving behind a million tiny pieces that barely registered in the grass.

Gavin reached out for me before I collapsed. "Shh. It's okay, Jo. You're safe."

"I killed him."

"No." He pulled back and grasped my chin, forcing me to meet his eyes. In them I saw sorrow, nearly to match mine. I realized it was for me. "Jo, he was already dead."

I tried to wrench away, but he held me tighter. "Listen to me. He was trying to turn you into something you don't want to be. Think of your mother, your father. Your friends. All the people you love. Who love you. All that would have been lost to you."

"No, Will was…"

"What was he doing right before you stabbed him?" Gavin asked softly. "Think." He gave me a shake. "Remember!"

I saw Will again as he'd been, distorted into a monster. I felt the cold, the void. My body shook and I buried my face in Gavin's neck and sobbed as if I would never stop.

"It's all right. I'm here. I've got you now," he said, holding me tightly.

After a long while, Gavin peeled me gently off him. Keeping his arm tightly around my shoulders, he led me back toward my apartment. As we turned toward the mailboxes, life suddenly returned to my listless form. I dug in my heels.

"What is it?"

I cranked my head over my shoulder and stared at the empty parking space in front of my building. Will's car was gone. Hope flared, lifting me briefly from my morass of sorrow, regret and guilt. And then it faded as quickly as it had come.

"Nothing," I said flatly. Arm Candy had probably valeted the Aston Martin home—wherever home was—like a good little underling.

But I had to wonder. Didn't I?

~*~

That night, I dreamed of Will. He was walking down a long flagstone hallway lit with golden spills of light at regular intervals by lantern-like wall sconces. At the end of the hall was an ornately carved wood door. Reaching it, he pushed it open and stepped into the room beyond.

It was a decidedly masculine room, dominated on one side by a large four-poster bed made up with navy linens. In the adjacent sitting room, a fire crackled in the grate, casting a glow over the floor-to-ceiling bookshelves, burnishing the leather covers and shades of gold and bronze.

Will unbuckled his belt and tugged his black shirt free of his slacks. As it sometimes is with dreams, Natasha appeared next to him as if she'd been there all along. Her eyes were luminous with concern. She reached her perfectly manicured fingers toward him. "Here, let me help you."

"I'm fine."

His fierce tone stopped her hands before they could undo a single button and they fluttered uselessly to her sides. Her tawny brows drew together in a worried V, and she bit her lower lip to keep silent.

Will continued undressing as if she weren't there. Slowly and precisely, he unfastened his cuffs, first one and then the other. Button by button, he opened his shirt, revealing a beautifully proportioned torso with the sort of long, lean muscles that would make a sculptor long for a block of marble and a chisel. With a shrug of his shoulders, the shirt fell free of his body.

Natasha sucked in a breath through her teeth. Or maybe the sound came from Will, as his fingers probed the puckering wound just to the left of his sternum.

"She is as good as dead!" Natasha whirled and headed for the door.

"No."

She turned back to face him, hands clenched, breast heaving with anger. "She tried to kill you! Even now, it is slow to heal. I demand retribution!"

"No." Blue eyes glittering like sapphires, he overrode her protest. "You are not to touch her."

"But—"

"She is mine." Suddenly, he turned to face me as if I were standing before him. His icy-hot gaze rocked through me like a thunderclap.

I sat bolt upright in bed, wide-awake and panting with fear. With trembling hands, I flicked on my bedside table lamp. Its yellow glow cut through the darkness of the night, but offered little comfort. I found my bathrobe—yellow and fuzzy—pulled it on over my boxers and T-shirt. Shoving my feet into slippers, I opened my bedroom door and padded down the short hallway into the living room, reaching ahead and turning on lights as I went.

I must have made more noise than I thought. Gavin was awake and standing by his makeshift bed on my couch, waiting for me. He had insisted on staying. I hadn't asked if it was because he was worried about me, or that he thought, after coming so close to being turned again, I would complete the transformation during the night.

I knew, if it happened, he wouldn't hesitate to kill me.

His short hair was rumpled, as were his clothes. The yawn he forced back spoke to his fatigue but his pale gray eyes were alert.

"He's alive." I swallowed hard against the dryness of my throat. "I had a dream... It was so real." My voice faded to a whimper.

To his credit, Gavin neither dismissed my words nor offered platitudes. "Have you dreamt of Will before?"

"After he first..." *Bit me*. Gavin nodded his understanding, so I didn't have to say the words. "But not lately."

Not since last winter, when I'd first doused myself in holy water. It was then the dreams had stopped and the wound on my neck had begun to heal.

"Tell me the dream."

I did, in fits and starts. When I finished, Gavin was silent a long time. Then he said, "You're shivering."

I was. My teeth started chattering. In two steps, Gavin was around the side of the couch, pulling me into his arms. He held me in the circle of his warmth until I stopped shaking. He bent his head and I could feel his breath, warm against my temple. "How about some hot chocolate?"

"It's the middle of the night."

I could feel the laughter rumble in his chest. "Has that ever stopped you before?" He stepped back and gave me a little tug toward the kitchen. "C'mon. I'll make it."

In no time, he had me settled at the kitchen table with its cheerful yellow cloth, covered in daisies. All the lights were blazing and the smell of chocolate filled the air as he spooned cocoa mix into two mugs and added hot milk.

"There's triple-chocolate cookies in the cookie jar," I said.

"Right." He opened a cabinet and china clinked as he reached for a plate.

"Just bring the jar," I said impatiently.

Gavin's face lit suddenly in one of his rare, full smiles. The room brightened as if it were filled with sunbeams.

"Somehow, Jo, I think you're going to be just fine."

My body relaxed as if someone had cut the strings that were tangled inside me. All except for one—that one whistled and vibrated like a warning. My hand lifted from the table and moved toward my neck to make sure the adhesive bandage was covered by my robe. I caught myself just in time and redirected my fingers to the steaming mug Gavin held out to me.

I gripped it tightly, fighting against the urge to check the damage Will had done to me before I'd pushed him away. I wondered for the hundredth time since I'd felt the prick of his teeth again on my neck, if he'd done enough this time to change me forever.

*I'm fine,* I told myself fiercely. I forced myself to drink some chocolate. The hot, sweet liquid blazed through me, taking the last of the chill away. And as Gavin sat down across from me, as he always did—hand reaching for a cookie, long legs stretched into the kitchen—I let myself believe it.

# About the Author

*L*iz Jasper's first novel, *Underdead*, won the 2008 EPPIE Award for Best Mystery. The sequel, *Underdead In Denial,* was published the following year to critical acclaim. Liz also writes young adult novels and is hard at work on the next book in the Underdead series.

Liz's first job was teaching middle school science. Apparently jealous of her students' place in the classroom, she eventually went back to school to earn a couple of master's degrees and now works as a financial advisor. With this career path, writing paranormal novels was not only natural—it was necessary.

Liz lives in California near hiking trails and good public libraries, in a house where chocolate is welcome and the resident cat gets fatter and lazier every year.

Find more about Liz at:

http://lizjasper.com

http://www.facebook.com

http://twitter.com/#!/AuthorLizJasper

Made in the USA
Lexington, KY
17 January 2012